FIRST FICTIONS

INTRODUCTION *A. O. Chater, Alan Coren,
Ted Hughes, Jim Hunter, Jason McManus, Julian Mitchell*

INTRODUCTION 2 *Francis Hope, Sheila Macleod,
Angus Stewart, Tom Stoppard, Garth St Omer*

INTRODUCTION 3 *Rachel Bush, Christopher Hampton,
Michael Hoyland, Roy Watkins, John Wheway*

INTRODUCTION 4 *Ian Cochrane, Vincent Lawrence,
Brian Phelan, Neil Rathmell, Irene Summy*

INTRODUCTION 5 *Adrian Kenny, Sara Maitland,
David Pownall, Alice Rowe, Lorna Tracy*

INTRODUCTION 6 *John Abulafia, Jim Crace,
Thomas Healy, Victor Kelleher, John Mackendrick*

INTRODUCTION 7 *Kazuo Ishiguro, J. K. Klavans,
Steven Kupfer, Tim Owens, Amanda Hemingway*

INTRODUCTION 8 *Anne Devlin, Ronald Frame,
Helen Harris, Rachel Gould, Robert Sproat*

INTRODUCTION 9 *Deborah Moffatt, Kristien Hemmerechts,
Douglas Glover, Dorothy Nimmo, Jaci Stephen, Deirdre Madden*

INTRODUCTION 10 *Anne Enright, Matthew Francis,
Hugo Hamilton, Tom Harpole, Carole Morin, Kathy O'Shaughnessy*

INTRODUCTION 11 *Rukun Advani, Lynne Bryan,
Sophie Frank, Kirsty Gunn, Jonathan Holland, Philip MacCann,
Anthony McCarten, Denise Neuhaus*

FIRST FICTIONS

Introduction 12

faber and faber

LONDON · BOSTON

First published in 1995
by Faber and Faber Limited
3 Queen Square London WC1N 3AU

Set in Palatino by Intype, London.
Printed in England by Clays Ltd, St Ives plc

This anthology © Faber and Faber Limited, 1995

The contributors are hereby identified as authors of this work
in accordance with Section 77 of the Copyright,
Designs and Patents Act 1988

'Disillusionment of Ten O'Clock' (page 177) is
reproduced from the *Collected Poems* of Wallace Stevens
by permission of Faber and Faber Ltd.

A CIP catalogue record for this book
is available from the British Library

ISBN 0-571-17261-X

2 4 6 8 10 9 7 5 3 1

Contents

Publisher's Note   vi
Biographical Notes   vii

LINDA REDSHAW
How We Triumphed over History   3
The Cave of Lovers   23
Animal Husbandry   36

VIKRAM CHANDRA
Shakti   47

ROSARIO FERRÉ
The Glass Box   89
The Other Side of Paradise   102
When Women Love Men   112

MATTHEW KRAMER
Sunset   129
The Great House   140
The South   154

SUZANNE CLEMINSHAW
Disillusionment of Ten O'clock   177
How Many Miles to Babylon   191
O Blessed Fall   207

Publisher's Note

First Fictions was first published in 1960 and quickly became established as the most influential anthology of its kind. The aim of this twelfth volume in the series is, once again, to introduce new writers to a wider reading public, and as before the number of contributors is restricted to give each the advantage of presenting a substantial amount of their work.

The five writers in this edition have been chosen for their distinctive voices. They all tell their stories in radically different ways, and yet thematically they share much. There are stories here that explore the dynamics of love and power between men and women, others that display the uneasy relationship between one class and another. There are stories about revenge, the desire for revenge, about suspicion and control and regret. The anthology opens and closes with two writers who have taken an ancient legend and a modern poem – Linda Redshaw with the myth of Tristan and Isolde, and Suzanne Cleminshaw with Wallace Stevens's 'Disillusionment of Ten O'Clock' – and carved them into stories all their own.

Biographical Notes

Linda Redshaw was born in Consett. She has worked as Information Assistant at MIND and in the House of Commons Library. She lives in south-west London with her partner and twins. This is her first published fiction.

Vikram Chandra was born in New Delhi, India, in 1961. He has studied in America at the Columbia University film school. His first novel, *Red Earth and Pouring Rain*, will also be published by Faber and Faber. He writes computer programs and currently lives in Houston, Texas.

Rosario Ferré was born in 1938 in Ponce, Puerto Rico, once a prosperous commercial port. Her mother came from a landowning élite and her father (who became Governor of Puerto Rico) belonged to a family of industrialists. She studied in America and later at the University of Puerto Rico, where she attended classes given by the novelist Mario Vargas Llosa. This is Rosario Ferré's first published fiction in Great Britain.

Matthew Kramer was born in 1961 in north London, where he still lives. He read Law and Politics at Cambridge University and now practises as a lawyer in central London. Previous stories have appeared in *Best Short Stories* and *Panurge*.

Suzanne Cleminshaw was born in Boston, Massachusetts in 1964, and raised in Ohio. She moved to England in 1990, now lives in Norfolk, and is currently writing her first novel.

LINDA REDSHAW

———

How We Triumphed over History

DAVID

Again she rings the little silver bell. It sounds so magical, like an actress laughing, trilling carefree, calculating she is admired. It tells me I must jump, pronto, and carry up the stairs one tall church candle, lit, the cleaned wig, the gold silk dress, and tonight's make-up, without, of course, setting fire to the lot. Can't pretend I'm not tempted. But as we both know, I'm not likely to find another job, not one that uses my special talents, anyway. All right, I admit she's doing me a big favour, about as big as the difference between living and dying, literally. That requires an exhausting amount of gratitude. Every time I see her I see her being too kind to mention it. As I stumble up the dark stairs, I wonder why we can't have electricity, at least in my part of the house, no one would know. And a television, it's over a year since I saw television or read a newspaper. I promise I'd keep them well hidden. She's told me she can't take the risk, that I'm so forgetful that one day some visitor would surely see. I say, you're too much the perfectionist, all day in libraries, reading Professor this, disagreeing with Professor that. If only you would trust me. Log fires in every room? So much work for me, and I'm the only servant, carrying dirty logs all day, couldn't I have a nice clean gas fire downstairs? The flames look almost like the real thing. And then she expects instant concentration for my specials. She laughs, tinkling girlishly, tinkling away. She has read in some book of a woman's laughter resembling a waterfall, and I hear her try to render this drop by drop. She sings, 'Ca-Ca Caliban, get a new master, get a new man.' I can't, can I? Where could I

3

go now? My face is sullen; I look at my shoes. Then she strokes me very gently, smiles the smile of those who have no doubts that the world is in love with them, of a film star or a queen graciously accepting her due, and whispers intimately, confidingly, that surely I know she can trust no other. She asks, how long we have been married? In essence, two years; in name, a couple more. Her voice loses its honey and turns acid. It's a rare thing, a great thing, for her to mention our marriage, such a favour these days, and I have spoiled it. Only one other person in this city even knows about it. She gives me a glance that says she is very, very disappointed in me, and regrets bestowing that moment of warm intimacy on one so unworthy.

I cannot even give her a name; she's had so many over these years. When we met, she was Kate, but not for long. She is sitting at her dressing table, by the fading light of her boudoir window, dreaming and planning the evening to come. Apple wood burns on the small fire, comforting even though spring breathes through the opened glass. I love her. Her hair has been many colours, so many it began to fall out. Since we thought of the wigs it has grown back downy, like a baby's first fluff. It has grown back golden, and given her a child's face.

'Put on my make-up,' she orders, 'and dress me. Then tell me what you see and hear.'

I look out of the tall window, and try to attune. Outside, on the grass, cherry blossom lies discarded like celestial dandruff. I try to go blank, cancel out my ego, my desires. 'I wish you would trust me,' I say. 'Trust my feel for things. You spend all your time on research, and the books aren't always right. The authors weren't there, you know.'

'Unlike you?'

'If you let me, I touch those who were.'

'Ah yes, David, you and your imagination. What use are your dreams when I have to answer to Professor X who believes the opposite of Ambassador Y? I've got to get it right. That's the whole point.'

4

'Then you could dispense with my services, perhaps?'

She looks worried now, and older. I take pity, and massage her beautiful shoulders. 'Who are you today?' I ask, knowing the answer from the dress, the wig. This is how we begin. Her eyes become heavy and languid as I make them up, slanting provocatively; I blot out the lashes. Heavy gold silk just touches the edges of her nipples – the trick is to reveal the breasts completely, without their creamy ripeness toppling out. Grandmothers wore this style, as well as young girls. You can see the successive portraits of Lauderdale and his beautiful wife at Ham House, where as he grows crueller and jowlier, she ages and flaunts more breast. What begins as seduction, seeing as much breast as possible, ends in convention, when you're no longer seeing bosom at all. Red and luxuriant, a coronet of flowing wig electrifies her body, she shivers with pleasure, and dances by her full-length mirror as the candles are lit.

'I hear courtesans cooing across St James's Park. They taunt any man who won't go with them into the bushes, and offer pretty boys instead.'

She claps her hands. 'And what do the men reply?'

'They blush and follow the friendly ladies.'

'Tonight is the age of the Merry Monarch, is it not?' she laughs.

She turns her head to the window and concentrates fiercely, but I know she will never see the figures I see. They smile and wave. They admire her beauty. Look, there's King Charles and his entourage, laughing. If she could only see, we could be married again. I've told her she's afraid to see, to let go. She fears madness. But I lost fear of that a long time ago. She uses my gift, then pretends it's all done by research, that I just carry the logs all day. The truth is in the way her eyes shine as I describe the callers down the centuries, how they look, how they feel. You think she is the one with the power? See how she panics when I mention leaving. I have more power than I realized. 'Imagination,' she laughs. 'Oh, David, you should

LINDA REDSHAW

have been a poet: you play games with your fantasies. Your
visions get me in the mood, that's all.' This is afterwards.
Before, she hangs on every word, asks for more, more detail,
until my friendly shades grow weary, and sometimes angry, as
if their kind empathy has been abused. Which it has. For a
very great deal of money. Enough for this grand residence
overlooking St James's Park, convenient for embassy staff,
politicians, visiting academics, gentlemen from gentlemen's
clubs, all specialists in history. My shades give through gen-
erosity of spirit, literally. We take for money, at least she does.
The scholars come up to her – the first is ringing now – and
touch her breasts and call her Nell. My wife. My darling wife.

KATE

After sunset, the girls took up position. They stopped chatter-
ing, and began to look very important. Every other voice
stopped, too, the way canned laughter suddenly dies, and
the loudspeakers brought the Elvis medley to a close. The
organizers had vainly begun with local folk songs, trying to
whip up a bit of community singing, but only the well-
rehearsed school choir remembered the words. I sang a little in
a feeble embarrassed way, and managed, 'She's a big lass,
she's a bonny lass, and she likes her beer, and they call her
Cushy Butterfield, and I wish she were here.' It's the only song
I recall: Cushy sounds so near my own heart. The children
sang politely of bar-room passion. I was thinking of a small
child burying her face in the bosoms of big Northern women,
of my own arms stretched out to embrace empty air. I was
thinking of my mother who one day was no longer there. I
sang louder. You know the way comedians come on stage,
get the audience to sing, and reap ecstatic applause for doing
nothing? Well, here we clapped for ourselves, too, feeling
beleaguered and knowing no one else ever would. Even
though we couldn't remember the words. Then Elvis took
over, and it was less of a strain for a while.

6

I was standing a little way back, in the road that runs through the works, the road that joins Front Street to Middle Street. After this imaginative beginning, chaos breaks out, with Bertha and Bessemer Streets, the relevant and the random, until it becomes the way to somewhere else. David sat by me, in the time when he too seemed on the way to somewhere else. I hoped the ceremony wouldn't excite him too much, or there'd be no sleep, only that awful moaning and voices all night, and whisky, and then sleep as dawn breaks. We did our living in shifts, David sleeping through the day, and myself putting in earplugs and locking my bedroom door at night.

A fine rain fell, clear rain unlike any remembered. It was the same rain as other places now, now the works had been shut down: thirst-quenching, fertilizing. The police had stopped all traffic, and what with the smell of hot dogs and onions, the warm breath of night, it felt like carnival, as if we were in another, more vivid country. I noticed that one or two police-men had their eye on David, and hence, on me. I wanted to say, I only stay with him because he can't look after himself. That's bad enough without guilt by association. Father O'Mally said, 'David is the cross you have to bear, Mrs Locke; God wouldn't burden your shoulders with more than you could carry.' When David smashed his stained-glass windows, and rang him up at 3 a.m. to accuse him of blasphemy, Father O'Mally didn't shout at God, the author of the burden, but at me. I dress David's feet in bandages when he's bleeding from walking barefoot in the road, to suffer like Jesus. We're shackled together in marriage like entrants in a three-legged race, falling on our faces, and getting up again.

Everyone was here: the neighbours we'd quarrelled with were quite friendly; grandparents held tiny bewildered babies in woolly hats to the moon. Even family pets came to bear witness. History was being made, and it smelt of hot dogs and onions, candy-floss and chips, and boomed in your head to the seasick whirling of the merry-go-round.

Clouds parted, and suddenly the moon was naked, as if

posing. The girls began to move. I recognized Kerry and Mandy from our street, and waved, but they were intent, they were anonymous now, moving to the group's rhythm, no longer their own. In white dresses, timidly bearing candles at arm's length, they looked like sleep walkers. Silently, they wove through the cooling towers. Their faces were dim in the moonlight; you saw only white dresses floating, and candles flickering against the solid, black-waisted spent volcanoes.

It was as if they half remembered other dances, other times. They were no longer here, but rapt, as if enchanted. They grew brave, one, then more, breaking free of the dance, now absolutely here, daring to touch with their free hand the epic, looming towers. They tossed white petals, as over black tombs. Some people wept. Terrifying wild beasts, who could burn and blast, were now harmless, toothless, to be stroked tenderly by children. And one by one, then all together, we ran to feel the cold dead metal. Suddenly time stopped, and we were all crying.

It was then I felt History nuzzling my ankles. He sidles in like nerve gas if you leave the tiniest crevice open: you can bolt and bar, but he'll seep through, smiling pityingly. Sometimes you feel his cold hand tighten round your throat, and you turn, and there's no face in his hooded cloak.

No one moved for some time. We held each other, apart from the embarrassed adolescent boys who stood with hands in pockets, spitting intermittently. David looked at me, 'I don't know why you're crying. You hated this place.' He sniffed the air as if tasting fine wine. 'Taste it. It tastes of oxygen. Don't you like breathing?' Then he began to dance. 'Red dust in my hair, red stains on my clothes, the smell of rotten eggs that gets right up my nose.' People were staring now. I could see him fumbling with his raffle ticket with an eagerness I found offensive, perhaps because I felt it, too. I wanted to see this great thing. A sick mind thought up this ceremony, especially the raffle. At first it was a joke – the EEC had decided the steel-works had to go, even though it was making a profit, so why not finish with a bang, a real bang? And after the feeble joke, a committee was appointed, a party organized, dynamite donated by a friendly arms manufacturer. Its momentum was now unstoppable, even after the thought occurred to the citizens that it was perhaps not in the best possible taste. If we've got to die, we might as well die partying, became the general feeling.

People came from outside, too, just to stand in silence. Some had been through similar bereavement without ceremony or official mourning, like a death without a body, without expression of grief. Redundant shipworkers from Sunderland, miners from Wales and Durham, and every citizen of the Red Dust Town. David bought twenty-seven tickets, one for each year of his life. I couldn't bring myself to buy one. Yet I'd come to see it, like everyone else. I felt confused. But I knew I had to be there, like the tiniest baby, to bear witness.

It was time for the winner to be announced. The towers were garlanded like sacrificial beasts. We waited, holding each other, a mass of people, staring upwards. A circle of fish-heads in star-gazy pie. Local celebrity Gayle Garland, goosepimpled in purple lamé, purred the winner's name down the microphone; I was still noticing the way Gayle's silhouette echoed the hourglass shape of the cooling towers when I realized I'd heard a familiar name. David had won, of course. Poetic justice. The investment of three weeks' benefit had not been in vain. He walked up to the button casual as a movie gunslinger; I could feel loathing and envy in the air. It was a wasted ticket. The crowd wanted someone who knew the significance of this act, not a mooncalf like David. But David knew more than anyone there. It was the cross he had to bear, that Father O'Mally's God had jokingly bestowed upon him.

He walked up to the button and pressed its red clown nose.

The towers began to glow, they were big women in red satin. They vibrated in ecstasy. Red towers taut as blushing corsets, their underskirts aflame with dynamite, whooshed heavenwards into history. Big Cushy Butterfield has lift off. The very earth booms in rhythm to her flight. She fragments into a thousand tiny fires. Dancing in formation across her lovely brow pulse tiny suns and moons.

Around me I saw ashes. There were toffee apples, hot dogs, beer; there were souvenir programmes and hot soup in paper cups. I'd even brought mulled wine in a thermos. Die partying. But we all wanted to go home, before that disappeared, too. David raised a solitary cheer. The crowd stared back, silent. I thought of Cushy's death, and her ashes, but I'd seen her dance across the heavens in her glorious vulgarity. My mother used to dance, until she danced away. David's voice began to throb melodiously. 'They'll be needing men to clear the rubble. You could ask at the job centre,' I said pointedly, but he only sang louder, exhilarated. I felt the same release, shamefully, secretly.

I led him home, happy now. Usually we had fund evenings which began with David saying cheerfully, 'I've seen the abyss.' And that's all he'd say for hours. Often I'd reply, 'Never mind, let's have a cup of tea.' I tried gentle raillery. 'I see the abyss too. It's called David and I'm married to it.' Of course his mother blamed me. 'He was normal until he met you.' I wanted to explain that he was fine until he caught History, that it fevered and possessed him. He says he's possessed, and it's true, it's fact. Honestly. If it's all my fault, why does he collapse whenever I try to leave him?

On the way home I looked forward to our usual whisky, our evening's entertainment. I'd lost track of how much we were drinking; the only stuff we can afford now tastes like urine. Perhaps it is urine, which would explain a lot. Haunting health food shops, his mother, Audrey, wrote a list of possible reasons for David's condition: me, of course, public enemy number one; allergy to the red dust from the steelworks (delete as no longer applicable); vitamin deficiencies; attack by mutant yeast; alcoholism I added, for although she's seen both of us drinking, I'm the one with the problem. No, no, it's History. We befriended him and loved him, until he betrayed our love.

David came whooping, eyes wild as at some marvel. He had seen fire; he had seen death; nothing excited him more than a good fire. I looked into those eyes. I saw fire and death. I was excited, too. It was almost sexual, and frightened me. He danced onto the sullen bus, where other eyes waited. His dance had neither rhythm nor shape: it might veer into violence or spend itself rocking into sleep. Being always aware, catching that flash of menace in time, like a mother watching for a toddler to run into the road, tired me so much. The other passengers fixed on us. David was the person who giggles at the funeral. We all want to do it, fearful of losing control. I grip him so hard we look like lovers. I clutch him to my cold heart and pretend he isn't there.

He isn't with me, but he's still twitching, like a phantom limb.

I could see a light in our window, and a shadow busily moving. I watched the self-contained movements through this frame, pretending it was television or theatre showing some kind of normal domestic life. It looked so warm, the fire flickering, a woman at the stove. It could be someone else's happy life. A nostalgic sadness flooded me. Then I opened the door and walked into a kitchen full of steam. It was my kitchen, but not mine now. Through the haze I made out a female shape. Audrey was here: she often 'popped in to help'. Her help was as innocent as the KGB. The steam made her beautiful, like a soft-focus lens. In one huge saucepan, I saw my underwear boiling; segregated, in another, David's Y-fronts. My pretty lacy things were torn beyond repair, punished for crimes like youth and life, his pants handled lovingly. 'Couldn't fit the bedding in,' she said, slightly defeated. 'Oh, it rarely needs washing these days,' I announce, as meaningfully as I can. An alpine incense floated decorously about the room; I thought I would suffocate in wholesomeness. My wine rack, which three hours ago had held several much looked-forward-to bottles of plonk, now contained arcane varieties of disinfectant, each with a distinct priestly role in the purification process. It was

11

death by Brillo pad. To wipe away the stain of me, the stain of her darling's illness.

We ate in silence, apart from David's intermittent cackling. Wondering whether the abyss had filled for the moment, whether it would yawn open like a disaster movie chasm in the wee small hours as usual, I observed our customary silence. I had begun to tense whenever anyone spoke, and loved silence above everything; but welcome solitude was quickly changing to loneliness. To think that a year ago, we were working, even David, we were happy. I thought, I do not have to stay with him. He has a mother and the NHS.

For so long I felt implicated in his madness, for I was the one History nuzzled as again I felt his embrace that evening. His touch was cold as my heart, and I felt this dark glamour again. Seducers don't return, but he is faithful in his way; he needs the warmth of human frailty to stay alive. Oh vampire lover I could begin to pity you, though you leave ruined lives and madness in your wake. Or kill you. Then this whole bloody country could breathe.

A year ago, we were working. No, not at the steelworks, then stricken, and later doomed by Brussels, but the industry of the future, the Heritage Centre.

I would go back and back. It drew me away from David, and propelled me towards him. The day after David blew up the steelworks, I returned. By now the attendants had exhausted their taunts, and my visits amused rather than agitated. Anyway, after David's abyss I could cope with pretty much anything, including a little petty hostility from former colleagues.

I went to see the banners again. They're displayed in the big house, Stonebrook Hall, among all that marble, among the reasonable Adam pillars, the tactful, elegiac light. Out of well-bred silence shrieked the banners, vulgar poor relations. Here they hung. Here are braziers of brotherhood. If I touch the redness of those banners, my frozen hand will burn. They hang like curtain samples in bargain basement shops, slightly soiled, reduced in value. I consulted the catalogue: delicately embroidered and neatly labelled examples of folk-art. Female fingers weaving male bonding. Here, see appliquéd the firm grasp of many hands in community; there, a radiant child pointing to a golden city overflowing with milk, honey and socialism. I examined the labels, written by art historians, as if words could control the violent hope of the pictures. Old fairground carousels with fantastical scenes of Venice and Rome, show cities of such longing, so beautiful that longing for them hurts, as you spin round and dare to open up your desires; they are no more visionary than the landscapes of these banners, these superseded banners. They hung obsolete as the medieval battle standards in Durham Cathedral; they drooped post-coitally; moths had eaten their dreams. I remembered the icon translated from Greek island church to interesting wall-decoration in New York exhibition. Last time I saw the banners in use I was lifted high over the shoulders of miners at the Gala, an infant passed from grasp to trusted grasp above the carnival crowd. Upward it wound, cramming the ascent to the cathedral, the streets like the whorls of a huge conch booming out an echo of dancing feet. I have touched the oak monument, oak coal-black, to miners who died in accidents over the centuries, their thin bodies fuelling other lives. I spoke aloud in the museum, without realizing, 'Hearth', seeing *homo neanderthalis* huddle in a circle round comforting flames that keep the terrible darkness away. Flames red as banners, red as the cry of a wild creature howling. A chieftain's hall, logs piled massively to warm warriors, minstrels and stories, while through a high window a swallow flies into the firelight and out again. Dark to dark. I stared at the reasonable pillars.

I loved the whiteness of the hall, as if everything had frozen, a chequer floor for human chess pieces. I loved the corpulent statues of aldermen posing pompously in togas, the hardness of the stone mocking the soft vulnerable flesh. Caught in mid-gesture, they argue forever some noble point. Perhaps they thaw at night, and come to life. No, no, they don't. And I should know.

We wanted to understand our place in history; how the town rose and died. Education took us away, but we wanted to go. And we kept returning, unable to feel really there: we tried genteel southern suburbs, but we never took in their neat rows of houses; only one imprinted landscape we saw wherever we looked, tall chimneys, towers and beacons. My father is a surveyor, intimate with every stone, the lie of the earth, where it is safe to build, singing his songlines away from the under-mining shafts and tunnels. To me the land is an old tired woman who has borne too many children, her bones poking through the sagging grass. I see rivers and waterfalls and moorland where the light falls away, and the foreground is dark, like an old woman remembering her childhood and for-getting yesterday.

So we worked at the Heritage Centre, rigorously academic at first, hating the syrupy proud glow of the other staff, as if simply being born in the north conferred a craggy nobility. Then I had the idea, and I wish I hadn't. I wish I could blame David, but he's the innocent victim. No, I was just a catalyst: he caught History like a virus, from me, the symptomless carrier.

My idea, my brilliant idea. I had tired of manuscripts, of always interpreting, of strange-smelling dust and classifi-cation. I'd learn so much, but never come really close to how they thought or felt. There was always that bloody glass screen between us. I was always waving through glass to shadows, knowing what they wore, how they spent their money; I knew more facts about them than my living neighbours, but they were as far from me as David is now. Sometimes in my dreams they touched my hand. For a strange, brief time, I fantasized about going to seances, but David laughed so much I felt ashamed. Instead, I thought up a respectable substitute.

We asked to be moved to the theatrical department. This was the most popular museum work, and difficult to get, especially for graduates, whose research gave useful academic prestige to an establishment nervous about rude comparison with Disneyland. For our audition, the casting director assigned injured miner on stretcher ('William') and inconsolable wife ('Amelia'). David lay like The Death of Chatterton, moaning softly. I mopped his brow and gave him sips of water, subtly inserting interesting statistics relating to fatality rates in the 1840s, and finishing with hysterics. It was a bravura performance, and a precedent for my later relationship with David. We got the job: miner and wife, the same performance ('exactly,' said the stage manager) every afternoon at three.

I sobbed over the limp body on the stretcher every day. In character I answered questions, many questions from fairly interested school children and their minders, on how we lived. What about pneumoconiosis? How long would we live? Did we keep pigeons or whippets? Did we have sanitary towels? Was one coal fire the only heating for a whole house?

In the mornings I wielded the poss-stick in the washing tub, in hairnet and sweat, then posed as one of the first woman doctors, with lethal obstetric equipment, in a room made impenetrable by aspidistra. Telling the children their teachers' Victorian heroes, like Wilberforce, had a drug habit earned me a reprimand. Although we enjoyed the work, after a time I told David, 'It isn't enough. I want to live here, live here properly.'

At first, he laughed, but it intrigued him. David had to lie on a stretcher in assumed agony for one hour twice a day, although alternating other roles, and was not a born actor: his boredom showed through in a few weeks. I'd begun to worry whether our supervisors had noticed, and that he might be sacked. My own role required rather more animation, but I longed for developments in the couple's story, to break the tedium: sometimes I wanted to shout, as he lay there moaning, 'Oh for Christ's sake die and get on with it.' And I knew I wouldn't be able to hold it back much longer. And why did Amelia have no children? Birth control was pretty rudimentary then, as I explained in great detail every day in my per-

15

sona of Dr Dorothy, in sensible Edwardian suit. I imagined scenes between them, the death of their child perhaps, the annual miners' outing to Scarborough or Whitley Bay. Perhaps he drank and beat her. Most of these visions seemed pretty negative: there must have been some pleasure and beauty. They didn't write their feelings down, and all I had were cholera statistics, accident statistics, and a few polished furnishings. I tried to love Amelia, but she was just a name in a parish register.

We walked through the proscenium arch into the banners' heart. Time flickered for a moment. Perhaps I felt the nuzzle of that dark mouth then. We collected discarded words, the rubble of our time. Community (there is no such thing, see also Society). Put them in a glass case. Memorize before they disappear: if words aren't polished by lip and tongue, they rust into history. We moved into the miner's cottage. Cold, we stole coal from the fake pit-shaft which the set designer had thoughtfully decorated with proper coal. Hungry, we took eggs from the Victorian farm, and vegetables from its wizened organic cabbage patch. But it was never enough. The proud shire horses gleamed in their polished brasses more brightly as we began to fade. Now ravenous, we looted the corner shop with its 1880s prices chuckled over by elderly visitors dragging unimpressed children. Inside the newly designed Victorian packets we found cardboard food; on the counter huge plastic hams glistened pinkly, bound with string as if so massive they must be forcibly restrained. In fairy-tales, when you're lured away by demon lovers, you feast on sublime delicacies that do not nourish, so that you sicken and waste away. But we ate our fairy food cross-legged on rugs woven by many women out of their lives: bright children's dresses telling of birthdays, faded well-worn coats from crueller winters than now. We made love by the fire on warm cloaks of banners.

I had ceased being a quick-change artist in some eternal rep. Our new life felt at first like method acting; the daily scene of the injured miner tore real tears from me. Sometimes I was sobbing too much, as if it were too real to bear, but I think vitamin deficiency must have had something to do with that.

At night, after the visitors had gone, we wandered through the greyly moonlit grounds, touching the rows of dead machinery that loomed out of the darkness. It glittered, seductive with danger, as if half sleepily watching our movement. This scrap metal fired the Industrial Revolution, it was power, it set the world moving. Now they were the Roman monuments barbarians thought giants had built. Every obsolete, ruinous thing seemed densely present, as if it ought to be a symbol, its rigid massiveness denser than reality. Its unarguable bulk made the moment recede, claimed more substantiality than any fragile present.

We walked into the white hall, leaving behind a graveyard of dying mammoths more alive than ourselves. Inside I lit candles; their pale narcissus light cooled the marble statues. But they spotlit the red pigment that pulsed on the banners so that your eyes burned. Air currents from the candleflame made them sway as if breathing, a red heart beating, red as howling, red as loss. Candles show only fragments – mine lay around me, further and further apart, my relics scattered. Ice-shards of waxwork eyes unblinkingly held me to account, caught forever, like the statues, in their one frozen gesture, the one essential moment summarizing a life. The candles flickered on a faint glow of white stuff or a favour from Elizabeth glowing against black velvet. David said, 'I will set you free,' and I didn't know whether he meant the waxworks or me.

He took down the glass partition. In our hands lay all history. I was Richard II, deposed, but wonderfully noble in my despair, my tabard embroidered with golden lions; I mourned Prince Albert movingly in acres of black silk and Victoria's monogrammed knickers, keeping a lock of John Brown's hair close to my heart all the while. One midsummer evening we dressed as Elizabethan boys, filling the night with madrigal. The fragile costumes fell to dust in our hands. David said, 'There was once a perfect summer, the kind where you

17

pause ... trembling before each action because you know you're stepping outside the sublunary world. It was the best ever grape harvest, the 1540 vintage. Hundreds of years later, a man gave all his fortune for a bottle of perfect wine. He took one exquisite sip, then the wine turned to vinegar in his glass.'

We ran up and down the past like an elevator, stopping by floors at random, trying each time for size. We were tourists of time. We were greedy for History. By now smelly and thin, cold, cold, I thought we were really there, David more so, but I was just shopping for History, flirting. Try a time, and throw it away if you get bored with it. History still stroked me like a lover, like many, many lovers, endlessly changing shape. Not substance. And he taught me his distaste for a flirt. I made love with Napoleon and Keats, and it was just David dressed up, but he was there, he was really free to become anyone in any time. I've never seen David so alive. He became History; his eyes glittered, but he wasn't seeing me. He stood at the top of the sky, watching ant-sized humans swarm across the centuries. And I was still me, a sick woman trapped in a cold northern town, dressed as Nell Gwynn with plastic oranges, and suffering from scurvy because I couldn't get real ones.

After summer we became greedier, for History, for the ever diminishing food supply. Then there came a time when History wasn't enough: we started inventing alternative histories. I remember the thrill of this power: we could wipe out countries, create new people. How petty and limiting facts seemed. How constrained the human life. Unattainable virgin Elizabeth married Leicester and sank into weary maternity. I thought of the sad white pile of baby clothes, desperately embroidered by Elizabeth to curry favour, love being impractical, with her Bloody sister; those uncanny, long alabaster fingers sewing feverishly to save her life. Mary's swelling belly was a cruel joke. What if she'd had a son? Anaemic now, my own belly began to swell, bursting through the sprigs of my Laura Ashley uniform. As replacement I sewed by hand a dress the colour of earth. It didn't look right. Visitors began to complain about our filthy undernourished state. The midden looked like a midden, they said. Our house was a pig-sty. All the other workers were showered and machine-washed and fed by the canteen microwave; they hoovered their cottages, and tended them with Domestos and Vim. I tried to explain how I used soapwort and orris root, offered recipes for household aids to visitors, but they took one glance, sniffed the air, and fled, disdaining my advice.

David was changing. His eyes glittered more, fixed on a distant place peopled by a cast of historical personages who had never even existed; or those who had existed, led colourfully altered lives. He would wake me up with his 'What if Queen Victoria hadn't been a haemophilia carrier?'

'Oh for Christ's sake go back to sleep.' I found myself withdrawing from him; I sensed a storm brewing. He started mixing roles, saying the wrong words: his dentist groaned at the cruel misery of the pit; his ruddy, smocked farmer palely brandished documents from the lawyer's office. There were complaints; there were warnings. I used to laugh, I thought he was playing practical jokes, but it was the beginning of his fever. And I had brought it on, with my brilliant idea, 'It isn't enough. I want to live here.'

At night he cried out more. Voices from over the centuries called to him like sirens, they tampered with his food, they were poisoning him. He stared into space for days at a time, and refused to play the stricken miner. 'I can change History. Play one person at a time? I am all History at once.' His eyes glazed at the effort of holding in his mind battles, arguments, casts of thousands . . . What an effort of will, to hold at the same time Danton and Stalin, battalions, the merest foot-soldier, the Terror. What blank eyes. A body breathing in present time, and a mind that no longer knew me. On the day of this outburst he was sacked. David's mother put him gibbering on a stretcher and they carried my poor wounded husband home.

My own job now became precarious, since we'd worked together as a team. The supervisor was about to move me back to research, when I miscarried over an exquisite chair cushion embroidered by Queen Victoria. Amelia had no children. I cried for many days. I stole a tiny white robe made by Elizabeth for the mockery child. It fell to dust. My employers noticed this pilfering, and it provided a welcome opportunity to send me packing. What kind of crazed father would David have made? But that is already an alternative history. I cried then for two deaths, father and child. And that is how we came to Audrey, to be cleansed of our various germs.

The day after the steelworks exploded was my last visit to the Heritage Centre. I used to haunt it, I felt ghostly away from it, at home with David. I thought I knew that place, but on that day, a keeper unfamiliar to me showed me through a door I'd never noticed. Underneath lay a thin slit of yellow light. The door led to a long, winding corridor; on the walls I could make out posters advertising exhibitions. Impatiently he beckoned, so that it was difficult to stop and note each poster in detail. I glimpsed the Lindisfarne Gospels, at least the intertwined animals suggested this, Renaissance Drawings, the Industrial Revolution, Early Women Photographers, Computer Graphics. Then some fragmented, shadowed, in a half-familiar language I couldn't seem to get hold of. Each poster stuck to a door showing a slit of yellow light underneath. I wanted to walk into them all, but the keeper indicated I must choose one only. Take a door, and you can't come out again. I couldn't choose, and the solicitous keeper ushered me on, he was kind, he stroked my sad hand. Further down the corridor, darker and darker until the posters glinted, far away, not fully-formed, metamorphosing as I looked. The keeper eyed me beseechingly; panicking, I tried to understand, but my head ached with migraine posters. Then he led me to the last room.

I knew it was History, that he'd return one day, although we'd been parted so long. No one else makes my neck shiver, then strokes and nuzzles all the pain away, the pain I know he created in the first place. I know I must accommodate or kill him. He speaks as to a young child, which I suppose is what I am, looked at from his great age. Cruelly, he hands me the baby's white gown, made perfect again.

He opened the door. The Prince of Darkness is a gentleman. He switched on the light. I was dazzled by mirrors, fairground mirrors, distorting my face, at times with hag-wrinkles, my red hair white in an instant, my body old and tired but not only this, not only this: see me grow young again, my child living and crowing at the sky. A dull, cowed woman dances into aria into colour, into meaning. I open up. I see desire in the mirror. Metamorphosis through mirrored light of such intensity I thought I would die of it.

I awoke outside. The air was clear, as if some constant static had been removed. Children sang as they played on the hillside. It was growing dark; I had slept for a long time, in every sense. I felt passivity melt away like the winner of a slimming competition.

So I got myself together, as they say. Of course I'd hoped to find David on my return, regenerated, transformed. This is not a fairy-tale. But when I saw advertised an MA in Heritage Interpretation in London, I signed up for it. As David agreed, what's the point of an obsession if you don't use it for a better life? My course taught me business skills, as well as sharpening my research technique. When David gradually learned to channel his visions, with expensive and prolonged analysis from Dr Bagel, I had a brilliant idea. How can I leave my wounded boy? This way, he is protected, has a home. His visions, though he won't admit this, can be erratic, so I've got to spend hours in the British Library getting the details right. You see, I privatized myself; I am walking heritage. Sex with Nell Gwynn? The foremost Restoration authorities have paid me thousands. Professor X gets the Nell his great book implies, the Nell he has constructed; she will not be the same as Ambassador Y's Nell. This is what David will never understand. What really happened is not the point. The point is to change it. David is so sentimental with his truth, his atmosphere, their real feelings. See my collection of silver, the por-

LINDA REDSHAW

traits of me (in the style of Lely, of Hilliard, of Gainsborough) that adorn my walls. I am celebrated by Historians and History lovers all over the world. See my town house overlooking St James's Park, where the real Nell lived. See David dressed as my footman, proud of his livery. I can do anything apart from Elizabeth's virginity. Listen, my first lover of the evening is ringing.

The Cave of Lovers

Tristan lay dying of a poisoned wound. I knew, I didn't need the messengers ineptly disguised as merchants, bobbing up wherever I tried to hide, pushing under my nose the secret love-token, or the white robe dipped in his blood. They followed me to my private chamber, to the battlements, to the hidden caves beneath Tintagel, that are only safe when the sea wills. There, they caught me, they were excited, listen, listen. Don't you want to sink your hands in these rich black clots? Last time, and the time before, you smeared it over your body, and said, this is my blood, clotted cream, and you licked it round your face and smoothed it over your hair like a child with a jam pot. Gleefully they started whispering the latest details. Well, this had to be endured. But I wasn't listening. I didn't need to. I heard his cries every hour; my head was bursting with the racket. I felt his pain in my loins, too, yes in that place, where else? Always that place, where the poisoned spear enters and shatters, the house of our sin. And always I had to heal it in the same way, while the gods watch and plan the next wound, the next comeuppance. The messengers talked while I watched the sea hating the rocks. They were covered in blue mussel shells like the moons on tiny finger nails, babies' nails clinging on for fear of drowning. I shuddered. Then the cries came back. I tried to run away pressing my hands to my ears to shut out Tristan's cries. By now they were unearthly, like nothing I've ever heard, they were desolation and loss, they were frightened. For God's sake! Why do you scream so loudly, when I feel the pain too, and I can keep my mouth shut? But it went on and on. I was demented with it pounding away, harsher than the sea that crashed against the castle walls each night as if trying to get me and drag me out on the rocks. What have I done, what sort of terrible crime is being punished? Love, only love, only love for Tristan.

So I had to go, to stop the noise, and because I always went in the end. All the court spies knew. A glimpse of another face at the mirror as I packed my hairbrush; the tail of a red cloak twitching behind a doorway. Of course they knew I knew they spied on me. They're so lax I ought to complain to my husband who employs them. You're not getting value for money, Mark. But I had not seen Mark since Tristan's last banishment from court six months ago, which puzzled me, for with his rival gone, I expected Mark to reclaim me for his bed. My spies (for marriage is a partnership in all things) tell me he sits in his chamber staring at the sea. Our land breaking apart, and Mark sitting by his window staring at the sea. And in my head sits Tristan, on the opposite shore, gazing out at the same waters, wondering where is the ship that carries fair Isolde, and his life.

No one tried to stop me leaving; in fact as I was putting on my cloak the door to my chamber opened suddenly, and there stood my husband. 'You are going, then?'

'Are you going to stop me?'

'No.' Then emphatically, 'I can't. I thought you weren't . . . I mean, you've left it very late. Perhaps too late. The ship is ready. I'll see you onto it.'

My lord is more understanding than I thought. He pities our love; he is reconciled to his twilit place outside the warm fiery glamour of Tristan and Isolde. I am a lover again as I think of my own place, my own power over Tristan's life or death, with a squeeze of my thighs, with a bunch of sweet smelling herbs. King Mark takes my hand, a little too roughly, I think, and runs towards the ship. He drags me down the steps cut into the cliff, too fast, I'm losing my footing, then bundles me in his arms and flings me on deck. There is something I don't understand.

'Did you talk to the messengers?' I ask.

'What messengers? I don't need messengers. Can't you hear him across the water? Can't you hear him howling over there . . .?'

How many times had I sped to Tristan's side, when he begged for healing? Tristan always had great need of healing.

The ship flew, and I wandered the deck, never quite breathing enough air, sicker and sicker until the vessel was a moving cage spinning from Mark to Isolde to Tristan in inexorable fatuous motion. It spun into space, outside time, it had symmetry, it was beautiful, it made patterns, like a dance: we come together, there are obstacles, we part. We couldn't get out, it wheeled so fast, a brilliant star twisted and twirled by the fatal magic of the love potion. There was only this movement, and nausea, and wanting stillness and air, then the dizzy dance began to throb, a beat to the music, then the throb became a pulse, my own pulse, then my pulse sounded louder than the dance and marked time with the gasp of my breathing. I stretched like a cat. I made a space about me that grew wide. It started inside me, growing in the beat of the pulse, in the rhythm of my breath. It split me apart like a fierce embryo. And now I was still. All else moving, I gave away my moving, the broken dance madly discordant, flying in all directions, in my stillness my free desire.

The messengers bore a code. Tristan would be watching for white sails, for Isolde: black meant no Isolde, and death. And I wished to renounce that power, that had made me glow like a god. Tristan was dying, not only of a poisoned wound but for love of me. You see if we parted for more than a few months, flesh fell from our bones. We faded. We needed our love-making with warm red blood. We shared one death and one life, after the love potion, in that order. Like the honeysuckle twined round the hazel-tree in perpetual embrace, that shrivel and die as they are prised apart.

The captain has hoisted his white sails, they flutter like the wings of turtle doves. We are making swift progress to bring Tristan delight. Here I come, my lover. Then it came to me from that stillness that again and again I must heal Tristan, with all my strength, no matter how tired I might be; draw into me the stinking poison, bring his body back to life with my own, taking his sorrows within me, so that I lay diminished and used up. I asked when he had ever healed me, stroked me like a mother and whether I had the strength to give him ease again? Was he not weary, too? And I knew that the honeysuckle was strangling the hazel tree. I would cut it back. One should be allowed to grow straight and tall to the sun.

I took a knife, and began to climb the mast very slowly, in the foot-holes I had seen the cabin boys use. I was shaking a bit, and my servants tried to pull me off, but this was my one chance, I was strong as a hero, I kicked them quite viciously. A little taken aback, they left me alone. The moon made me white; it caught my dress and took me high to meet it. I was light as a seagull, shivering with delight, with the fierce proud air, with the space that went on forever. I didn't look down though I could hear snatches of voices calling me, but I watched the wheeling stars and felt my breasts rise and fall in a new rhythm. Then I reached the white sails, and raised my knife. Tristan's anguish tore through me, as if I were about to sink the knife into his heart. Tingling through thighs, toes, earlobes, belly like a parody of . . . I'm sorry Tristan. No, no, I am not sorry. Though the ship lurched, I would not let go. In my dreams at Tintagel the sea bore me through windows and doorways to the rocks as though I had done a great wrong. It gathered and tossed me, and I noticed I was wearing my wedding dress. Sometimes Tristan pushed me under, sometimes Mark, and I stumbled in my layers of silk and lace, further under, so that my dress became the moonlit water and the lace its foam, and I lay down with my eyes open seeing cold sea-creatures, sinking down and down to a mirror castle where bright fish swim and church bells ring under the sea.

How free I felt up there on the mast. I cut away the white silk and tied in its place my black shawl. Let it flap for Tristan. Let it flap like the wing of a great black crow.

At once the sea began to seethe. We all felt its anger. Shot through with fire, it turned on itself, it convulsed. It bellowed; its chops foamed; it was wounded and mad. The crew crossed themselves as if this were a portent. Once before it had snarled at me in such a way, when Tristan and I had unwittingly drunk the love potion, and the appalled Brangane, my maid, threw its dregs into the sea. Then what a tantrum it inflicted on the ship bearing Tristan and Isolde all those years ago. How many years? Is it thirty now? Did you not know that we are old? It seemed to me now that the sea had taken into itself my passion for Tristan, as before it accepted, not without a fight, the fatal love potion.

Soon it was calm again. It rocked me playfully to sleep. It laughed and sang. It was tender and kind and loved me.

Tristan was dead, as I had hoped, by the time of my arrival. I was somewhat surprised by the ostentatious black bunting that lined the road from the harbour to his castle. The crows were here, too, black wings of flags flapping in doorways, women actually tearing out their hair. Worse, some had slashed their garments so fiercely that I could see their flabby breasts lolling out as they ran hither and thither, not knowing where to go now their lord lay cold. Was it Tristan alive or dead they found so erotic? Anyway, he was mine. What right have you to grieve like this? He was my lover. You didn't even know him. Grown men stood sobbing noisily beside shuttered shops. Reluctantly, I caught what they were saying: remembering a kindness by Tristan, an act of justice, getting work for some poor labourer, or a good marriage for a daughter. I didn't want to listen. I had imagined all he had done was love me. I thought it filled up all his time, consumed and broke him, like it did me. Then I shut it out. Mother of God, these people barely knew Tristan. He did all these things to show off. Didn't you know how vain he was? And he sang endlessly about his feats in arms on that harp of his, twanging away and beaming smugly. I almost laughed, their grief was so deranged, so theatrical. And I felt uneasy at the way it drew keener attention to my own lack of grief. At first I thought, they're too busy prancing about in this ridiculous way to notice me, but soon realized I was the star of the occasion. They were mourning for me too, imagining my great epic tragedy. One by one they queued up to touch me in silence as if I were a rare white unicorn. This moved me strangely, and I felt more tenderness for a crowd of strangers Tristan loved than I ever felt for Tristan. Now no longer Isolde but an amputee of Tristan-and-Isolde.

When I reached the castle gates, the distraught citizens ran to arrest Tristan's wife, my rival, Isolde of the White Hands. We had never met, although spies related her hatred of me. I did not hate her: pitied her situation, and I was curious about her love for my lover. Indeed, I envied her, as I envied Mark: what is it like to know love without potions? Love given freely, not wrenched out of your blood by poison, draining, burning you up. And you can keep your children. Can you tell me who suffered most in Tristan and Isolde: you, who loved Tristan passionately, yet lay untouched beside him; Tristan, who had my love but rarely my body, knowing Mark had my body but not my love, knowing Tristan had my love; or myself, who had my husband's body and love (neither of which I wanted) and Tristan's love and body (infrequently)? Now which was most unhappy?

Expectant, the crowds followed me to the death-chamber. I saw in their faces that certain things were expected. I knew from this heightening of gesture, this feeling that now there are rules, the right action must be ritually performed. In a corner of the chamber five poets stood with quill pens ready. So Tristan had passed into myth and seemed likely to drag me with him. From now on, the fleshly, breathing Isolde would be lost by the wayside. He had taken my life away. The moment has come to embrace his beautiful body, stroke his wet eyelashes, wash his cruel wounds. The moment has come to die weeping in his arms. I approach and take up one exquisite ivory hand. I am ready to kiss his god-like face rotting already in this feverish heat. Go on, they are waiting. Clasp your pretty boy: no matter he's a stinking gangrenous carcass. Die in torrid necrophiliac embrace. Even in death he could control my life, but then the thought came to me that now I was a myth I could do anything I wanted, and no one would believe it, because they'd prefer the perfect symmetry of tragedy. The poets would write what they wished whatever poor Isolde did.

Isolde didn't die.

Just a little embarrassment that I hadn't done the expected thing, and then a fierce anger, so that if I stayed there would be a bloody lynching. I faded out of the room and into my own life. Through the corridors and castle gates I heard snatches of tinkling harps; enterprising bards had already tied up the loose ends for me. They looked surprised as I ran past, but did not pause in their singing. My black-sailed ship lay waiting in the harbour.

You must credit me with some bravery: I knew there was a strong chance I might die. The potion still coursed through my veins. Tristan and I were old, I should have been well past the menopause, but you would have sworn I was a pretty rosebud of nineteen. I looked then as I looked on the day I drank the love potion. Oh, I was a unicorn alright, a talking white deer, a green-girdled changeling from fairyland. I shimmered, I brimmed, I dazzled with life: with beauty that cut through the thrilling murmur of witchcraft. Everyone wanted to gaze on the unicorn. Whether progeny of Hell or no, surely such grace showered down as a gift from Our Kindly Lady?

One life; one death. Well, Tristan had died, and I was still here. But the potion raged still, it was vengeful, it had been cheated. It would fight back.

Brangane came with me on the ship; she took charge as my own will faltered. The ship drifted listlessly for a few days, fetching up on King Mark's shores. I would go home to the husband I wanted to love, who had loved me without coercion for thirty years, through my endless betrayals, and the treason of his subject and heir. Mark hadn't wanted to marry; he tried to keep the kingdom for Tristan, his ideal knight. Of course, he changed his mind when Tristan told him of my beauty, hoping to make his dear lord happy, and himself less exposed to the plots of courtiers. Let me come home to my lord. But the potion scorched me, and I was forced to seek shelter in a convent famed for the healing powers of its sisters. Might they heal me, who had spent long weary years tending Tristan? Could I put my head in a woman's lap, and be stroked lovingly back to life? My own mother made that potion, the witch, and it could never be undone; it was the most binding magic, the binding of souls. And I would lose so much. Under its influence every sensation heightened. Cornish rain on my face felt like a god kissing me. A leaf's intricacy could drive you mad. Tristan and I were not celebrated conversationalists. All we seemed to say were things that seemed profound at the time, like, 'Look at that cloud', or 'Can you scent Byzantium on the wind?' Most people left us alone. It must have been obvious we were lovers, in the way we spoke the same words, the way our languid movements echoed like call and reply. We swapped clothes. I wore his sword and he my dress sometimes. And we thought no one noticed! We thought we were being discreet. Ignorant and helpless, we flaunted our love under Mark's nose. And we were the two people he loved most in the world. Oh this grand love makes you act out great cruelties.

The nuns took me in as a penitent adulteress. I did not hide my sins, and there was little point in hiding my identity. The great tragic lover Isolde was somewhat superfluous, not to mention a bit of a problem now there was apparently no tragic lover Tristan about. Even cloistered nuns had heard my story, and lined up giggling and pointing at my door.

Here began the worst time of my life, and I rued the day I crawled up that mast to fix on that black sail, and begged for the taste and smell of Tristan's body as if it were the elixir of life. For days, I vomited black bile. Huge insects climbed over my body, biting my legs, my arms; the worst bites burned in secret sexual places, as I'd known they would. I began to age, years in seconds, dizzyingly swooping down to catch me as I ran about the cell, like black crows, like black sails. My beauty fell away like ill-fitting clothes. I banged on the cell door, and begged sweet Lord Jesus to release me. But He sent fiends with burning brands. Fierce torments even for a penitent. 'Pity me', I cried, but He turned His face away. In His name, the nuns set fire to my eyes, they covered my skin with a leprous rash, scourged my poor body, as I confessed the sin of lust. For twenty days I lay wretched and close to death.

One day I heard singing outside my window, wafted over from the chapel on a balmy spring wind. The sun poured through, and I could faintly smell hyacinth. Oh, not the grand swooning perfume that would have made me lose consciousness in the time of the potion, but a gentle, delicate sensation. I must work hard and be attentive or I will find these senses so subtle I won't feel at all. Looking out of the window, I saw greenness everywhere. On the table someone had left a bunch of hyacinths in a bowl of water for me. The tiny florets curled like Tristan's hair.

There were other smells too. I used a pail of water to wash away the excrement in my straw. I washed my crusted clothes. I wept that a great queen should have lain in such filth, but it was mine and I must wash clean my life. Presently, feeling a little stronger, I asked for a mirror knowing the shock would be more than I could bear. Most of my hair had fallen out, and my bones poked through my skin. 'You gorgeous creature,' said Brangane, as she came to collect me. 'There'll be queues of lovers all the way home.' Home. And where would that be now? With my husband?

I will make it all up to him now. He will have the real Isolde, not a fake magic doll. What I can give him now comes from nature, from the earth that he stands on, not the stars he can't touch. He will welcome this honest, living, ageing, breathing, mortal love. How much better than sham quackery and witchcraft.

When I walked out of the convent I was surprised how the world had diminished, how drab its colours had become. I knew it would be like this. But once the world shimmered for me and I was a god. I took Brangane's hand. 'Remember the cave of lovers,' she said.

Ah, la foissiure a la gent amant. We found it after Mark banished us, past wasteland and desert. We found a marvellously carved door, barred against all who are not lovers, but for us it swung open at our approach. Inside, a great cavernous vaulted ceiling, like a cathedral. I know now it was blasphemy, Brangane, but then it seemed a holy thing to love. Veined green marble formed the floor, and near a window, the only furniture, a bed, of course, flashed red, purple, yellow crystal, as deep as stained glass. How these false trappings echo the monuments of our faith. At its head, white candles glowed softly. So still. Far away from the world, our kind refuge. And while we lived there we had no need of food. We feasted on each other's body like the blessed holy sacraments.

'Yes, I remember the cave of lovers. Leaving it was like the Fall, like being driven out of Eden. And yet it was a hideous place.'

'Hideous?' Brangane looks disbelieving. Her own love-life has been somewhat mundane.

'We were gods, Brangane, we glowed; our lovemaking in that cavern fuelled the sun; we felt its pulsing make the world grow green and swell the harvest; and all we did was lie there, gazing into each other's eyes, day and night, ecstasy day and night, craving more and more. And all around the stars wheeled in feeble imitation. I felt queasy with it, as if I had gorged myself on sweet delicacies, as if strong fists forced them down my throat. And the more we made love, the more my senses tingled, so that, what with this craving for Tristan, not being able to stop, I whirled round and round in ever fiercer sensation, pleasure was pain, but I couldn't stop, nor could Tristan. Outside, the kindly birdsong deafened me; the water in the gurgling stream felt like acid on my hand. Tristan's kisses left weals like whiplash wounds, and I wanted more and more, and I howled with desire fulfilled by torture. I kept thinking, this is all I want, and this is the greatest prison I could ever imagine, both at once. Can you imagine craving someone's body so much you think you will die without it, forced to make it your own life, while thinking, I don't actually like this man at all? You will know women who cry "Oh, you cannot imagine what he did to me this time", and you hear again and again the lists of insult and violence, and when you say "leave him", they turn in amazement and sigh "But I love him." '

I much preferred my husband.

My father was a king of Africa. I remember a shaded courtyard and lemons dangling like tiny suns, and women clapped their tinkling jewelled hands as I danced. Then we boarded a ship full of soldiers, and ran away from the sun as fast as we could. There were no more lemons and the sun was so sad we had gone that it started crying and never stopped. There was no more dancing, only a grey mist so deep I could barely see my hands, and the people in our new land moved labouredly as if under water. My jewels weighed heavy here in Ireland, but I had no wish to be without them, drenched by the insolent muttering rains. And my unsmiling servant-women, always scraping black mould from the castle walls with kitchen knives. That rasp of scouring like someone fighting to breathe.

Then Tristan came, with his harp. He taught me to read and write. He bore music and poetry across the sea. He taught me to play the harp exquisitely. He was like a young lady demurely parading her accomplishments. And everything I could do was taught by Tristan. He made me into someone else, he was a toymaker moulding the perfect doll. When I found out who had taken away my old self, given me a voice to sing where before I was mute and ignorant, I hated my knowledge, my beautiful voice, my delightful manners. 'I have civilised a savage,' he said, admiring his handiwork.

But he was a killer. He stabbed my uncle, whom I loved dearly.

Then my mother made the potion. She put into it all the scents of Africa. When I drank it I saw the lemon trees, heard the tinkle of women as their hands clapped for me. Lions nuzzled my face, and Arabia rained desert sand over my whole body. I danced back to my own land, lay on its loving breast, and listened for the sound of drumming, the leap of the gazelle. All the longing of my growing up melted away. And now I felt as a child, the hot sun rippling through my spine, bringing me out of Ireland's sullen dream of mist. But I was perceived as woman, all woman, all sex and doom and tragedy, by Tristan and everyone else. They looked at me and chorused, 'Sex and death, sex and death', like demented parrots as I was just coming alive, a long-suppressed giggle breaking out as I danced and tumbled. That is why I hate Tristan.

Mark loved me freely, without the violent straight-jacket of drugs. Do you not think his a greater love than Tristan's? He loved Tristan as friend and heir. He tried not to see when we flaunted our dalliance under his nose, even when every courtier so kindly shouted it. He pretended not to see my swelling belly or to comment on those yearly disappearances, those flimsy tales, and my slim return. Oh, the kindly woodcutters' wives I've supplied with infants. I never checked whether those apple-cheeked smiling women twinkled so wholesomely at the child or the money. For all I know they were drowned mewing in buckets or cast onto Cornish rocks. Mark tried to believe the best of us. 'Brangane, he never found out I'd tried to have you murdered because I thought you'd spill the beans. I am sorry.'

'This love is so ennobling, makes you do wondrous deeds, does it not?'

Don't pout at me. Myths aren't to be pouted at. The source

of my love was poison. It coursed through my veins and taught me infanticide and murder. That was my stinking wound that Tristan should have healed.

'Shall we go back to your husband?'

We went, but he did not know me. I feared he'd say, Look you expect me to love a skeleton, a freak with all its hair fallen out, while Tristan had the most beautiful woman the world has seen? I expected horror and revulsion. I am a penitent; I accept punishment. But this listless indifference? Once, in the cave of lovers, as I lay with Tristan, I saw Mark's face at the tiny window. He was watching with the longing face of a poor shut-out child. Shut out, irrevocably. I could see from his hand movement he was masturbating, gazing at us, and masturbating. When he had me as his queen he rarely wanted me, you know. He wanted Tristan wanting me, I think. When I returned to Tintagel, I found him slumped in a chair, pulled close to the window, staring intently at the sea. I started to speak, and he shushed me, putting a finger to his lips and pointing to the grey waters. He was listening, listening for Tristan's cries, looking out as if he could see them, looking past the rocks studded with mussel shells like babies' fingernails that cling to keep from drowning. Whether I came back beautiful or hag-ridden didn't seem to matter at all. I wasn't even relevant. He just sat there lost in the sea, listening fiercely, listening for Tristan.

Animal Husbandry

It is good to sit here in the dark. I will wait to light the lamps, but just now I can hear the river being swallowed by the cold black lake, and the scurrying of small creatures outside the cottage. It must be late: I have forgotten the time. It is good not to think, not to see anything through the glass. Last night, when I lit the paraffin lamp, the windows seethed suddenly with swarms and swarms of moths coming at me, trying to smother me in a vast tormented blanket.

I know your tricks. And the stray dog that howls at the door, scratches and whimpers. Get away! Your friend has gone now. He'll not be coming back.

If only I could have seen him, at a distance, just as the man, not even seeking to know his name or spoil his beautiful solitude, just watched the taut body poised to dive into the lake, or climbing up the crags, panting at the summit and staring at the horizon as if he owned the world. With his explorer's profile, his lovely completeness. Ah, yes. I wouldn't dare intrude. And I can't help seeing him as the monarch of the glen, oh God, it's such a serious picture, this misunderstood loner, standing high and free and cold-showered and white and Aryan, high and free over everyone else, running as fast as he can from the contamination of other people, that I have to laugh.

To think I've followed that manly profile since school, fasci- nated by the rich stillness of his silence. I spent hours, years, imagining what was going on in his head, especially since his rages were so inexplicable. I learned to soothe, to anticipate

36

trouble. If I could work out what he was thinking, if I could really understand him, I'd be able to make his life so happy, there'd be no need for this reckless, blind anger. I could smooth his brow and he'd love me. As I loved him. But did I really? Trying to predict his mood, deflect his wounded rage, cosset and understand him made me so tired I had to give up work and have a lie-down every afternoon. Did I never think that his silence meant he had nothing in his head worth saying?

In the evenings I'd prepare supper, and his few friends sometimes dropped by to rave about the crimes of the human race. They were all vegans with plastic shoes, but they didn't mind a jar or five. They looked like fierce Old Testament prophets, lamenting and cursing all night. I didn't say much, usually. Everything I thought was heresy. Every word I spoke was dangerous. It was better to keep quiet for an easy life. Basically, animals could do no wrong, they were noble and lovely and furry and lived in harmony with their environment. Whereas Man . . . (And they left Woman out of it – her doings seemed irrelevant or frivolous, or even worse, and I was personally implicated in the crimes of Man from the way they scowled at me as an unbeliever . . .) And, of course, animals never kill for pleasure, only when they need food, unlike evil old Man . . . 'But . . .', I started to say, and they'd already moved on to something else. I was thinking of the way a cat torments a mouse for pleasure, and, better, of the adult male animals who have to be kept apart from the newborn. I tried to tell them about Jane Goodall's film showing one group of chimpanzees gleefully practising genocide on another. I thought they'd be interested.

'Look, this is Science, this is fact . . .' I got well into my clinching argument, a programme I'd seen on the wild dogs of the Serengeti, but they kept interrupting, shouting, so I stopped. They gave me a pitying glance, as if I were deranged or brainwashed, and asked for coffee. I've always been a good hostess. 'You're so middle-class,' they said with contempt. But they still expected to be brought coffee.

When I came back from the kitchen, they'd moved on to birth control in the Third World and the dangers of overpopulation. Man was up to his tricks there, too, and using up all the earth's resources. My dear husband would start his daring monologue, saved up till the whisky took effect, on famine in Africa being no bad thing because there are too many people there anyway. He loved it when a hapless Oxfam collector rattatted at the door. He explained that aid organizations ought to be banned, it was a waste of money that could help fight vivisection or save the whales. You heard an appalled gasp as the samaritan fled.

'Aren't you being just a little bit inhuman?' I began, but they asked for more whisky. Their conversations made me feel so stupid, so ill-informed.

When we had the Vegetarians for Abortion Rally, I tried to understand. 'But I thought you were against harming living creatures? You hate those women who use animal placenta creams to keep their skin looking young.' This was a mistake. My husband practically foamed at the mouth and rolled on the floor like Laurence Olivier playing Othello.

Whenever I got pregnant, I was so happy. Perhaps this time he would love me. It was made from him, after all. But it was human, so it had to go. The baby or him. And I didn't dare choose the baby. I had no job, and years with Harry had worn away my selfhood until I wandered round transparent, without edges. I drifted like a wraith. When it snowed I was amazed to see I had made footprints.

I loved him. He put me in hospital a few times when I was pregnant. Broken ribs, nose, usual sort of thing. He didn't talk much but he could make his feelings clear. The last abortion nearly killed me. I just couldn't stop crying. I knew it would make him worse, but I was raw with loss. When I came out of the clinic I tried to slash my wrists. There was a lot of blood on the bedcover and carpet. Harry refused to react. That would only pander to her, I felt him thinking. He came upstairs with a bucket of soapy water and a J-cloth.

'Look at the mess you made. Clean it up.'

'I think I'll need more than a J-cloth.'

I thought of another nature programme, about a mother chimpanzee and her son. She loved and spoiled him, the last child of her old age. She carried him on her back, like the other children, though he grew heavier, he grew adult, he grew bigger than her, and there she still struggled, carrying him until she was older and older and his weight broke her back and killed her.

The doctor gave me tranquillizers and sympathized with my bad luck in walking into so many ladders and falling down so many flights of stairs. Harry was his patient too, and a smarter dressed, more polite patient than Harry you never met. Shame about his clumsy wife. Carefully, I gulped my tablets from a dainty china cup patterned with blue dragons chasing pink roses, the last of a wedding present set I'd smashed accidentally through our marriage. Harry had resignedly swept up the broken pieces. He refused to buy any new ones since I'd wasted the others, so we took turns drinking from our one cup.

When he disappeared at night sometimes, I knew he was with another woman. Of course I was jealous. But Harry's nature was solitary; I knew there'd be fierce couplings on mountainsides, the women rolled in pine needles, bruised, muddy, resinous; they'd feel like Leda possessed by a wild force of nature they half feared, blindly giving themselves and bewildered when the spent god pushes them away and runs with the wind at his back.

All these affairs. All this glamour. It's the silence that draws them. As though words are too easy, are not worthy of the profundity of his soul. All this sexuality, and none of it directed at me. Since the last abortion, he had refused to sleep with me. Afraid I might try trickery, because I dearly wanted a child. How could that be the only reason, though? He could buy condoms, he could have a vasectomy. No, no, he drew away from me. Even using my body would be too much acknowledgement. He might find himself kissing me. It could be mistaken for affection. He'd get on well with old Onan: he'd rather spill seed on the barren ground than give it to me to make a child from love.

You ask how I could love such a man? Open your eyes. Women everywhere do. Why did Callas love the brute Onassis? He was the only man to give her *le petit mort*, to bond her in pleasure. I can't break these bonds, they bite too deeply into my flesh. I think perhaps only death can break them.

And I can't break my longing for a child.

Can you choose these loves? Does free will come into it at all? A surge of hormones, your own body betraying you so its genes survive. Your body isn't interested in your uniqueness, your selfhood, just its own immortality. No matter if it destroys you.

Soon I will be forty. In my family we have early menopause. Tick, tick. I took big risks: I am braver than I thought. I had to conceive without Harry's knowledge. I always do, but it's even harder when you're not having sex. Unfortunately there was no other man: we were living in the country being at one with nature and avoiding the contamination of human contact, so that limited the field at bit. I made seduction plans. A feast of the senses. Enough wine to make the memory of the night hazy, but not so much that he couldn't rise to the occasion. The crudest black lacy lingerie. Harry usually scorned the gentle accoutrements of love: 'Animals don't need suspender belts,' and regarded these as decadent. You don't know what deca-dent is, Harry. What a memorable night for me. It was almost like being loved. Even better, the morning a few weeks later when the home pregnancy kit turned blue as a jay's feather, as the boundless sea, as the soaring sky.

The next stage brought more danger. We went on holiday. Harry always liked the Lakes, and this summer booked a self-, or rather, me-catering cottage, on a spectacular mountain peak, like the backdrop of a theatre specializing in melodrama.

'A millionaire couldn't have a better view,' said Harry with satisfaction. He stared motionlessly from mountaintops for hours, being at one with the usual and thrusting out his god-like profile, while I dragged heavy shopping bags up the steep overgrown path, peeled potatoes, and tried to concoct delectable fare from the decadent tins of the tourist shop.

'This the best you can do?' he would snarl, unimpressed, but I didn't care. I had a baby hiding until the time was right. My belly was still flat. The baby knew it had to lie low. We had plenty of time.

While Harry walked stern and solitary, I wandered about in vague circles, not too far from the house. One morning I came across an old quarry, full of slimy brown water. A steep descent, but I balanced carefully, to protect my treasure. Everywhere, frogs copulated, hundreds of them, as the sun shone indulgently. The pond was the colour of treacle, thick and teeming. I sat on a carpet of wild flowers and breathed their life. I lay with my legs open to the sun and prayed for my child, for my own life. Faintly, I heard laughter: flash of a woman leaping the stream, holding a bow taut, running on. A panting, younger laugh from a cave behind me. I jumped up, climbed into the cave, but it was empty, just a sad echo chamber to my cries. As I got used to the darkness, I saw a fleeting shape flicker by, light as a gazelle. As it ran, it dropped some trinkets: a shell comb, blue glass beads from a broken necklace, and a posy of the same flowers I had lain upon a few minutes before.

Each day I came, and each day the child would leave another token. A favour for me to wear. A purse, some smooth grey pebbles, a jay's feather. An ammonite, curled like the spine of my child inside me. Each day I grew stronger, and ran to hear clear flutey laughter, teasing and healing and daring me.

I decided to tell Harry. I'd been dreaming of the wild dogs of the Serengeti. In the film, the leader of the pack, a bitch, begins to hate another bitch. She tries to humiliate and destroy the weaker animal, and singles her out of the pack for punishment. What her crime is, we never learn. She is broken for the fun of it. Whenever her rival has puppies the leader drags them away, one by one, and kills them. Every time, the mother gamely wags her tail at the leader as if to say, no hard feelings, then gives the gesture of submission – what is it again, backside in the air? – because if she doesn't, she's finished, and she must endure it until the leader gets bored and chooses another victim.

I knew Harry would be so angry he'd lose control. Blows to the stomach this time, casualty (far away), miscarriage immediate. At the least. A real carpet-chew. Flaring nostrils, foam at the mouth. At least he wouldn't have the element of surprise. I decided to tell him while we were swimming, at sunset, in the lake beneath our little terrace. A perfect end to the day. The water blazed like arterial blood and the air was so soft it was like a blessing. I wasn't disappointed, as he pulled my face under the water, and then my legs were tangling in tendrils of slimy weeds. Snakily, they insinuated their way up my body, until their heavy mass was dragging me down; startled, I recalled that the last time I'd felt this sensation was when the full rich skirts of my wedding gown, the layers of crisp, thick lace, the heavy dull satin, the hooped underskirt, the garlanded bows where the folds gathered up like a milkmaid's dress, had made it impossible to stagger and totter after Harry onto the carriage whose horses would gallop us away to a new life together. 'If you can bloody walk without falling over,' Harry had shouted that special day. I woke up, dancing among the weeds as I'd danced on my wedding day, working my legs free, kicking like a can-can dancer, kicking up through the water at Harry's manly groin, kicking his startled face as he fell backwards in amazement.

I wait to hear your animal friends howling at your death,

Harry, echoing through the mountains. They are as silent as you are.

I've put on some Mozart. I've turned it up as loud as I can, so you can hear, Harry. When it has finished I will read you a speech from *The Winter's Tale* about great creating Nature. A pity you are blind in the deep dark water so you cannot see the colour plates in my book on Leonardo.

I'm going to throw stones at that whining stray dog.

It is good to sit here in the dark. Wafting from the Aga, the air is thick with venison in red wine. Just under the violins, I hear the squeals of mice caught in my traps. I have counted the money you left me, and am full of admiration for your thrift.

I will carry my daughter on my back as long as she needs, we will cast a single shadow with hard, clear outlines. I will protect her with the savagery of a tigress.

Nature is red in tooth and claw.

VIKRAM CHANDRA

Shakti

We had been talking about Bombay that evening. Somebody, I think it was Patel, was telling us about Bahadur Shah, who gave the island to the Portuguese for their help against the Moghuls. 'At the beginning of everything great and monstrous,' said Khanna, 'is politics.'

'You're forgetting the other half,' Subramanium said. 'Remember, the Portuguese gave the island to the British as part of Catherine of Braganza's dowry.'

'Meaning what?' I said.

'Meaning this,' said Subramanium. 'That the beginning and end of everything is a marriage.'

What you must understand about Sheila Bijlani is that she was always glamorous. Even nowadays, when in the corners of parties you hear the kind of jealous bitching that goes on and they say there was a day when she was nothing but the daughter of a common chemist-type shopkeeper growing up amongst potions and medicines, you must never forget that the shop was just below Kemp's Corner. What I mean is that she was a shopkeeper's daughter, all right, but after all she saw the glittering women who went in and out of the shop, sometimes for aspirin, sometimes for lipstick, and Sheila watched and learned a thing or two. So even when you see those early photographs from the Walsingham School – where she was, yes, the poor girl – what you should notice is the artistic arrangement of the hair, which she did herself, and the shortness of the grey skirt, which she achieved every morning with safety pins when she reached school. Even in those days there was no argument that Sheila had the best legs at Walsingham, and so when she finished with college and next we heard that she was going to be a hostess with Air France, it all made sense, I mean who else would you imagine pouring champagne for a movie star in some Frenchly elegant first-class cabin or running down the steps of the Eiffel Tower, holding her white stilettos in one tiny and graceful hand, it had to be Sheila.

Air hostessing in those times didn't mean tossing dinners at drunks on the way back from Dubai or the smell of a Boeing bathroom after a sixteen-hour one-stop from New York. Remember, travelling abroad was rare then, and so all the air hostesses were killingly beautiful and Xavier's graduates and they all had this perfume of foreign airs which they wafted about wherever they went, and Sheila was the most chic of them all, the way she smoked a True could break your heart, placing it ever so delicately between her lips and leaving just a touch of deep deep red on the very tip. And the men came around, the princes and the *jamsahebs* in their convertibles promising adventure, the cricketing knights in their blue blazers of glory, the actors' sons offering dreams of immortality. We used to see Sheila then in a flash as a car roared around the curve on Teen Batti, and we would sigh because somewhere there was a life that was perfect and wonderful.

So we were expecting a prince for Sheila, at least, a flashing star of some sort, but she disappointed us all when she married Bijlani. He was USA-returned and all; but from some place called Utah and what was electrical engineering anyway when you had Oxford cricketing royalty on the phone, but Sheila liked Bijlani and nobody knew why. He was square and later fat and mostly quiet and he told everyone he wanted to make appliances, which was all very well and good but four-speed electric mixies weren't exactly dashing, dammit. They met at a party at Cyrus Readymoney's and Bijlani was sitting quiet in a corner looking uncomfortable, and Sheila watched him for a long time, and when she asked, Readymoney said, 'That's Bijlani, he used to be in school with us but nobody knows his first name. He wants to make mixies.' Then Readymoney, who was dressed in black, snapped his fingers and said, 'Let's boogie, baby,' but Sheila looked up her nose at him, what I mean is she was a foot shorter than him but she somehow managed to look him up and down like he was a worm, and she said, 'Why don't you go into a corner and squeeze your pimples, Cyrus?' and then she went and took charge of Bijlani. Now you must understand that when nowadays you see old Bijlani looking hugely regal in a black silk jacket, it all started that night when Sheila took him out of his corner and tucked in his shirt at the back and took him around, never mind his sweating, and kept him by her side the whole evening. I don't think he ever tried to understand the whats and whys of what happened, I think Bijlani just took his blessings gratefully into his bosom and built mixies for Sheila. Everyone made fun of him at the start, but they went and got married and people rolled their eyes, and a year passed and then another and another, and then they suddenly reappeared with an enormous flat on Malabar Hill, and there was a huge intake of breath clear down to Bandra and now the story was that she had married him for his money. If you tried to tell someone that the first mixie was built with Sheila's money from a thousand trips up and down an Air France aisle, the next thing you heard was that she was paying you in cash and kind and more to say nice things about her. Her success drew out the venom up and down the coast of Bombay, let me tell you, it's a wonder the sea didn't curdle and turn yellow.

So now Sheila was on the hill, not quite on the top but not quite at the bottom either, and from this base camp she began her steady ascent, not quickly, she had patience and steadiness. It was done over years, it cost money, and the hill resisted, it fought back right from the start. In that first year Sheila threw cocktail parties and lunches and Derby breakfasts, and it

became clear to her that the top of the hill was the Boatwalla
Mansion, which stood on a ridge surrounded by crumbling
walls, overlooked by the frame of a new apartment building
coming up just above. The Mansion wasn't really on top of the
hill, and it was dingy and damp, but all the same Sheila knew
it was where she had to go to get to the real top, the only one
that mattered. For the first year Sheila sent invitations to Dolly
Boatwalla every other week and received typed regrets one
after the other, she saw Dolly Boatwalla at parties, and finally
she was introduced under an enormous chandelier at a plastics
tycoon's birthday party. Dolly Boatwalla was long and horsy-
looking, she looked down an enormous nose and murmured,
'*Ha-aaloo,*' and looked away into the middle distance. Sheila
understood this was part of the rules of current diplomacy and
was happy all the same, and even when the next weekend at
the racecourse somebody by mistake introduced them again
and Dolly said '*Ha-aaloo*' as if for the first time, Sheila didn't
mind a bit and took it as part of her education. Sheila smiled
and said, 'You look wonderful, what a lovely scarf.' She was
willing to let Dolly have her way, and if Dolly had been a little
less Boatwalla and a little more sagacious, she could have
adopted Sheila and taught her and patronized her in a thousand little ways, but Dolly saw only a little upstart, which
Sheila was, but Dolly didn't see the ferocious political will, that
hidden glint. This is how wars start.

How it all really began was this: finally Dolly accepted one
of Sheila's invitations. Actually she had no choice but to
accept, which may be why she went from being coolly conde-
scending to openly sarcastic. And it started. What happened
was that Sheila had finally been able to join the Lunch Club.
Not many people in Bombay knew that the Lunch Club
existed. Most of the people who knew what it was also knew
that they couldn't be in it. The women in the Lunch Club met
once a month for lunch at one of the members' houses. After
lunch they played cards. Then they had tea and went home.
That was it, nothing very exciting on the face of it, but if you

knew anything you knew that that was where marriages were arranged and sometimes destroyed, deals were made, casually business was felt out, talk went on about this minister in Delhi and So-and-So's son who was school captain at Mayo. It was the real stuff, you know, *masala* grinding, how the world works. So Sheila's name came up, naturally, several times, and every time, Dolly sniffed and said, Not our type, really, and that finished off Sheila's chances. But then Sheila made friends, fast ones, and they pushed it, they liked her, for her money, for her nippy wit, for her snap, and maybe it was also that some of them were tired of Dolly, of her Boatwalla sandwiches served soggy but with absolute confidence, of her pronouncements and the delicate way she patted her pursed lips with a napkin after she ate pastries. So they insisted, and it was clear there would be either agreement or a direct struggle, and Dolly decided that it wasn't worth risking defeat, so finally she flung an eyebrow towards the roof, sighed, and said, 'All right, if you must, can we talk about something else, this is really so boring.'

So this was how they all gathered at Sheila's home. Her new house, that is. It was a white two-storied mansion, really, with a bit of lawn in front and a little behind, and of course even though it was big money for the time it was nothing on the sprawling Boatwalla jungles from colonial times, when you could buy land on the hill for nothing. Still, a house was something, actually it was a lot, and the Lunch Club oohed and exclaimed as they came up the short flight of stairs and into the front room, Sheila had it absolutely right, there were the big double doors inlaid with brass and then a carved wooden elephant's foot with walking sticks in it and a Ganesha that was chipped and old and grey stone and it had to be some major antique, two huge plants on either side, and a diffused white gleam through a skylight, and in the halo, changeless and eternal as the day that Bijlani threw his future kingdom at her feet, was Sheila, her skin glowing, her hair as dark as a Malabar wave on a moonless night. She welcomed them silently, smiling as they chattered around her, she led them through a long hall, past a study with a huge brown desk and a brass lamp, past a room full of leather-bound books and brown and red Kashmiri rugs, and finally into the dining room, where on a stone-topped dining table gleamed twelve place settings in silver. Here finally Sheila spoke her first words of the afternoon, 'My son,' because a young boy was standing near the table peering at the fantastic ikebana flower arrangement at its centre. Sheila ruffled his hair, and he turned his head to look at her, and the ladies murmured. He was certainly very good-looking. Bijlani's stolid bulk had passed into a sort of slow, unblinking expressiveness in his eyes, a kind of silence, and he had Sheila's sharp features. 'Say hello,' Sheila said, and he did, shaking hands with each one of them. Mani Mennon laughed over her shoulder as he gravely bowed over her hand, 'Better watch out for this one.' Meanwhile Sheila leaned into the corridor and called, 'Ganga! Take Sanjeev to his room, will you?'

Ganga came in, a short wiry woman with her hands still wet from dishes. She had her red sari pulled between her legs and she pushed back a strand of loose hair with one hand. As Sheila walked Sanjay to the door Ganga took his other hand and they smiled at each other over his head. 'Isn't he so cute?' Mani Mennon said, and as she did, Sheila turned and saw the look on Dolly's face, a kind of absurd pursing of the nostrils, an unmistakable look of offence, as if she had just begun to smell something bad. As everyone went towards the table Mani Mennon hung back and whispered at Sheila, 'She has *French* maids.' It was true. They weren't actually French, usually Keralans, but all the same the petits fours at the Boatwalla Mansion were served by maids in black dresses and those frilly things around their heads. Mani Mennon rolled her eyes. She was Sheila's main supporter in the Lunch Club, her sponsor, and she hated Dolly Boatwalla but was absolutely silenced by her, robbed of speech and presence of mind by Dolly's height and ruthlessness and way of commanding a room. Mani Mennon was short and funny and plump and couldn't think of any reasons why she should be silenced by Dolly, but always was anyway. 'Boatwalla bitch,' Mani Mennon hissed. Sheila shrugged and took her calmly by the elbow and led her to the others.

'Have some quail,' she said. The food was unusual, small and spicy, made by a Lucknow cook from a Nawabi family. The tastes were light and chased each other across the palates with such foreign essences that they had to exclaim that it was all perfect, because they had never tasted anything like it before. Dolly held a silver fork at an angle and sawed at a tiny wing, and even she was puzzled and pleased, you could see that. Afterwards they sat on the sofas, luxuriously sunk in the pillows and lingering over the sweet dish, a concoction of almonds and cream so light you barely felt it on the tongue. Dolly began to be funny. She sat on a couch by herself, one leg bent over the other, in her cream pants suit, all long lines from the silk sheen of her leg to the nose, which was a little bony but very elegant. She told cruel stories about people doing silly things or embarrassing themselves or just being stupid and not knowing about something that everybody knew. Dolly had a great sense of timing and was a good mimic and it was impossible not to laugh at her stories. They sat in a little semi-circle around her and laughed. Sheila laughed, and Mani Mennon laughed. Mani Mennon whispered to Sheila, 'She must tell stories about me too,' and then she laughed at a story about a Punjabi woman at the club who pronounced *pizza* like it was written and who dressed her daughters in too much gold.

Finally everyone grew quiet in an afternoon haze of contentment. There was no doubt it had been an enormously successful lunch, and Dolly had been allowed to dominate it completely. Now it was almost over, and there was a quietness in the air as everyone relaxed with the thought that it would actually get over without any horrendous tension, and as they walked towards the front door everyone was exhausted from the relief and strange disappointment of it all. Then Mani

Mennon startled everyone by squeaking, 'Hussain!' They were passing by the room with the bookshelves, and what Mani Mennon had noticed on the wall opposite the hallway was a large canvas, the chariot of the sun, gold and red. She went fluttering into the room with her arms held out, and stood swaying in front of the painting. It was quite overwhelming, with its rich swirl of colour and the horses as if they would burst from the canvas, and everyone clustered in front of it. Dolly hung back in the hallway but then everyone crowded forward and she was alone, so she came forward reluctantly and stood behind them all. 'It's your second one, isn't it, Sheila?' said Mani Mennon. 'It's wonderful. Look at those yellows.' And then, seeing Dolly behind the others, she said, smiling, 'It's a Hussain, Dolly.'

Dolly tilted her head back. 'Is it?' she said. Her head tilted further. 'Oh. Is that what it is?' She smiled. 'Freddie has a few of those at his office.'

Sheila was standing next to her. Without a word, Sheila turned and walked back into the hallway. They followed her, and she walked to the door, opened it, and held it open. They walked past, saying thank yous, and she smiled, but her eyes were opaque and she never took her hand off the door-knob. Dolly walked past and murmured, 'Thank you so much, darling.' Sheila shut the door and the click was very firm and crisp and everyone knew then that something had started.

Sheila sat in her office among the books and tried to think about what she had felt in that moment. It hadn't been anger, more a kind of recognition. In that instant she had felt suddenly outside her body, standing somewhere else and looking at both of them. What she had seen was that she was herself perfect, she was petite, she had an acute sense of colour and line and so her clothes fell on her exactly and well, her features were small and sharp, her hair was thick, and her vivacity came from her intelligence. Dolly was not perfect, she was long everywhere, she was sallow, she wore old jewellery sometimes missing a link here and there, today she wore a tatty green scarf over her shirt, and that was just it. Sheila was perfect and she knew that however hard she tried she could never achieve the level of careless imperfection that Dolly flaunted. It had nothing to do with perseverance or intelligence and it took generations. It couldn't be learned, only grown with the bone. It was absolutely confident and sure of itself and easy. Dolly had it and she didn't: looking at it honestly Sheila knew this. She knew it and was absolutely determined that if it took her the rest of her life she would defeat Dolly. That it had come to open conflict she knew, and she would not stand losing.

'*Mem Sahib*.' Ganga was standing in the doorway, leaning against the side, a hand cocked on her hip. She was wearing a dark-red sari with a gold-stamped border. Ganga was dark and very thin, she flung herself at her work with such velocity that it was necessary to put the glassware by the side of the washbasin, otherwise as she sped through the plates crystal would inevitably crunch somewhere in the pile. Ganga had been recommended by Sheila's next-door neighbour. She worked, as nearly as Sheila could tell, in another dozen houses up and down the hill, and she sped from one to another without a pause the entire day, after which she stood in a local train for an hour and fifteen minutes to get out to Andheri, where she lived. It had taken Sheila six months to get her to eat lunch, which she did squatting in a corner of the kitchen and holding a plate directly in front of her face for greater efficiency.

'It was a good lunch?' Ganga said.

'Yes,' Sheila said. For the first year they had known each other, Ganga had been courteous but dry, her face always expressionless and impossible to read. Then one day, on her way out, seeing Sheila sitting at her desk in the study as usual, she paused in the hallway, her whole body still pointed at the front door, to ask, What do you do in here? Accounts, Sheila had said, for our business, pointing to the ledgers piled up and the sheets of paper that folded out to cover half the room.

Ganga had nodded silently and gone on her way, back up to her normal speed with the first step, but since then she would stop in the doorway, one foot in front of the other, leaning sideways, one elbow angled out, and they would talk for a few minutes.

'Well,' Sheila said. 'It went well.'

Then they talked about their children. Ganga had a daughter named Asha. Then Ganga tightened her *dupatta* about her waist and it was time for her to leave. 'Going,' she said, clipping the word now, and she went.

When Ganga got home it was seven-thirty. She put down a small packet of *jira* and set about making dinner. There was a single lightbulb in the single room, and Asha was sitting under it studying, or at least flipping the pages of a book. Asha was dressed in a flowered shirt and a skirt that reached her ankles. Her hair was pulled back and neatly oiled, and around her plait she wore a single string of white *mogra* flowers. She was sitting cross-legged with her spelling book in her lap, her chin in her hands, and now she darted a quick look from huge brown eyes at her mother.

'All right, all right,' Ganga said. 'Come eat.'

They sat near the doorway and ate from brass plates, which were old but shiny. Outside, people were still passing, and occasionally somebody would say something to Ganga. The lane was narrow, and whoever walked by had to brush close to the door. Across the lane there was a narrow gutter which flooded in the rains, and behind that more shacks made of wood, cloth, cardboard, and tin. Later, when it was dark, Ganga would sit in the doorway and talk to her neighbours. Most of them were from the same village in the Ghats near Poona, but to the left where the lane curved it became a mostly Malayalee locality. Today they mostly talked about a man in their own community who drank so much that he finally lost his watchman job. 'He's a fool,' Ganga said. 'You always knew that.' It was true. They had all known him and they had always known that.

Ganga had arrived in Bombay eleven years before with her husband, who had come back to his village to marry, and since then she had lived in the same place. Ramesh, the husband, had been a mill worker in the days before the labour disputes and the big lockouts. He had been a Marxist, and he was killed, stabbed, in a quarrel with another union the year after Asha was born. Ganga remembered him mostly as a melancholy sort of man who seemed to cultivate his own sadness. It was only in the month after his funeral that she found out that he was said to have killed two men himself in the same union fight. But anyway now the mills were closed and the years had passed. Now it seemed that Ganga was going to move, and this was the news she had to give her neighbours. Two stops up on the Kurla line she had found an empty plot, and she planned to build her *kholi* there.

'*Pukka?*' said Meenu, her neighbour, her voice a little breathless because brick would cost more, and everyone knew that Ganga worked so much that she must have money, but nobody knew how much.

'Yes,' Ganga said. 'Ten thousand for the land, five for the construction.'

'Fifteen,' Meenu said.

'Yes,' Ganga said. 'I don't have it.'

'How will you manage?'

Ganga shrugged. She didn't tell them what she planned because she wasn't sure she would get the money, and she didn't want to sound sure before she was. That afternoon it had occurred to her to ask Sheila for a loan. Sheila had said that the lunch had gone well, but the concentrated expression on her face, the set of her shoulders as she sat among her books was not that of a happy woman. Looking at her then Ganga had realized that this was after all a woman of business, somebody who wanted things from the world, and had realized that she should ask Sheila for the money. She wanted to wait for a few days, let the thought sit in her stomach, because she had learned from the world to be careful when one could, since often there was no time for care. Now she had a month from the owner of the plot to come up with the money, and so she waited for a week. It still made sense, so one day after lunch she asked Sheila, and Sheila said, 'Of course,' went into the bedroom for a few minutes and came back with a stack of notes. It was no fuss. They talked terms and it was decided that Ganga was to pay it back monthly over six years.

But leaving was a fuss. They had lived in that nameless lane for a long time, Asha since she was born, and Meenu organized the people up and down the street to give them a send-off. They rented a television set and a video player and they watched films all night long, and it was very very late when Asha finally fell asleep with her head in her mother's lap. Ganga sat in the darkness, an arm over her daughter, and felt the loss as a tightness in the stomach, a kind of relentless wrenching, and the coloured light from the screen flickered on her face as she wept. But the next day when they loaded up their belongings into a handcart she was crisp and organized, and she led the way, holding Asha with one hand and a bundle with the other and tireless in her stride, until the men pushing the handcart leaned against it and begged for mercy.

Their new *kholi* was small, but during the rains it was dry, and Ganga kept it in good repair. There were some two-storied houses on their street, built very narrow on tiny plots, and at the end of the lane there was a grocery shop built like a cupboard into a gap between two walls. Also there was a pan seller who sold cigarettes and matches and played a radio from morning till night. Their years in this street were ordinary, and Ganga continued her work as before, coming and going with a regularity that her neighbours began to depend on.

Finally what disturbed their life was Asha's beauty. When she was fifteen a local bootlegging *tapori* fell in love with her.

He was at least ten years older than she was, a grown man with some reputation in his chosen trade of gangsterism and some style, he wore tailored black shirts always, and he fell in love with her ripeness. She was not tall, but there was a certain weight about her body, a youthful heaviness that she made a great show of hiding. She was a student of the movies, and always had flowers in her hair, white or yellow ones. His name was Girish, and he fell in love with a glance that she threw at him coming out of a morning show of 'Coolie'. After that he spent his time sitting on the raised platform at the end of their lane, waiting for her to pass, polishing his dark glasses on his shirt. When she did she never looked at him, but the force of his yearning caused her to duck her head down and blush darkly, amazed and a little frightened and feeling something that was not quite happiness.

Ganga knew nothing about this until the neighbours told her. She had seen him sitting on the platform, spreading out a handkerchief before he sat down, but she had paid no attention because it had nothing to do with her. The evening when she found out, she sat in her doorway for a long time. When she shut the door, she came in and found Asha sitting on her charpoy, reading a film magazine. As she watched, a wisp of hair fell across Asha's cheek, and the girl pushed it back behind her ear, only to have it fall forward again. Idly, Asha flicked it away, the hair was heavy and thick and dark brown, and as Ganga watched her daughter's fingers move across her cheek and linger, the danger of it all pressed her heart like a sudden weight. She knew instantly and completely the violent allure of the black glasses, the coiled stance that projected danger, the infinitely dark and attractive air of tragedy.

'Tomorrow I will take you to your grandfather's,' Ganga said, louder than she had intended.

'What?' Asha said. 'In the village?'

'Don't argue,' Ganga said. 'You're going.'

But Asha wasn't arguing, she was silent, caught somewhere between heartbreak and relief. Her sobs that night in her bed weren't full of grief or even of sorrow, but of the tension of weeks. She left quietly and obediently with her mother, and in the train she smiled at the mountains and the zigzagging ascent of the tracks and the birds floating in the valley below. But in the village – called Asan – she grew sulky at the endless quiet of the long afternoon. Ganga was in no mood for sulks, having spent an unexpected 200 rupees on the tickets, and she put Asha to work straight away, in the kitchen and with the cows in the back. Ganga's father was small and very lean, as if every last superfluity of flesh had been burned away by season after season of a farmer's sun. She had brought him two shirts from Bombay, which he would wear on very special occasions. She spent two days in the village, straightening out the house and seeing to the repair of a waterway that came down the hill into their land. When she left she hugged Asha briefly, and she felt the youthful sigh more than she heard it. 'Don't be silly,' Ganga said. 'What have you seen of suffering yet?'

It was afternoon when she opened her door in Bombay. She went in and put down her bundle, smoothed down her hair once in a single movement, tucking back and tightening all at once, and then she reached forward for the *jhadoo*. She was sweeping under the bed with it when she heard the voice: 'What have you done with her?'

When she turned he was looming in the doorway, tall and silhouetted. The sunlight was blinding behind him, and she could see the glint of the perpetual dark glasses at the sides of his face.

'What,' she began, and then her throat closed up from fear. She stood holding the *jhadoo* in front of her with both hands, handle up, clutching it.

'If you married her to someone else,' he said hoarsely. 'If you married her.' He moved in the doorway slightly and Ganga's head reeled, her eyes dazzled. 'If you married her I'll kill you and her. And myself.'

He came in, closer to her, and now she could see him clearly. 'Where is she?' he said. 'Where?' But his head was moving from side to side and she understood that it was very dark in the *kholi* for him. He reached up and took off the spectacles and she saw his eyes, red-rimmed. He was very young, and under the sleeve of his black shirt his wrist was thin and bony.

She spoke: 'Don't you have a mother?'

A tear formed slowly and inexorably on his eyelid and rolled down his cheek, and she knew he could do exactly what he had said. She looked at him, into his eyes and the seconds passed.

'Go home,' she said.

A moment passed and then he turned and stumbled out of the doorway. She stood still, holding her *jhadoo*, for a long time, looking towards the door, until the light changed outside and evening came.

On the hill, it was generally agreed that the Shanghai Club was Sheila's master-stroke. There was a whole faction which insisted that Mr Fong was only a front man, that the money behind Shanghai was actually some of the Bijlani's industrial lucre, that, having diversified from mixies into plastics and transportation and pharmaceuticals, they had resources to spare. Of course there was no proof for any of this, but what was clear and needed no proof was that the whole thing started when the Bijlanis were blackballed at the Malabar Gym. Sheila and Dolly had conducted a ruthless but fiercely polite war for years, in which the victories were counted in receptions given and famous writers annexed and huge sums collected for causes, and the casualties were the bruised egos of the partisans of either side, who cut each other in Derby boxes and flicked razor-sharp looks over shoulders at openings. But there were some rules, a certain code of conduct that kept it all civilized until the incident of the blackball.

The Bijlanis had applied for membership to the Malabar Gymkhana, a little belatedly but they were busy people, this was understood, and their son was now old enough to want to play tennis and rugby at the Gym, and the passing of the application was a foregone conclusion. And then came the blackball, which was actually not a black ball but a little slip of blue paper at the quarterly meeting of the membership committee, and the blue paper had on it the single word. 'No.' Everyone looked at each other, astounded, but everyone avoided looking at Freddie Boatwalla, because the process was anonymous but of course who could it be but him? There was nothing to be done about it, the rules were clear and ancient and unamendable, a blackball was a blackball, if you weren't in you were out, there was no middle ground. The chairman burnt the slips according to the rule but those who saw the blue paper said the letters were blocked out and firm, and even before the meeting was over the members were talking about the indisputable fact that Freddie had after twenty years of membership suddenly put himself up for the committee, why now unless there was a plot, a plan, and that this was an unprecedented escalation. Freddie left the meeting without talking to anyone and afterwards he was seen drinking a stiff whisky-and-soda downstairs in the Jockey Bar. The bartender said he had come in and made a phone call first and then asked for his drink. Sitting outside on the long patio with the lazy ceiling fans and the field beyond, the commentators related this and said no more, the implications were clear.

Now everyone waited for the inevitable response from Sheila, and nothing happened. It was unbelievable that she had accepted defeat, and yet this was what some believed, and others insisted that it was merely a tactical feint, this doing nothing, watch and wait. The months passed, and in the fullness of time a Mr Fong announced that he was going to start a place called the Shanghai Club, and nobody noticed. No one knew who Mr Fong was, and there was no reason for anyone to ask, and nobody was interested in his club. Then it was known – nobody knew where this came from – that the Shanghai Club would admit only women as members, and furthermore only by invitation. That to do the inviting there was a committee of ten prominent women who were to remain anonymous – and suddenly the phones started ringing all over Bombay. Who was the committee? Nobody knew. Then the first invitation arrived, in a plain white envelope without a stamp, hand-delivered at the house of Bubbles Kapadia, of the Ganesha Mills Kapadias. 'We are pleased to offer you a charter subscription to the Shanghai Club', it said. 'We request the pleasure of your company at the opening on January 26th'. At about the same time in what must have been a sublimely timed leak, it became known – seemingly in the exact same minute from Nepean Sea Road to Bandra – that Sheila Bijlani and Mani Mennon were one-fifth of the committee, and that only a hundred memberships were to be offered. Now there was wild conjecture, endless lists were drawn up and debated, memories were searched for histories of friendship and betrayal, and suddenly that plain white envelope was the most coveted thing in the city. Mr Fong received so many calls that he changed his home number seven times, and still he was woken up in the middle of the night by desperate pleas from councilmen and captains of commerce. 'I'm afraid I can't do anything about it,' was his standard reply. 'I don't control the committee. They tell me what to do.' The Chief Minister himself made a resigned call to Mr Fong on behalf of the Pallow Toothpaste heiress, who sent a hundred and fourteen baskets of fruit to various houses in a scattershot attempt to flush out the committee. Nothing worked.

The white envelopes came in a trickle through October and November, and nobody could tell where one would show up next, and the exact count was tabulated and maintained with increasing tension as the months passed. Those who got one let it slip casually: 'Oh, guess what was under the door today?' and those who didn't affected not to care: 'I can't believe everyone's so crazy about this stupid Mr Fong's club.' Some pretended to sniff at the kind of people who were getting invitations: a policewoman – an inspector, but still; a documentary filmmaker; several journalists, some of them of the television variety. And when Ramani Ranjan Das, the erotic poetess, was invited, a whole faction of the Gym set, at the very north end of the patio, declared very dramatically and at great length that they were withdrawing from the Shanghai race, until Bubbles Kapadia asked how they knew they were in it. In the dead silence that followed Bubbles flicked her ash onto the table, drew long and at great leisure on her green cigarette holder, then got up and turned and disappeared in a great white cloud of triumphant smoke.

Of course Dolly behaved as if the Shanghai Club did not exist and never would. It was at the Gym, at lunch, that somebody first brought up the subject in front of her. The words dropped and suddenly silence spread around the table like a ripple. Everyone waited, but Dolly was staring into the middle distance, her eyes calm and genial, absolutely imperturbable, as if she was suddenly a stone-deaf idol, elegantly dressed. She had not heard it, even though the softly spoken words were heard from one end of the oak table to the other. After a while she picked up her knife and fork and cut a tiny little piece of quiche and ate it slowly and with pleasure. As the weeks passed and the hysteria mounted and the rumours flew and everyone talked about nothing but the Shanghai Club, she continued not to hear anything. She was absolute and unshakeable. The commentators argued: She must really be upset, some said, she must go home and cry in the bathroom. Nonsense, said the other, stronger, school of thought, it is all truly beneath her, she doesn't care a whit. As January 26th drew nearer she grew more and more to resemble a kind of stately ship in sail, constant and beautiful, unmoved by choppy waters, and her supporters grew delirious with admiration. It was true: she was magnificent in her dignity. One of the north-patio commentators said, in a tone which mingled exactly equal amounts of envy and quiet pride, 'After all, she *is* a Boatwalla.'

All this was true until the evening of January 15th. Bijlani came home, drew Sheila into their bedroom, locked the door, and related a strange and wondrous tale. He had been sitting, as was his custom, on the balcony of the Napier Bar above the Dolphin Club swimming pool, sipping at his nightly Martini. He did this every evening after his fifteen laps and massage, with the cane chair creaking gently under his bulk and the breeze in his hair. On this evening, he was startled out of his meditation by a man's voice: 'Hello, T. T.' Bijlani had acquired, over the years, with his increasing financial weight, with his famous and many-faceted magnitude, a name and a dense, magisterial composure. So his quick turn of the head, his spilling of his drink, was unprecedented but understandable – the man who stood uncomfortably over him, shifting from leg to leg, was Freddie Boatwalla.

Bijlani waved him into a chair, and when he sat Bijlani could see his face clearly in the light from the door. Freddie had always been thin, but now, in the single light against the darkness, he looked like a paper cutout, one of those black shadow figures from another century, nineteenth or maybe eighteenth or something. Bijlani knew their shipping company had been through some ups and downs, but who hadn't, it was no cause for this kind of deterioration. Bijlani waved to a bearer. 'Drink?' Bijlani said.

'Thanks, old boy,' Freddie said. 'Gin-and-tonic.' He crossed his legs, and Bijlani had a moment of hideous bilelike envy: Freddie's crease above the knee was absolutely straight, without needing a tuck or pull or even a pat. The white pants fell just so, like everything else. His name was actually Faredoon Rustam Jamshed Dara Boatwalla, but he had always been Freddie, son of Percy Boatwalla, grandson of Billy. There had been a great-grandfather, whose name Bijlani could never remember but who stood in full life-size glory in a niche near Crawford Market, haughtily ignoring the pigeons swarming around his feet.

'Nice evening, isn't it?' Freddie said.

'Very.' Bijlani was remembering the story about Freddie that everyone told again and again, that he had in the golden days of his youth bowled out Tiger Pataudi twice in two consecutive innings during a match at Cambridge.

'Heard about your pharmaceutical deal with the French. Good show,' Freddie said.

'Thanks.'

'We've been thinking in that direction ourselves. International hookups. Collaborations.'

'Yes.'

'Negotiating with an American party, ourselves. Difficult.'

'Really?'

'Oh, very. Arrogant sods. Full of themselves. But really it's the only way.'

'I'm sure.'

'Change, you know. Adaptation.'

'Absolutely.'

Freddie's drink came and they sipped in a silence that was not exactly companionable, but at least businesslike. Above them the lights of the tall buildings made a rising mosaic, and a swimmer's slow splashing in the pool beat a sleepy rhythm to and fro. Freddie put his glass down.

'Thanks for the drink. Have to be getting along. Dinner, you know.' He stood up., 'Can't stay away. Family. You know how these women are.' He laughed.

Bijlani tilted his head back, but Freddie was against the door now and it was hard to make out his face. 'Family,' Bijlani said. 'Of course.'

'You know, old boy, you ought to re-submit.'

'What's that?'

'Your application, I mean,' Freddie said. 'At the Gym. I'm sure that whole business was a mistake. Error. Lapse. Awful. Happens. Resubmit. We'll take care of it.' And with that he was gone.

When Bijlani told Sheila about this conversation, she sat very still for a moment, so immobile that she might have been frozen. Then only her eyes moved, and she looked up at

Bijlani. 'How interesting,' she said at last. 'Let's go down to dinner.'

That Freddie and T.T. had talked was known by everyone half an hour after it happened, and there was much speculation about what had actually been said. It was clear that some sort of deal had been made, that negotiations had happened, and now Dolly-watching took on a strange, fresh piquancy. When she received her white envelope, what would she do? Would she say something casually about the Shanghai Club at a lunch? Would she now hear the words that had rendered her deaf and blind? Everyone wanted to be there at the event itself, whatever and whenever it was, because it was completely unprecedented and sure to be delicious in many ways. But nothing happened. Dolly remained casually unaware and went about her business, and the days passed. It was now awfully close to the Shanghai opening and everybody was wound tight, what with fittings and appointments and plans. In those last few days you only had to say to someone, 'Has anything happened?' and they'd know what you were talking about.

But of course nothing did happen. Sheila told no one anything either, she was infuriatingly and politely private and unrelenting. Only Mani Mennon knew, because she had been there on the afternoon of January 25th, in Sheila's study, looking through a list as Sheila worked with a calculator and her endless files. 'Memsahib.' Ganga came in, picked up her half-pay from the desk, and paused long enough to watch Sheila make a notation in a long list of her installments. As Ganga left, Sheila smiled at her. The phone rang, and Sheila picked it up and said, as she had many times that afternoon, 'Sheila Bijlani.' Then there was a moment of silence, and Sheila stared at the receiver as it went on, from awkwardness into significance, and she looked at Mani Mennon and both of them knew instantly who it was.

'Hello,' the phone finally said, a little staticky and hissy. 'This is Dolly Boatwalla.'

'How are you, Dolly?'

'Very well, thank you. How are you?'

'I'm fine.'

There was another little moment there and then Dolly cleared her throat. 'I've been very busy, what with the children being at home. Trying to keep them amused is so trying. Freddie told me he saw T.T. at the pool.'

'Did he? Yes, he did.'

'Keeping fit, that's good. I have to practically send Freddie out with his clubs. Listen,' now a little laugh, 'have you heard anything about this Shanghai affair?'

Sheila took a deep breath. One by one, she relaxed her fingers on the receiver and settled back into her big leather chair. She wriggled her shoulders a little. Then, completely calm, she slowly said the word she had been saving for so long: 'No.'

'Ah.'

Mani Mennon began to laugh into a pillow, holding it to her chest and shaking violently.

'Well, it was nice talking to you,' Dolly said. 'I hear the children coming in. I should go.'

'It was nice,' Sheila said. '*Namaste.*'

Mr Fong stood at the door of the Shanghai Club in a dinner jacket and a bow tie, his hair solid black and with a sheen, looking dashing and mysterious and exactly right. Inside, if you looked closely, you could see that the club was really a little too small, that the tables were the same kind that Bhendi Bazaar furniture-makers copied from Danish catalogues, that the drinks were a little diminutive for so much money, that everything was quite ordinary. But it was all transformed that night by an extraordinary electricity, a current of excitement that made everyone beautiful, a kind of light that came not from the dim lamps but from the air itself. Ramani Ranjan Das wore all white, white *mogra* in her hair and a white *garara* suit and a silver nose ring, and she came with a film director twenty years younger. The police inspector wore slacks and turned out to be quite charmingly shy. Sheila wore a green sari and came a little late. She and T.T. sat in the middle of the crowded, smoky room and the air was filled with a pleasant chatter against the faint strains of music, and though it was photographed and written about, nothing ever really caught that feeling. It felt new, as if something was starting, and it was somehow oddly sexy, it was certain that at least six new affairs and two engagements started that night, but that wasn't all of it. It was the certainty of it, the feeling that for a few hours there was nowhere else in the world to be and nothing else to do, it was that cusping of time and place and history and power and effort that lifted the Shanghai Club that night into romance and made it unutterably golden.

We thought then that Sheila was invincible, but we had forgotten that even the strongest will in the world is easily defeated by its own progeny. Inevitably, Sheila's son came back to Bombay a poet. Sanjeev had been gone a long time, first to school at Doon and then to the States – he went not to his father's college but to Yale, where he took many classes in photography and art history, and broke many hearts with a dark curl of hair on his forehead that gave him a look of sad nostalgia. He had learned to ski, and had an easy physical grace that was quite different from his mother's nervous energy, her focus, and his father's thumping walk. He was indolent and he had a little smile just a little tinged with arrogance, but we all forgave him that, he wrote such lovely poetry. Mani Mennon was the first one outside the family to meet him that summer, and she watched him for a long time, and then she said to nobody in particular, in a tone of wonder, 'You know he looks always like he's just gotten off a horse.' When she said that she had said everything. Bijlani said to Sheila, 'I don't know what to say to him and he's not quite what I expected but he's very wonderful.' Sheila nodded, overwhelmed by her love. She treated her son like a jewel, standing between him and the world, willing not only to give him anything but to take whatever he wanted to give, a poem if that was it. She already understood that getting what you wanted from the world meant that your own struggles became grubby and irrelevant to your children, which was as it was, that was after all why you gave them what you didn't have. But like all parents she never really believed he would fall in love.

This is how it happened. A week after coming home, Sanjeev wandered away from the house, feeling rested in the body but exhausted by loneliness. He said later that he was discovering the strange terror of coming back to a familiar city and not knowing anyone, and he thought that seeing the playing fields of his childhood, the streets and the corners, would fill the gap in his heart. So he wandered off the hill and down to Pastry Palace, and as he crossed the flyover bridge he was trying to recall the excitement that once really had made the place a palace, that teenage feeling of seeing a cluster of friends and knowing that everything was possible. But now it just looked ordinary. It was disappointment that made him trudge on down to the Palace, a bitter determination to see it all through.

So there are opinions and opinions about what happened next. Some say it was just this – that he needed a way to reconnect, you see, hold on to something. Others contend contemptuously that it was just the narrative force of history that forced them into their headlong affair, that it was the ferocity of the feud that made them long for each other. 'What a bloody cliché' we heard on the balcony of the Gym. 'What atrocious taste to allow themselves.' The best of us believe that it was merely love. But of course nobody really knows what happened, except the essential facts which tell us precisely nothing: that afternoon, seated at Pastry Palace with her friends, was Dolly's daughter Roxanne, eighteen years old, finishing at Cathedral that year. She was a fair girl, with the milky Boatwalla complexion, dark straight hair, dark eyes, a little plump, sweet and quiet and a little shy, very charming but nothing spectacular, you understand. She and Sanjeev had known each other by sight before, but the last time he had seen her was when she had just turned thirteen. They talked, we know this for certain, but nobody knows what happened next, did they meet again at Pastry, how did they call each other, was it at a friend's house, what exactly went on. Certainly Sheila didn't know. What she did know was that three months later, at the end of the summer, Sanjeev told her that he wanted to marry.

When she heard who it was Sheila didn't flinch. She asked calmly, 'Did Roxanne tell her mother yet?'

'Yes,' Sanjeev said. 'We thought she should.'

Looking at his face, Sheila suddenly felt old. He was confident of the future. He knew there was a problem but of course he had the essential belief that the wars of the past were fought because of benighted ignorance, that good sense would after all prevail. She wanted to tell him that the past was responsible for him, for his beauty, but of course there was nothing to say, no possible way to explain. After a few minutes of her silence, he asked, 'Are you angry?'

'No,' she said. It was true; she was baffled. She had no idea what to do next. But as the afternoon passed, as she and Sanjeev sat together in her office, she couldn't endure doing nothing. She picked up her phone and began to make calls. After the first few it became clear that Dolly did know what to do: she had left the city with Roxanne. They had left by the four-o'clock flight for London. They had been seen being driven to the airport, and the report was that Roxanne had looked tearfully out of the window all the way, but this, Sheila was sure, was dramatic value added on as the story passed from phone to phone. In any case, they were gone.

Now Sanjeev looked stunned and wanted to go to London. 'Don't be silly,' Sheila said. 'How do you know you'll find them there? And what'll you do when you find them, tear her away?' Dolly had two other daughters, one married in

71

London, one in Chicago, Roxanne could be anywhere in the world.

So they waited. Sheila was sure that Dolly wouldn't leave Freddie alone for too long, not at this time, she would return soon. Sheila had no idea what she would do when Dolly did return, she thought about it often but could come up with no satisfactory plan. In the meantime she looked after Sanjeev, who was causing havoc as he suffered. He grew thinner, and with the dark circles under his eyes his forelock of hair was completely irresistible, women old and young pined after him, they left him notes and waited for him in the pubs he was known to frequent and they pursued convoluted paths to introductions to him, but it was all useless, he forgot them a minute after meeting them, he saw nothing and heard nothing except the memory of his Roxanne. Sheila understood that every minute he spent apart from Roxanne bound him more irrevocably to her, and she also understood that if she as a mother told him to forget her, Roxanne would become as unforgettable to him as his own childhood. Sheila had to keep quiet. It was a trap finely honed for her by the years of victory. Even now she had to appreciate the justice of its bitterness.

After sixty days Dolly returned. Bijlani had friends at customs, so they knew even before she was through the green channel that she was back, that she had come alone on a Pan Am flight from Frankfurt. Sheila let forty-eight hours pass, and then on a Saturday afternoon she asked for the car. She sat alone in the back as it went through a couple of left turns, up a long upward slope to the left, and arrived at the Boatwalla Mansion. She could have walked in about ten minutes, but in all the years they had lived so close to each other she had never actually seen the Mansion. The lane that ran up to the gate was shadowed with branches that came over high walls, so that when you actually got to the gate you were surprised by the expanse of lawn beyond. The gate itself was wrought iron, with some kind of coat of arms at the centre, but Sheila noticed with a quick forward leaning of surprise that the marble on the left gatepost was unmistakably cracked. The car went by the gateman, who saluted the Mercedes and let it through without question, and as it swept around the circular drive she saw the whole place clearly for the first time – the white columns, the ornate windows, the façade with its grand curls and flourishes, all of it stained and patchy. The front door was opened, incredibly, by a maid in a black uniform, and suddenly Sheila had to hold back a laugh, but then she noticed that the woman had a head of white, very fine white hair, and that she was peering at her with a concentration that was absolute and unwavering.

'Please tell Mrs Boatwalla that Mrs Bijlani is here,' Sheila said, stepping past her. The woman's stare held for a moment, her hand still on the door knob, and then she turned and shuffled away. 'Mrs Bijlani,' Sheila called after her curved shoulders, but the maid did not turn her head. The only light came through the open front door, catching a myriad of motes that barely moved. In the dim dark, Sheila could see two ottomans against the wall, under a picture of workmen toiling on a dock. The carpet was worn and, near the door, stained with patches of deep brown. There was a very slight smell of damp. There was no light switch that Sheila could see, and so she waited near the door. Finally a sibilant scraping came close and the maid appeared out of the darkness.

'Madame is not in.'

'It's very important,' Sheila said. 'Tell her that it's very important.'

'Madame is not in.'

The woman was saying it without impatience, standing with her hands loosely holding each other in front of her white apron. Sheila had no doubt she would say it again. Sheila nodded and turned away. She heard the door click gently before she was halfway down the steps. As the car pulled away she looked back at the house, but there was no sign of life in any of the windows. Before the car went through the gate her strategy was clear in her head, fully formed. The thought came to her that way, precise and whole. She was going to buy the mansion. She would buy them out complete: lock, stock, ship, and house. Finally it came down to this vulgarity – that they had the pride and she had the money. She sat alertly in the back of the car which she had earned, paralyzed no more, her mind moving quickly. It was, after all, she thought, only inevitable. It was time and history.

Sheila and T.T. sat together late that night, figuring the exact liquidity of their cash. That had always struck her as a strange phrase, because money was if anything hard, impersonal. But now she saw how it could be like a stream, unpredictable and underground, and she was going to turn it into a torrent that would flow up the hill instead of down, crumbling the bloody Boatwalla gate like paper. It was going to burst out of the hillside under the mansion like a fountain from the interior rock, surprise, surprise. It was two o'clock when they stared down at a figure at the bottom of a white pad, at the long string of zeros they had spent a lifetime accumulating.

'Is it enough?' Bijlani said, rubbing his eyes. 'Is it enough?'

'It's enough,' Sheila said. 'Let's sleep.' They went up the stairs to the bedroom, and Sanjeev's light was on under his door. She resisted the impulse to knock and went on, but when the lights were off she couldn't sleep. She could see the shapes of the companies they owned, how they fitted together, and she moved the segments against one another like the pieces on a chessboard, looking for the nuance that would give them the edge four moves down. She got up once to drink water and was shocked by the hour gleaming at her from the bedside table. Again she tried to sleep, but now it was only the zeros that spun before her, symmetrical and unchanging. *Shunya shunya shunya*, the words came to her in her father's high voice teaching her some forgotten childhood lesson: *shunya* is zero and zero is *shunya*. She felt very tired.

The exhaustion passed but something else remained. As they began their bid, which Sheila insisted was not hostile but necessary, as they began their slow and audacious assault on Boatwalla Shipping International & Co. (since 1757), she found that all the pleasure was gone. The takeover was the most complicated puzzle that she had ever faced, and she was perfection itself, her memory was prodigious, her stamina unquenchable, and her charm of course was gleaming and soft and unstoppable. But she felt the gears grinding inside her. She told herself to remember whom she was doing it for after all, she looked at her son's face and remembered the way he'd learned to walk by clinging precariously to her sari and his jerky little steps, but still every morning she lay awake in bed gathering the vitality, a little from here a little from there, for the great effort to get up and war with the day. But the only true thing was that her taste for the game in itself was gone. Suddenly it felt like work, but even when it was over for the day she could only sit silently, staring sometimes at the television, feeling lost. She tried to hide it, and Sanjeev, who had begun to write page after page of poetry, never noticed, but T.T. was uneasy. He said nothing but he looked wary, as if he had smelled something dangerous in the shifting air but wasn't quite sure of what it was, where it came from, what it meant.

It was now, in this Sheila's time of ashes, that Ganga came to her one Sunday. She was wearing a new, bright-blue sari, and with her was Asha, also in a sari, a green one. It was a formal call: they stood in Sheila's study, the mother a little in front.

'How pretty you look, Asha,' Sheila said.

As the girl blushed, Ganga spoke. 'She finished her nurse training last week.'

'Very good, Asha!' Sheila said, touching her on the shoulder.

'She's getting married next month,' Ganga said. 'We came to give you the card.'

Sheila took the envelope, which was huge, a foot square. Inside, the card was red, with a gold vine that went around the borders. It invited the reader to a ceremony and reception at the Vivekananda School Hall, Andheri.

'Will you come?' Ganga said.

Sheila was looking at Asha. For some reason she was thinking suddenly about her first flight on an Air France plane, the leap of her stomach when the machine had escaped the ground. 'Yes,' Sheila said. 'Of course.'

'Bring Baba, too.'

'Yes, I will.' Sanjeev hadn't left the house for days, even weeks now, and Sheila was sure she couldn't get him to come out of the edifice of his grief, she had already stopped asking him, but she said, 'We'll all come.'

Ganga nodded. 'Come,' she said to Asha, who smiled over her shoulder at Sheila. She ran down the hall to keep up with her mother, the silver *payals* at her ankles tinkling with every step. Sheila sat down slowly at her desk. The girl's eagerness hurt her, the small musical sound pressed against her abdomen and gave her a feeling of discovering a new emptiness. She remembered – remembered driving in a bus, in the early morning, to the airport, the red lights far away in the cool blue dawn, a plane thundering overhead with its running lights twinkling, and the glad feeling that it was all an invitation, a promise. They used to sing together, sometimes, Hindi film songs, from Marine Drive to Bandra, and sometimes in Paris on the road to Orly, with the French drivers smiling at them.

Now Sheila waited, with her hand on the phone, collecting herself before the next call. There were a lot of calls to make. The takeover was not going as planned. The Boatwallas had conducted the sort of political manoeuvring that had been expected, and that was easily countered – in fact it was welcome, because it revealed their connections and their understandings of their own predicament. It had become clear as the weeks passed that Boatwalla International was even more overextended than T.T. and she had thought. The interest on their debt alone was barely within the Boatwallas' means. But when it seemed that they must surrender or be reduced, there had come a sudden influx of cash. Like a transfusion it had revitalized them, fleshed them out and made them capable of resistance: Freddie appeared on 'Business Plus,' pink and ruddy under the studio lights, and declared that it was all over, they were safe. Sheila knew they had borrowed money, lots of it at unheard-of rates of interest, but when she tried to find out who had lent it there was no answer. Her sources all over Bombay and beyond dried up like the city reservoirs in May, there was no information to be had. She and T.T. called in their favours and doled out some more, but still, nothing. If they could get a name, everything would be possible: politics could be made to interfere with the vital flow of money, fine legal quibbles could bring down the whole ponderous sickly-white elephant, once in a similar situation they had even purchased outright and cleanly the entire lending corporation. But without a name, without that vital secret, they could do nothing, everything was meaningless.

So now she picked up the phone and looked at it, at the numbers on the keypad. There was a time when she had handled it like a fine instrument, her fingers used to fly over the keys without her looking, it had been her delight, her sitar and her stiletto. Now she just stared at it. I can't remember people's numbers anymore, she noted with a kind of dull surprise. Then she opened her book and began dialling.

When they drove out to the Vivekananda School Hall a month later the problem was still with them. Boatwalla International stayed perversely healthy, like a patient sprung from the deathbed and made up with rouge. And for Sheila and T.T. the outcome was not quite a draw. In the eyes of the market, the stalemate was their defeat. It was not only for this that Bijlani was silent and distraught; his uneasiness was the trouble of a man whose life has lost its accustomed centre. Sheila knew that her own doldrums becalmed him even more than her, but her best attempts at revitalization seemed false to her. She could feel the muscles of her mouth when she smiled. There seemed to be no way out, so she endured from day to day, and he with her. Now they sat, apart, in the back seat behind the driver Gurinder Singh, who besides having been with them for a long time was also a friend of Ganga's.

When the car drew up outside the Vivekananda School, Ganga was waiting outside for them. She welcomed them in the midst of a jostling crowd. As they walked in, a pack of children in their shiny best raced around them, staring unabashedly. The hall had been done up with ribbons, and there was a *mandap* at the middle, with chairs arranged in untidy rows around it. 'Sanjeev was busy,' Sheila was saying as they walked up to two ornate chairs, thrones of a sort, really, all gilt and huge armrests, that had been placed in front of the *mandap*. They sat down and Ganga took her place by her daughter, who was sitting cross-legged next to the man who was becoming her husband. The priests were chanting one by one and in chorus, and throwing handfuls of rice into the fire. Asha smiled up at them with her head down, looking some-how very pretty and plump and satisfied. Sheila nodded at her, thinking of Sanjeev. He was not at all busy, in fact he had been sitting on their roof with his feet up on a table, but he had said he was tired.

It was the first time that Sheila had ever seen Ganga sitting absolutely still. She seemed at rest, her knees drawn up and her hands held in front of her. The priests droned on. Mean-while, nobody paid attention to the ceremony at all. Children ran about in all directions. Their parents sat in the chairs around the *mandap* and talked, nodding and laughing. Occasionally somebody would come and stand in front of the thrones and stare frankly at Sheila and T.T., whispering to friends. Sheila had her chin in one hand and she was lost in the fire and the chant. Then suddenly the ceremony was over and the couple were sitting on a dais at the end of the hall, on thrones of exactly the same magnificence as those provided for the Bijlanis. Sheila and T.T. were first to go through the recep-tion line, and Sheila hugged Asha and T.T. shook hands with her husband, whose name was Ramesh and who was a schoolteacher. Then Sheila and T.T. sat on their thrones, which had been moved to face the dais, and food was served. Everyone was eating around them. Sheila ate the *puri bhaji* and the *biryani* and the sticky *jalebis*, and watched as Ganga moved among her seated guests, serving them herself from trays carried by her relatives behind her. She gave Sheila and T.T. huge second helpings and they ate it all.

After the food, Ganga gave gifts to the women at the wedding. She walked around again and gave saris to her nieces and aunts and other relatives. She came up to Sheila, who said without thinking, 'Ganga, you don't have to give me anything.'

Ganga looked at her, her face expressionless. 'It is our custom,' she said. Sheila blushed and reached up quickly and took the sari. She held it on her lap with both hands, her throat tight. She felt perilously close to tears. But there were two girls, sisters, seven and eight, leaning on her knees, looking up at her. She talked to them and it passed, and finally she was sitting on one side of the room, away from the lights, not on a throne but on a folding chair, tired and pleasantly sleepy. T.T. was on the other side of the room, talking about the stock-market scandals with a circle of men. Ganga's father sat beside him, quiet but listening intently. Sheila thought drowsily that T.T. looked animated for the first time in months.

Then Ganga walked up. She paused for a moment and then sat beside Sheila, on a brown chair. They looked at each other frankly. They had known each other for a long time and they liked each other well enough, but between them there was no question of love or hate.

'How did you manage this, Ganga?'

'I sold my *kholi*.'

'You sold it?'

'For 30,000 rupees.'

Sheila looked around the hall. A song was ringing out, and a group of children were dancing, holding their arms up like Amitabh Bachchan in *Muqaddar Ka Sikander*.

'Thank you,' Sheila said in English, gesturing awkwardly at the sari that she held in her lap.

For a moment there was no reaction, and then Ganga smiled with a flash of very white teeth. 'We got them at wholesale,' she said. 'I know someone.' She pointed with her chin at a man Sheila had noticed earlier bustling about, herding people from here to there. 'Him.'

'That's good,' Sheila said.

'You speak English well,' Ganga said.

'I learned it as a child.'

Ganga settled herself in her chair with the motion of someone who is very tired. 'I have heard that Boatwalla speak English.'

'You work for her, too?'

'For longer than for you.'

'I didn't know. I didn't ask.'

'I didn't tell you. I wash dishes and clean the kitchen. Their other people don't do that. I never see her.'

'I see.'

'Except now and then, once or twice every year, when she comes into the kitchen for something.'

'Yes.'

'But she never sees me.'

'You mean you're hiding?'

'No, I'm right there in front of her.'

'Then what do you mean?'

'I mean that she doesn't see me. If she's talking to someone she keeps on talking. To such high people the rest of the world is invisible. People like me she cannot see. It's not that she is being rude. It's just that she cannot see me. So she keeps on talking about things that she would never talk about in front of you or somebody else. Once she saw me, but it was because she wanted to get water from the fridge and I was mopping the floor and she had to step over my hand.'

Ganga's voice was steady, even. Sheila lifted the packet on her lap a little.

'Even then she kept on talking. Once, I heard her say bad things about her elder daughter, the London one.'

'Ganga, do you . . .?' Sheila stopped.

'Understand English? A little, I think. I've worked for you for twenty years, haven't I?'

'You have indeed.'

'Last week, she came in to shout at the cook about the bowls he used for the sweet after lunch. Her husband lagging behind her. These people, she said. She sent the cook to get all the bowls in the house. She said something about meetings, and her husband wrote down something on a piece of paper. How she talks in English, chutter-chutter-chutter, like she's everybody's grandmother in the world, she asked something about the American business, then she said something about a Hong Kong bank, all the time going here and there in the kitchen.'

'Bank?' said Sheila.

Ganga straightened up at the sound of Sheila's voice.

'Yes. Bank.'

'In Hong Kong?' Ganga said nothing in the face of Sheila's sudden needle-sharp focus. 'Ganga. Did she say the name of the bank?'

'Maybe.'

'Do you remember it?'

'Is it very important?'

'Yes. Very.'

Ganga threw back her head and laughed, and two children running by stopped to gawk at her. 'It was Fugai Bank. Foo Ga. Foo Quay.'

In the car, Sheila reached out and took T.T.'s hand. She said nothing and looked out of the window as they went down the length of the city. Gurinder was playing cassettes of old songs, he was humming along with the music, his mood lightened by the food and the amiable chaos of the wedding. Bombay's night hadn't yet quieted down, and everywhere there were people, and at some intersections the cars and scooters honked

at each other madly. As the car came around a curve, Sheila
saw a family sitting by the side of the road, father and mother
and two children around a small fire. There was a pot on the
fire, and the flames lit up their faces as they looked up at
the car going by.

At home, Sheila walked ahead as T.T. gave Gurinder a
couple of notes. She could hear their voices murmuring behind
her, a cricket chirping and the rustle of the wind in the leaves.
She had said nothing to T.T., and the name of the bank balanced precariously in her stomach, not unpleasant but not
quite welcome, there was something moving in her, something
not quite born yet and still unknown. The anticipation kept her
awake, and finally, much later, she left her bed and went up to
the roof. Now everything was dark, it was a moonless night,
and the scrape of her *chappals* against the cement was loud. She
found a garden chair and sat in it, her hands held together in
her lap. Sometimes a freshness billowed up against her face,
barely a breeze but cool and moist. It came again and she
was remembering her father. She remembered him as a small,
balding man with a potbelly, dressed always in *chapals* and
black trousers and a bush shirt in white or brown. He kept the
shop open till late in the evening and opened it early, so that
Sheila saw him usually at night, when he ate his dinner alone.
When she was growing up she had always thought he was a
simple man. But once a year he liked to take his family away
from the city, to a resort or a hill station, for a week, two weeks.
She remembered waking once while it was still dark, she was
ten or eleven, they were in some place on the banks of a river, a
small hotel, she couldn't remember the name of the river. But
she remembered the cold lifting off the water when she went
outside and saw her father sitting in the sand on the river edge
below. In the dark she could see the white of his *kurta* and his
head shining above. She walked through a garden with
flowers and down the steps that led to the river, and sat beside
him, her leg resting on his knee. He smiled at her, then looked
away, across the river where the water melted into mist. She

shivered a little. There was white speckled into his stubble, which she knew he would shave later with a Parkinson razor. His name was Kishen Chand, and he was a small man. Later, after he was dead and she was older, she would remember his gaze over the water and think that nothing and nobody was simple. Later, she would remember the old story of schisms and horrors, how he had left half his family murdered in Lahore, two brothers, a sister, a father. They had a shop which was burned. Partition threw him onto the streets of Bombay but he still spoke of his Lahore, his beautiful Lahore. It was something of a family joke. She huddled beside him as the river emerged from the grey light. She remembered her geography lesson and whispered to her father, Is this a sacred river? It must be, he said. It is, he said. What is that smell? she said. He said, Wood smoke. She asked: Smoke? He said, Fire. What fire? she said. He said, Cooking fires, hearth fires, hay fires. Funeral fires. Ceremonial fires. Even the firing of refuse, of things that are thrown away. Home fires and factory fires. It's starting to be day and there are fires everywhere. And she saw the white smoke drifting slowly across the surface of the water.

Sheila heard a footstep and lifted a hand to her face. It was wet with tears. She wiped it with her sleeve and when she looked up she saw that the sea, far below, was gold. She stood up and felt the light hot on her face. Sanjeev came up beside her and subsided lankily into the chair. She smiled down at him. He had a book in his hand and looked very handsome in a kind of tragic way.

'You were out late last night,' he said.

'Yes.'

'You went on to one of your parties?' His mouth was pouty with disdain.

Sheila laughed. As she looked down she could see on his T-shirt a blond, scruffy-looking man and the single word 'Nirvana'. She said, 'Sanju, you're my son, but it would take a lifetime, two lifetimes, to tell you all the things you don't know about the world.' As she walked away, she ruffled his hair.

In her bedroom, she laughed to see the mountainous bulk of her husband under the bedclothes. She pulled at his toe. 'Come on. We have work to do.' He followed her down the stairs, rubbing his eyes, to the office. He sat in front of her as she leaned back in her chair and picked up the phone.

'What are we doing?' he said.

She put her feet in his lap. He rubbed them, smiling, because in her flowered nightgown and with her hair pulled back she looked like a child, and she looked at him sideways from lowered eyes, naughty and a little dangerous. Her fingers moved so quickly over the keys of the telephone that the beepings came out as a kind of music. She grinned. 'Ah,' she said. 'I thought we might make a few calls to Hong Kong.'

What we remembered from the wedding was not the scale of it and not the celebration, not even how beautiful the couple was or the speculations about their honeymoon in France. It wasn't even the sight of Sheila and Dolly walking hand in hand into the reception. It wasn't the sight of Tiger Pataudi and a very boozy Freddie re-creating their second innings so that T.T. and Mani Mennon could judge whether there had indeed been a flannelled Pataudi leg before wicket. It wasn't at all the news that Ganga had bought a large shed in Dharavi where she was going to put in a cloth-reclamation factory. After it was all over, what stayed in the mind was a strange moment, before the double ceremony (one for each religion), when the two families had moved into the centre of the huge *shamiana*. On one side we could see Sheila's aunts, large women in pink and red saris with bands of diamonds around their wrists and necks, and on the other Dolly's relatives, in particular one frail, tall old lady in a white sari and a pair of pince-nez glasses, with pearls at her neck, and all these people looking at each other. Then all the talking died away, there was a curious moment of silence, it was absolute and total, even the birds stopped chirping in the trees. Then two of the children ran through the *shamiana*, it was Roxanne's second cousin who was chasing Sheila's niece, both squealing, and the moment was broken and everyone was talking. Yet there had been that strange silence, maybe it was just that nobody knew what to do with each other. But I think of that moment of silence whenever I realize how much changed because of that marriage. What I mean is the formation of the Bijlani-Boatwalla Bombay International Trading Group, then the Agarwal loan scandal, the successes of the BBBI, the fall of the Yashwant Rao Ghatge government and the meteoric rise of Gagganbhai Patel, and what happened after that we all know. But that's another story. Maybe I'll tell you about that another evening.

ROSARIO FERRÉ

———————

The Glass Box

I've always known that I, too, was one of the chosen. I've always trusted my dreams because I know that behind them lies the door to immortality. I've always trusted my hands, their power to create magic bridges with cables, with spiderwebs, with steel girders, with sticks of dynamite, with whatever comes to hand which may make better communication possible. They've been looking for me for a long time now, although so far they haven't been able to find me. When they do, they won't show much sympathy. They'll point their guns at me and won't even bother to search for the proper identification: driver's license, fingerprints, work papers would all, in my case, be unwarranted.

My great-grandfather landed in Cuba still dressed in his old frock coat, tuxedo pants, and opera hat, and snorting 'God, it's hot,' as if in Panama it had been cooler than in Havana. In spite of his fallen-wizard's mien, having crossed the Atlantic by Ferdinand de Lesseps' side gave him an aura of prestige. They had been good friends, had shared the same dreams: to open a channel of communication between the Old World and the New; to be able to sail from France to India without ever changing course; to reach at last the Orient's swirls of silk, the forests of cinnamon and cayenne, the urns of musk and aloe. But if Ferdinand had dreamed of digging a channel in the virgin continent which would be the geographic feat of the century, Albert had dreamed of building the most beautiful bridge in the world, a bridge which would open and close its arches like alligators making love.

89

Upon the failure of De Lesseps' company in 1896, Albert decided not to return to Europe. His vision of a bridge that would bring universal communication to the world had failed, but when he landed in Cuba his curled whiskers were still those of an unpenitent dreamer. As soon as he arrived, he set himself to designing metal bridges, which spread fragile spiderwebs over the tops of mango and bamboo thickets. His bridges offered the islanders a refreshing change from the heavy, turdlike pontoons built by the Spaniards on unimaginative dirt roads. His fame spread so that he soon got to be known throughout the island as 'the Frenchman of the flying bridges', but Albert never thought much of it, as building bridges was simply his way of making his dreams come true.

Around that time he met the girl he eventually married. Ileana couldn't speak French and Albert could barely manage to make himself understood in Spanish, but she had been deeply impressed by his whimsical gaze, as by the tenderness with which he strung strange webs of threads between his fingers, when he attempted to illustrate for her benefit his method for designing bridges. She would cook potage St Germain for him and brush his top hat every morning, before kissing him goodbye on the running board of his blue-fringed surrey. While Albert was always studying the topographic contours of the island's rivers and waterways, Ileana would spend the day with her aunts and cousins. Together they would oil rifles and guns, count bullets, and prepare bandage rolls and gauze pads, which they would hide under the lid of the family's grand piano. Albert had married into a family of Cuban rebel-patriots, but because he lived in his own world of dreams, he never found out about it.

One day Albert was told that the French lawyer in Paris to whom he had been sending his savings for years had disappeared mysteriously, taking everything with him, and he began to feel crestfallen. The political unrest of the island was making it more and more difficult for him to build his bridges, and he soon found himself out of work. The heat now mortified him more than ever, and he began to dream obsessively of the snow-covered landscapes of his childhood, which he would never see again. It was then he put together the first icebox ever to be built in Cuba, after melting the steel gridirons of one of his unbuilt bridges. He used to sit in it for hours on end, dreaming of the icy bridges and elegant steeples of Paris, as his parched skin at last found relief from the heat.

One morning Ileana couldn't find Albert anywhere. She looked all over the house, coffee cup in hand, calling for him to come for breakfast. She found him sitting frozen inside his icebox, dressed in his old frock coat, tuxedo pants and frayed silk opera hat, his eyes wide open on the same ghostly landscape, spanned by bridges of all sizes and types, which he had described to her on the day they met.

Ileana took her only son, my grandfather, to live in Matanzas with my rebel great-great-grandmother. The Cuban Revolution was burgeoning: Cacarajícara, Lomas del Tabí, Ceja del Negro; each new uprising threatened to set the island's landscape on fire. Jacobito must have been around seven years old when a traitor's bullet downed 'El titán de bronce' in the battle of Punta Brava. Maceo was an old friend of the family's: 'He stood up on his stirrups, dropped his machete, and came tumbling down from his horse. There you see the Ceiba tree, those are your cousins, colonels of the army, there he lies dead in your cousin's arms, after they picked him up from where he had fallen, behind enemy lines.' Ileana would point out these images to her son again and again, leafing through an old, thumb-worn volume of Cuban history. 'They were true revolutionaries, your cousins were. They defied volley after volley to recover the body, and later galloped for three nights and three days to bury the body as far as possible from the enemy's vengeful arm.'

Jacobito was never impressed by the family's heroic deeds. He was more interested in the colourful fairs and marketplaces of Matanzas, where he would gaze for hours on the betting wheels of the snow-cone vendors, on the grinding wheels of the knife and scissors sharpeners, on the horse-betting wheels, and on the huge, multicoloured blinking Ferris wheel, on which he could never ride because he was too poor. He was, in short, so obsessed by everything that had to do with wheels, that when he turned fifteen his mother sent him off to a small town off the southern coast of Puerto Rico aboard a banana sloop, where a distant uncle had a foundry where the catherine wheels of nearby sugar plantations were cast. Puerto Rico was a much poorer island than Cuba, but peace had suddenly made her relatively rich, as business there was going on as usual. There he would not only be safe from the haphazard surroundings of Matanza's fairs, but he would also be out of reach of the fierce reprisals of the Spaniards, who had by then wiped out most of the family.

Jacobito went ashore at Playa de Ponce, machete in hand, pants rolled up to his knees, straw hat pulled down over his eyebrows, and without a shirt to his name. 'I became a machinist's apprentice at El Phoenix, Uncle Theo's foundry, and I immediately took the idea of an immortal bird which rises again from its ashes. I learned fast; I was soon casting the dizzying catherine wheels of the sugar mills and helping my uncle make a profit by them. I loved the work at El Phoenix, because the wheels of the sugar mills reminded me of the spinning wheels of the snow-cone vendors of my faraway hometown. The catherine wheels whizzed, the flywheels whisked, the steam cylinders whistled as they pulled on the axle that pushed on the flywheel that squeezed out the sugar syrup, and before I knew it the Marines had landed in Guánica.'

Gallantly done up in his braided fireman's uniform, Jacobito rode Yumurí chest deep into the Caribbean, in order to greet Commander Davis properly. The Dixie, the Annapolis, and the Wasp formed a string of leaden silhouettes against the sleepy seascape of La Playa. The Spanish troops withdrew from the village without firing a single shot, and the key to the city was

handed over to Commander Davis in a musical *kermess*, held
to the tune of the fireman's fine brass band.

The next day, when the rest of the troops were about to land,
Jacobito drew near to the commander and, with the help of
an interpreter, tried to warn him not to set up tent near the
Portugués's dry riverbed, as this was a treacherous river given
to sudden violent floods. 'Our town is a peaceful town,' he
told him, 'you have nothing to fear. Set your tents up in the
city square, so that we may get to know you better and you
may mingle freely with us.' But the strangeness of the place,
the blinding heat, the toads plastered like cardboard cutouts
on the dusty streets, the eccentric firehouse with its quizzical
red-and-white stripes half melting under the sun, the
cathedral's silver-titted belfries, the Masonic Lodge with its
huge eye staring at them from under its whitewashed steeple,
were all too intimidating for the young volunteers from
Pennsylvania and Illinois, and the Marine columns were
ordered to head toward the riverbed.

Commander Davis thanked Jacobito for his well-meant
advice. 'How did you come into such a splendid specimen of
the Tennessee Walker?' he asked Jacobito politely. Jacobito
didn't understand what he meant, until the interpreter pointed
to Yumurí. 'He's not from Tennessee, no, sir; this horse is
Puerto Rican by birth, a *paso fino* of the finest breed. He's the
son of Batallita in Mejorana, a direct descendant of our
country's champion Dulcesueño, but if you like him he's
yours, sir, please accept him as my gift, so you'll know what a
real horse is like.'

The commander didn't understand the business about the
lineage very well, but he gladly accepted Jacobito's unexpected gift. 'His name is Yumurí. I named him after a famous
Indian chief who beat off the invaders in my country. No, sir,
of course it wasn't here, it took place in Cuba, where I was
born, and the invaders were the Spaniards, they were a very
backward people, sir; it was a long time ago.' 'You don't mind
if I change his name, do you?' the commander asked, looking a

93

bit staggered. 'No, of course not, name him whatever you want.' 'How about Tonto, that's a nice name; it's very popular in New Mexico; they use it a lot in rodeos, corridas, and horse shows.' Horse, rider, and Panama hat all spun around of a piece, a rebel weathervane suddenly whipped by the wind. Jacobito didn't even turn his head to take leave of the commander as he rode away. 'Tonto! I'll never let him name you Tonto! I hope the river drowns them, Yumurí, it's what they deserve.'

In spite of such an inauspicious beginning, the fact was that Jacobito's dreams all came true thanks to the Marines' arrival. He was at once commissioned to build modern metal bridges that would span the bamboo thickets at every difficult bend of the island's rivers, to melt huge quantities of bluish-reddish-white-hot steel, which were then poured into the immense moulds of the catherine wheels that were needed by the great sugar mills, which were mushrooming up on the island at the time, built by foreign investors. Thus, Jacobito's house was the first in town to be lit up with General Electric lightbulbs, to have a Frigidaire icebox with the condensing coils on top, a Hot Point electric stove, a sexy black tile bathroom with black American Standard toilet and shower tub, an Electrolux vacuum cleaner and a Sunbeam electric fan that was so noisy it made you feel you were sitting under the nose of a Pan Am DC3. He loved to ride through the dusty streets in the town's first Model T, scaring horses and people alike. One day his admiration for the foreigners reached such a pitch that, after witnessing the daring acrobatics of an American parachute fiend who jumped from his open cockpit to the canefields below, he climbed up on the high gabled roof of his house and hurled himself courageously into space, clasping an open umbrella in his hand.

The whole town followed his wake to the cemetery. His friends, the members of the fireman's band, walked slowly behind his casket, blaring their horns without letup, their tears mingling with their brass lit-up smiles as they sang:

The Glass Box

Happy days of love
will never come again
let life be savoured now
by happy and sad alike.

He wouldn't have liked a solemn funeral; he had never trusted solemn people. And so they buried him in his fireman's uniform, his plumed helmet under his arm and his patent-leather boots shined like new pennies. In compliance with his last wishes as a Freemason, there was no cross at his grave. Grendel, his dog, was laid out upon it, ears alert and fluffy tail raised in farewell forever, as he had been preserved long ago by Jacobito himself, enshrined in a bath of cement.

As a child I used to think about all these things, whenever I sat enthralled, listening to my grandfather's stories. He always told his stories in front of a curious glass box he had had made in Cuba to counter the nostalgia of exile. The hills of coarse green grass made of dyed hay, the little thatched roof huts, the latticework balconies, the cotton-swab clouds stuck to the painted blue sky of the barrio in Mantanzas where Jacobito had been born would then all come to life. Farmers with burlap bags over their shoulders would suddenly start walking down winding paths, would start tending their vegetable plots or milking their cows, proud that the land they cared for belonged only to them.

I always suspected the box held an unanswered secret. After my grandfather was gone I would stare at it for a long time, standing unsteadily on tiptoe on one of the wicker chairs in the parlour (the box was always on a high shelf, out of reach of the children). Discouraged because I couldn't decipher what the box was trying to tell me, I'd go out of the house angrily, slamming the door behind me and refusing to play with my cousins, who milled around yelling and running in the yard. I didn't know why I felt so angry and soon I'd forget all about it.

After my grandfather's death, my grandmother took over the family affairs. My father, Juan Jacobo, was the youngest of

95

her six sons, and also the most gifted. Once he took the strings out of the family's grand piano and put them back in such a way that it ended up having a Japanese five-tone scale. My grandmother began to worry when she saw her husband's extravagances begin to crop up in her son. Jacobito, for example, had a passion for lavender African lilies, but he couldn't settle for planting a row or two of them in his garden. To him, planting lavender lilies meant planting an ocean of lilies, so they would overflow from one island town to the next, and he could build new bridges to cross over them.

His grandfather's old dream of universal communication haunted him, and he went into politics as the only way to carry out Albert's vision of a bridge that would span both the Northern and the Southern hemisphere. 'Last night I dreamed I was building the most beautiful bridge in the world,' he told me one day, 'a bridge of silver strands that stretched from North to South, from East to West, and the strands kept coming out of me as if I were a giant spider and not an engineer. Isn't it strange? My bridge joined the world into a single nation where there was no war or hunger or poverty; thousands of birds came to nest in our forests, and those who sighted us from afar would cry: "This island is indeed an Afortunada because it has helped us find peace." '

At that time the island was torn by an ever-more violent struggle between statehood and independence. Politicians squabbled endlessly about status, becoming richer by the minute, while the country became poorer and poorer. Juan Jacobo believed his bridge would be the answer to the country's problems. He advised the people to forget about the age-old feud between statehood and independence and to concentrate on eliminating poverty. He travelled to Washington, where he convinced Congress to help turn the island into a 'showcase for the South.' The island would be the first place on earth where Latin American faith in the values of the spirit would blend with Anglo-Saxon respect for the law, faith in democracy, and technological progress.

Soon millions of dollars in federal funds began to pour into the island. Playing his tune in every town square like the Pied Piper of Hamelin, Juan Jacobo won the country's poor to his campaign, so that they followed him everywhere. He promised them lampposts, public telephones, air-conditioned buses, Christmas bonuses, municipal orchestras, homes for the aged, even free meals for the orphaned and the poor. Foreigners who visited the island couldn't get over the spectacle of Juan Jacobo, the millionaire, being the champion of the city's poor, idolized in every shantytown from La Perla to Chichamba.

But Juan Jacobo's dream of turning the island into a universal bridge was doomed to failure. Latin American countries, envious of the island's progress, thought it was being used by the United States for covert purposes; they looked down on the islanders for having sold out to North American interests. In the United States, the islanders were still considered Latin Americans, and were never seen as completely trustworthy. The professional island politicians, on the other hand, did all they could to fuel the status controversy. It did them no good to have a united country working together to banish poverty; the controversy between statehood and independence was for them a lucrative affair. In view of the growing mistrust in his dream of a universal bridge, Juan Jacobo began to feel dispirited. A bridge, he thought then, was, after all, something to be trod upon by those who knew where they were coming from, or at least where they were going. But the people of the island had no idea of either, and therefore it was better if it was never built.

Juan Jacobo renounced his dream and devoted himself to strengthening the family fortune. With the help of foreign capital he built more and more factories and became richer by the day. Of all the family members, he was the only one to keep a heart unspoiled. Like King Midas, everything he touched turned to gold. He even went so far as to feel a certain nostalgia for poverty, but he needn't have worried because gold went through his hands like a sieve. His fingers were hardened with gold dust but the clothes he wore were always somewhat threadbare; his cuffs frayed and the hems of his pants trailed baggily after him. The scent of fresh lemons which filled the room every time he took out his handkerchief to mop his brow, the gesture of his hand poised fleetingly in the air when he began to speak – everything about him suggested the genteel politeness of a cavalier gentleman of a bygone age. Before he was forty he had lost everything he owned, trying to help out his friends in need.

On the day he met Marina, an ocean of lilies stirred up waves of passion in his eyes. He married her after a short courtship, during which she let him know she would be both master and mistress of the house. She was the one to spruce up the family each year at Easter time. On Easter Sunday she would decorate the hallways with ferns and poinsettias, have the servants polish the floor and the furniture, and then tell us children to get the good china and silverware from the cupboard. We would then set the table for twelve and go out to the slums in search of our dinner guests. When we came back, the dwellers of the glass box would have suddenly come to life. I can almost see them as they stretch their limbs to move about dispiritedly, dragging their bare feet across the tile floor Mother made me scrub so hard this morning. They leave their burlap sacks on the floor along with their bunches of bananas and plantains, and gingerly begin to sit at the table, as if they didn't know how to move, how to lean on the carved chairs without splintering the mahogany roses, how to place their weatherbeaten hands on the snow-white tablecloth. My mother blesses the food from the head of the table. My aunts and uncles begin to pass the porcelain platters among the guests, the steak and onions, the rice and beans, with painstaking care, so as not to let a single grain of rice, a single drop of sauce, stain the immaculate white tablecloth. Little by little heads begin to look up from sunken chests, glances are exchanged with more confidence, a toothless mouth timidly rehearses a grin, and the dwellers of the glass box seem happy once again.

Every Christmas, on Three Kings' Day, my mother's Easter ritual would be observed in reverse. We would then be sent by our parents to the slums, to be the guests of our guests. On those occasions we loved to pretend that we were entering grandfather's glass box, as we jumped from plank bridge to plank bridge, puddle to puddle, balcony to balcony, frightening the pigs, the chickens, the guinea hens, the billy goats, just for the pleasure of hearing them bleat until the moment came to pass out our gifts solemnly among the children, wrapped, as always, in glistening silver foil, with huge poinsettias tied on with red bows.

The gift-giving ceremony would last all morning, but by noon we'd be sitting patiently in a rusty zinc shed. The shed was punched full of holes, and the sun lit restless fireflies over our heads as the aunts, uncles, and parents of our young friends began to spread out a splendid banquet before us. Platters heaped with baby goat stew, steaming cauldrons of rice and chicken, suckling pig served on plantain leaves and decorated with fire-red hybiscus, 'mazamorra', 'majarete', and 'mundo nuevo', the stream of dishes was endless. We'd never be able to eat it all; we were already stuffed to the gills. 'We've had enough already, thank you, it was delicious.' 'You can't mean it, dear, you haven't tried anything yet. Taste this last bit of "longaniza", this littlest bit of "butifarra", we made it especially for you.'

We knew we had to sit there and eat it all up; there simply was no getting around it until all the platters were empty and the mongrel dogs under the table would begin to lick our bare legs clean. Only then would the slum children stop watching us without blinking; only then would we be able to get up and play hopscotch, marble-in-the-hole and hide-and-seek with them, to the tune of the guinea hen's 'yapaqué, yapaqué'; only then would we be allowed into the latrine, where it was such fun to go standing up, cooling your behind thanks to the breeze that seeped through the chinks in the wall; only then could we fly the kite, skip the rope, spin the top, tralala, fiddle dee dee, come and make merry together, you and me.

Many years later I came back to the island, having finally acquired my engineering degree. Mother and Father had been dead for some time, having died tragically in an airplane accident. The witnesses to those Biblical banquets – uncles, aunts, and cousins – had expanded the family business to new heights. I had no money of my own but I asked them to give me a job and until now I have led a peaceful life. I dress carefully every morning, blue serge suit, white shirt, striped tie, and head for my uncle's office. By now I am well versed in the rhythm of production and depreciation of factories; I am what you might call completely assimilated into the environment. Today, however, I've made up my mind finally to find out the secret of the box. I'll slip into my grandparents' old home during the family auction; I'm sure no one will pay attention to me. My relatives, faced with the crisis the family business has recently been going through, are too desperate to notice. Several days ago they agreed, because of impending bankruptcy, to auction off the house and the family heirlooms, which they had till then so reverently preserved.

I step silently across the hall and walk rapidly towards the dining room. To my right, the haggling and wrangling goes on, all family loyalties severed where profit is at stake. 'How much do you want to pay for the silver candelabra? Ten, fifteen, sixteen hundred? Will anyone pay two hundred? They're worth a lot more than they were appraised for, after all; we're not going to take advantage of each other, are we? Grandfather's clock, how much do you want to pay for grandfather's clock? It still chimes and grandfather's been silent dust now for some time. Going, going, gone for two hundred and fifty, that's a good buy, let me tell you, much better than the moth-eaten piano nobody wants.'

I place my hands over my ears and walk into the darkness of the living room. The uproar of the auction still hasn't reached this part of the house; the old wicker armchairs with carved headrests are still in place, as if waiting for ghosts to sit on them; the glass box is still on its high shelf, covered by a fine layer of dust. I lift it up tenderly with an ease that surprises me; I always thought it was heavy and it's so light. I tuck it under my arm and walk out into the street with it.

I feel I must hurry; I haven't much time left. My bridge will be the last one ever to be built by my family: it will be at once beautiful and frightening. I mingle with the crowds for a few minutes, until the bus to Playa Ponce goes by. I let out a sigh of relief as I sit next to a lottery vendor and listen to him advertise today's lucky number, an islander's 'one-way ticket to Paradise'. Once I reach the wharf, I get off the bus and quickly locate the schooner in which I am to sail. I look toward the elegant suburb where our family house still stands. Because I'm relatively safe now, I can wait patiently until the detonator hidden on the same shelf where the glass box used to sit finally goes off. I feel happy at last. I know I'll find peace, once the burning arches of my bridge spread out towards the north and towards the south.

Translated by Rosario Ferré in collaboration with Nancy Taylor

The Other Side of Paradise

Methinks her fault and beauty, blended
together, show, like leprosy, the whiter,
the fouler.
The Duchess of Malfi

It's been exactly a year since they began delaying their return home, as if they were afraid to confront the last trace of pain on her face, the last distress her memory may still cause them, when they sit down once again on the living-room couch. It's understandable that they've lacked the courage to return after what happened, that they've needed almost twelve months to wind a protective mantle around their hearts before they could come back. Now they can finally look at the wedding album, hold the photographs carefully, like soft, shiny panes of glass between their fingers, so that they won't be cut by the pain. The album's pages are as spotlessly clean as the walls and floors of our house. I scrub them every day in her name, getting down on my knees to wax the pink marble tiles, sticking my arm in the toilet bowls to scour their white porcelain throats, going down on all fours to brush the thick pile of the carpets until I leave them fluffy and clean, soft as the down on the pubic mound of the teenage girls I love to watch when I walk down Ashford Avenue.

Thus I humble myself day after day for her sake, so that she may go on living on cream and custard, so that she may go on sitting in seventh heaven like the angel she has now become, dreaming her seventh dream on top of seven cushions filled with eiderdown feathers, her forehead stamped with the seventh seal; may the Lord keep her forever by Him. The photographs are the only thing that's left of her now, of her shoulders and of her thighs, of her fingernails on which the light of the venetian blinds which I dust every day still falls, of her skin that gleams like newly applied wax and which I buff every day when I polish the floors of the house. Only they will answer to our need for remembering, the bride par excellence, kneeling on the silk cushion of the prie-dieu with the lighted taper in her hand, praying before the diamond-studded monstrance which holds the consecrated Host, as though she could guess the martyrdom that awaited her. This is why I must cherish the album like a holy object; put it away at night in a safe, cool place, so that the photographs will never melt in the noonday heat, so that they may never crumble from age and moisture into a mound of treacherous dust. I must preserve her thus, encased forever within dove-white covers, as she stood that day at the top of the stairs, the train of her wedding gown melting before her in a pool of snow, so that we may both one day be eternal.

My master and mistress are always coming and going; they spend a few months here but soon they start packing again, and they take off for France or Spain. They have peace of mind when they travel; they know that the house is safe under my keeping, that I'll never let it fall into disrepair. When they come back it's usually unexpectedly and for no reason at all. Something, a piece of news read while cruising far out to sea which may or may not have to do with the family's investments, the drought torturing the plains of Africa, the rapid rate of cholera deaths in India, will make them look up from their steaming cups of coffee at breakfast, point out the event that threatens them on the printed page, and comment, in their slow soft drawl, that it's time for them to return home. It's always fear that makes them want to come back to where they belong, to where they can sit once again in their dining-room chairs, to sip slowly, from familiar silver spoons, the soup I always prepare them at dinnertime. Here is the space where everything is known by heart, where they can go on living without danger when they grow old and must suffer the infirmities of age; because here they know every nook and corner, every cushion on the sofas and every crease on the rugs, every chip of the chinaware and every crack of the crystal water goblets, which could painfully injure their skins, their hands, or their lips. But this time their homecoming is bound to be different.

Marriage bed embroidered with pastel-tinted butterflies or funereal catafalque crowned with twisted braids of gold, it was all the same to her; she let them scheme for months, until they managed to marry her off. They spent days on end planning parties during which they would parade her like a perfumed, barely ripening fruit, delicately sliced so that she'd ooze the last drops of candour amongst her friends. When the guests would comment on her beauty at these parties, I invariably pointed out that it was not because her hair, her lips, or her eyes were anything extraordinary, but because of the way she carried herself when she walked, as though her body were a ladder up and down which angels were used to travel.

One day her parents introduced her to Juan Tomás, a young man of undeniable good manners, good income, and an impeccably cruel smile. After a month of insisting on the advantages of such an alliance, of placing his photograph on her bedside table so he'd be the last person she'd see at night, of inviting his relatives to coffee or tea, she consented to give away her hand in marriage, wrapped in the same mantle of indifference which enfolds the statues of Greek gods. She had arrived at the conclusion that no one else would come, that no one else would dare defy the family taboos and come knocking at her door. When I remember it all I wish I could cry, but I feel only sand would trickle out of the corner of my eyes. I turn the pages of the wedding album and it feels like everything is swimming inside me; the memories it holds are about to perish, erased by my welled-up tears.

The first sign I had of their return was when I saw that the almond tree that grows next to the house had begun to abort its harvest. It dropped the buds of its pink blossoms on the blue porcelain tiles of the terrace, so that it was soon mantled by a sea of grey cocoons which began to turn black at the ends. I swept it all away and left everything as clean as before, but the tree went on aborting. That same day I took out all my savings, went out on the street and bought the album. I took it to my room and sat on the bed with it, surrounded by the wedding photographs. It was difficult to find the right album. It had to have a cover of white kidskin, of the same kind as the full-length wedding gloves I myself had buttoned to her wrists that morning. I held the album to my chest as I sat there, remembering how the kidskin had swathed her arms as she rested them on the carved back of the Victorian chair where her first wedding photograph was taken, and I also thought of how she would have looked after the ceremony if it hadn't been for me. She would have lain on the marriage bed with her dress a peeled lily thrown on the floor, aborted there like a useless almond bud; abused, mistreated by an uncaring husband and yet still pure and undefiled, dreaming of the other side of Paradise. I gave a sigh of relief when I thought I could at last do something about it, carry out what my conscience, or perhaps it was my instinct, had long ago told me I must do.

When I first came to work in this house I learned that I didn't have to go on living in the outside world. Here the common world of men is nothing but a faraway murmur of voices, a limp screeching of ambulance sirens, a treading of steps which come and go from the door without any clear purpose. Before I came here I had lived in quest of love, obsessed with the idea of finding it one day at the bottom of a pair of handsome virile eyes. I have always searched for perfection, be it in a woman or a man. But I had only felt attracted to men, and those I met in the San Juan hotels where I

worked were always afraid to touch me; they were afraid to
give themselves in love because their hearts were eaten up by
fear of a sickness which is rampant today on the island, but
which I have always taken the greatest care not to contract.

Then one day I saw her as I was walking down the street
and I thought she had come out of a dream. She was so beautiful I found it hard to look straight at her; her skin was so
perfect it had something mysterious about it, which forced
you to look away, shielding your eyes with your hands. I
immediately followed her down the street to the house. A few
minutes later I knocked on the door and someone came to
open. I said I was looking for a job as a butler and I presented
my credentials; I had worked in the best hotels and had had
several years experience as a headwaiter; working for a single
family, in a private home, would definitely mean half of what I
had made before but it hardly seemed to matter. They gave me
the job and that very day showed me to my room at the back of
the house.

When I buttoned on my humble white cotton jacket I felt as
if I were buttoning on a pair of starched, homemade wings. I
looked at myself in the mirror and saw that the unpretentious
uniform, so different from the elegant livery I had worn before
in the hotels, was very becoming to me. I must be excused for
saying so, but I am a very handsome, albeit a sad man. We gay
people are never able to revel in the name; on the contrary,
our condition usually condemns us to melancholy, as it is our
ability to change, to transform ourselves like chameleons into
whatever we like, which most often sentences us to loneliness.
If you can be many people's soul mate, life becomes a swirling
carnival, and you go from room to room like Poe's revelling
chevaliers in 'The Masque of the Red Death', one of my
favourite short stories, which I read once in the master's study.
I pulled on my cotton gloves, a must for all correctly dressed
house servants on the island, and was grateful, from then on,
my fingerprints would be erased from everything I touched,
that the gloves would put a convenient distance between my

body and what I would have to do. That night I felt like Don Quixote on the eve of his knighting by a handmaid turned prostitute; I spent the whole night praying, kneeling by the side of my iron cot.

The next day the master and mistress informed me of my household chores. As I had more experience than the rest of the household staff, I had to organize the menus, supervise the purchase of foods and wines, oversee the chores done by the maids, serve the table at dinnertime, and answer the telephone every time it rang. But, seeing that I was what they thought of as hopelessly inverted, they also entrusted me with the responsibility of caring for their only daughter, who was about to get married soon. She's still an innocent child, you see, they said – and she's at that age when girls do not know how important it is to arrive at the altar with their maidenly manners intact. So please stay near her as much as possible and, without her noticing it, keep us well informed as to her whereabouts.

The first time I saw her up close she was sitting at her place at the dining-room table. As I bent towards her with lowered eyes, my right hand bent behind my back the way strict etiquette demanded, and offered her the silver tray heaped with viands with my left, I knew that she was looking attentively at me, and that she had instantly guessed how I felt about her. She had recognized me because she had dreamt about me every night the same as I had dreamt about her; she had run after me on the other side of the glass walls of dreams; she had tried many times to kiss me without success, desperately pounding on the glass with her fists.

During the days that followed our first meeting we finally managed to cross over this wall, and lived on the same side of paradise. The wedding was to be soon, and I was ordered by the master and mistress to supervise the preparation of the wedding banquet. During the day we would spend hours together, stirring the sauces which were to be poured over the roasts; whisking together the egg whites until they became hard as cloud banks, so they could be poured into the bowls of golden butter and flour which would later become cakes; ironing sugar into caramel panes of glass over the custards as if we were ironing it over our own flesh; sealing the lid of the apple tarts as if we were sealing our own eyelids with the tips of silver forks. When the presents began to arrive, I carried them one by one to her room. I loved to stand in front of her when she opened them, as she slowly let the silken wrapping paper drift to the floor, or as she undid the ribbons with her delicate fingers, letting them fall here and there like silver curls.

But no matter what I did, my devotion was never enough for her. She would stare at me coldly, a look of disdain on her face, and berate me because my household chores would never be perfect. When I carried the breakfast tray up to her room in the morning, for example, she would make a grimace and complain that the coffee was like dishwater and the jellied preserves rancid. When she was ready to take her bath of eucalyptus leaves, she would scream at the top of her voice for me to come and help her, and then she would parade naked before me in all the terrible array of her beauty, revelling in my supposed impotence. When she was about to get dressed, she wouldn't let anyone else shine her patent-leather shoes, which she enjoyed seeing me wear at certain moments. On those afternoons when she felt most bored by the seclusion her parents had condemned her to before the wedding, she would order me to dance for her Morel Campos's danza, 'From Your Side to Paradise'. I listened to her ranting but never lost my patience. I knew, deep down, that she loved me, and it was just her way of letting me know. So it was that, on the morning of the wedding, I entered her bedroom while she was still asleep, and did what both of us knew we had to do.

As soon as I learned the master and mistress were returning home I began to clean the house with tireless energy. I had learned about the suicide from the press and knew they wouldn't be alone, but that they would arrive accompanied by a large number of visitors from town. Friends and family would all gather at the house after their trip from the airport, milling behind their limousine in a slow wake. Now I hear the cars arriving, people climbing slowly up the stairs. The wedding album is lying on the table; too obvious for it to go unnoticed. They've formed a queue at the foot of the stairs and are coming up in pairs, all of them gossiping about what's happened. All the ladies have gone to the beauty parlour and their hairdos are stiff with hairspray; a woman goes by with a head of curls that resembles a pasta salad; a patent-leather helmet goes by, knotted tight at the base of the neck; a beehive moist with perspiration breathes by. They're all wearing new clothes; black silk, linen, cotton. Jewels, of course; it's a formal occasion; the urchin pearl pin on the suit lapel, at an angle that most becomes the face; the matching urchin ring with diamonds trembling on the tip of its quills.

As they begin to sit down in the living room, conversation is lively; it flits this way and that like a cloud of flies on a hot summer day. The ladies have begun to perspire; sweat stains their black granite-stiff skirts and blouses; they gossip about the accident with so much gusto, it seems as if every elbow and nail were about to sprout a tongue. I serve them iced lemonade, iced tea, or coffee. The gentlemen have dropped on the sofa like heavy sandbags moist from the heat; the sofa cushions, when people sat on them, exude a mouldy smell of feathers that haven't been sat on or bolstered for a long time. They order me to bring them whiskey, rum, aspirins with milk. Some of them mill around the master and mistress. 'We read about it in the papers,' they say, 'before anyone had a chance to call us. It said she was alone in the car and hadn't even taken off her wedding gown before it happened. She drove the car on the road to Fajardo, and sped headlong into an empty delivery truck parked at the end of the highway. Juan Tomás found the note later, when he returned to the bridal suite in the El Conquistador Hotel where they had checked in.' And: 'The funeral was so sudden and unannounced, no one had a chance to go and comfort you. And right after that you left the island, poor dears; you've been away for such a long time.'

All of a sudden someone discovers the album lying on the coffee-table. The master and mistress look at it in surprise and are about to pick it up when one of the mourners reaches for it first and takes it from the table. 'At least you have the beautiful photographs of the wedding to remember her by,' they say.

'There aren't any photographs to look at,' the master says in a voice that trembles slightly; 'we destroyed them before we left for Europe; it was all too painful to remember.'

'But you seem to be wrong, someone must have saved these after all,' the visitor said wonderingly as he caressed the album, weighing it carefully in the palm of his hands before he dared to open it. And then it was already too late, the album had begun to circulate from group to group, from hand to hand; blinding them with your beauty in the first photograph, where you were still standing next to Juan Tomás at the altar; drinking champagne at the dinner table; and later attesting to what had really happened; proclaiming that you had slipped away from the party and had met me secretly in my room, where I'd helped you to undress, your naked body swathed in angel wedding silk and surrendered into my arms. And then came the rest of the pictures: the one where you had your back to the party and said goodbye to the guests as you stood next to Juan Tomás on the stairwell, still dressed as a bride and yet already an adulteress, having given yourself to your slave-servant. The mourners begin to get up shamefacedly and start to leave the house; a rumour has begun to go around the living room and all of a sudden the whole house buzzes like a threatened beehive. They begin to shake their heads as they fall into disarray, shaking hands and pretending as if nothing had happened but already forming a disordered squadron of retreat. 'There's nothing to be done about it now but find the courage to go on living,' they mutter to the master and mistress as they go out the door.

A few days after their return the master and mistress

decided it was no longer advisable for them to keep the house. They ordered it demolished and went to live in a modern condominium, with central air conditioning, Jacuzzi bath, electronic oven, and rubbish disposal, none of which they had had at the house. I was, of course, on the spot decommissioned of all my duties, and unceremoniously kicked out. I left without a cent to my name and feeling a bit discouraged because of the incongruities of the world. Why shouldn't someone like me be allowed to live his dream, to strive to make perfection possible? Now there's nothing left of her but the razed lot where the house used to stand, and of course the wedding album, which I sneaked out of the living room without their realizing it. At night I sit on my bed and look at it, recreating the images of the perfect bride, be she kneeling before the Host in its diamond-studded monstrance, or on her prie dieu of Chinese silk. One day, as I was turning the pages, I suddenly stopped and looked at her eyes, which were gazing at me in wonder behind the mist of her veil. At that moment I realized I had reached the end of my quest. She had been my true soul mate, and our mating had made me accept myself for what I really am.

Translated by Rosario Ferré

When Women Love Men

La puta que yo conozco
no es de la China ni del Japón
porque la puta viene de Ponce
viene del barrio de San Antón
  'Plena de San Antón'

For we know in part
and we prophesy in part.
But when that which is perfect is come,
then that which is in part shall be done away.
When I was a child, I spake as a child:
But when I became a man, I put away childish things.
For now we see through a glass darkly;
but then face to face; now I know in part;
but then I shall know even as also I am known.
  St Paul, Epistle to the Corinthians,
  also known as the epistle of love.

It happened when you died, Ambrosio, and you left each of us half your inheritance; it was then that all this confusion began, this scandal spinning all over like an iron hoop, smashing your good name against the walls of the town; this slapped and stunned confusion that you swung around for the sake of power, pushing us both downhill at the same time. Anyone would say that you did what you did on purpose, just for the pleasure of seeing us light a candle in each corner of the room, to see which one of us had won. At least that's what we thought then, before we sensed your true intentions. Now we know that what you really wanted was to meld us, to make us fade into each other like an old picture lovingly placed under its negative, so that our own true face would finally come to surface.

When all is said and done this story is not so strange, Ambrosio; it seems almost inevitable that it should have happened the way it did. We, your lover and your wife, have always known that every lady hides a prostitute under her skin. This is obvious from the way a lady slowly crosses her legs, rubbing the insides of her thighs against each other. It's obvious from the way she soon gets bored with men; she never knows what we go through, plagued by them for the rest of our lives. It's evident in the prim way she looks at the world from under the tips of her eyelashes, as she hides the green-blue lights that swarm beneath her skirt. A prostitute, on the other hand, will go to similar extremes to hide the lady under her skin. Prostitutes all drown in the nostalgia of that dovecote-like cottage they'll never own, of a house with a balcony of silver amphorae, with fruited garlands hanging over the doors; they all suffer from hallucinations, such as listening for the sounds of silver and china before dinnertime, as though invisible servants were about to set the family table. The truth is, Ambrosio, that we, Isabel Luberza and Isabel la Negra, had been leaning more and more on each other; we had purified each other of all that defiled us; and we had grown so close that we no longer knew where the lady ended and the prostitute began.

You were to blame, Ambrosio, for the fact that no one could tell us apart after a while. Was it Isabel Luberza who began the campaign to restore the plaster lions of the town square, or was it Isabel la Negra who misspent the funds in making herself beautiful for the rich boys of the town, the sons of your friends that used to visit my shack every night, their shoulders drooping and dragging themselves like pigeons gripped by consumpton, staring hungrily at my body as though at a promised banquet; was it Isabel Luberza, the Red Cross Lady, or was it Elizabeth the Black, the Young Lords' President, who used to shout from her platform that she was living proof of the fact that there was no difference between Puerto Ricans and Neoricans, because they had all come together in her cunt; was it Isabel Luberza who used to collect funds for Boy's Town, for the Mute and Deaf, for Model City, dressed by Fernando Pena with long, white lambskin gloves and a silver mink stole, or was it Isabel the Slavedriver, the exploiter of innocent little Dominican girls, put ashore by smugglers on the beaches of Guayanilla; was it Isabel Luberza the Popular Party Lady, Ruth Fernández's long-lost twin in political campaigns, or was it Isabel la Negra, the soul of Puerto Rico turned into song, the temptress of Chichamba, the Jezebel of San Antón, the sharpest-shooting streetwalker of Barrio de la Cantera, the call girl of Cuatro Calles, the slut of Singapur, the vamp of Machuelo Abajo, the harlot of Coto Laurel; was it Isabel Luberza, the lady who used to breed pigeons in La Sultana cracker tins under her zinc-gabled roof, or was it Isabel la Negra, of whom it could never be said that she was neither fish nor fowl; was it Isabel Luberza, the baker of charity cupcakes, the knitter of little cloud-coloured *perlé* booties and blankets for the unwanted babies abandoned by their mothers on the front steps of the Church of the Sacred Heart, or was it Isabel the Rumba, Macumba, Candombe, Bámbula, Isabel the Tembandumba de la Quimbamba, swaying her okra hips through the sun-swilled Antillean streets, her grapefruit tits sliced open on her chest; was it Isabel de Trastamara, the holy Queen of Spain, patron of the most aristocratic street in Ponce, or was it Elizabeth the Black, the only lady ever to have bestowed upon her the order of the Sainted Prepuce of Christ; was it Saint Elizabeth, mother of Saint Louis King of France, our town's patron saint, lulled to sleep for centuries under the mountainous blue tits of Doña Juana, was it Isabel Luberza the Catholic Lady, the painter of the most exquisite scapularies of the Sacred Heart, still dripping the only three divine ruby drops capable of conjuring Satan, was it Isabel Luberza the champion of the Oblates, carrying a tray with her own pink tits served in syrup before her, was it Isabel Luberza the Virgin of the thumb, piously thrusting her pinky through a little hole embroidered in her gown; or was it Isabel la Negra, Step and Fetch It's only girlfriend, the only one who ever dared to kiss his deformed feet and cleanse them with her tears, the only one to join the children as they danced around him to the rhythm of his cry, 'Hersheybarskissesmilkyways', through the burning streets of Ponce, was it Isabel the Black Pearl of the South, the Chivas Regal, the Queen of Saba, the Tongolele, the Salomé, spinning her gyroscopic belly before the amazed eyes of men, shaking for them her multitudinous cunt and her monumental but- tocks; spreading, from time immemorial, this confusion between her and her, or between her and me, or between me and me, because as time went by it became more and more difficult for us to tell this story, it grew almost impossible to distinguish between the two.

So many years of anger stuck like a lump in my throat, Ambrosio, so many years of polishing my fingernails with Cherries Jubilee because it was the reddest colour in fashion at the time, always with Cherries Jubilee while I thought of her, Ambrosio, of Isabel la Negra; because, to begin with, it was unusual that I, Isabel Luberza, having such refined tastes, should like the shrill and gaudy colours that negroes usually prefer. Years of varnishing the contours of the half-moons at the base of my fingernails, of carefully brushing around the edge of the cuticle that always stung a bit as the nail polish fell on it, because when I saw the defenceless soft skin of the cuticle caught between the tips of my cuticle trimmers it always reminded me of her, and I'd usually cut too deep.

I think of all these things as I sit on the balcony of this house that now belongs to both of us, Ambrosio, to Isabel de Luberza and to Isabel la Negra, this house that will now become a part of our legend, of the legend of the lady and the prostitute. I can already see it turned into a brothel, which is what Isabel la

Negra plans to do. Its balcony of long silver amphorae will be painted shocking pink; its balusters aligned along the street like happy phalluses; its snow-white, garlanded facades, which now give the impression of cakes coated with heavy icing, spread stiff and sparkling like the skirt of a debutante, will then be washed in warm colours, in chartreuse green fused into chrysanthemum orange, in Pernod blue thawed into dahlia yellow; in those gaudy shades that persuade men to relax, to let their arms slide down their sides as though they didn't have a care in the world, as though they were about to sail out on the deck of a transatlantic luxury liner. The walls of the house, which are now elegantly gessoed, will be painted a bottle green, so that when you and I stand in the main hall, Ambrosio, everything will be revealed to us. We will then see ourselves unfold into twenty identical images, reflected in the walls of those rooms that we will rent out to our clients, so that they may have their indifferent orgasms in them, so that we may see them repeat, to the end of time, the ritual of love.

And so here I am, Ambrosio, sitting on the balcony in front of your house, waiting for them to come whisk her away, waiting to see Isabel Luberza's wake wind its way to a grave that was destined to be my grave. The sacred body of Isabel Luberza will file past my door today, a body which had never before been exposed, not even a sliver of her white buttocks, not even a shaving of her white breasts. Isabel Luberza renounces, Ambrosio, as of today, that virginity of a reputable wife which you had conferred upon her. It makes no difference that she had never before stepped into a brothel, that she had never before been slandered in public – as I have been so many times – that she had never bared any part of her body, food for the ravenous eyes of men, except her arms, her neck, or her legs from the shin down. Her body now naked and tinctured black; her sex covered only by a small triangle of amethysts, including the one the bishop once wore on his finger; her nipples trapped in nests of diamonds, fat and round like chick-peas; her feet stuffed into slippers of sparkling red rime, with twin hearts sewn on the tips; her heels still dripping a few drops of blood. Dressed, in short, like a queen, as I myself would have liked to be dressed, if it had been my funeral.

When they bring her out, swaying under a mountain of rotting flowers, I'll be waiting right there, Ambrosio. I'll walk up to her then and I'll scent my own body with Fleur de Rocaille perfume; I'll whiten my breasts with her Chant D'Aromes powder; I'll do my hair just like hers, spiralled in a cloud of smoke around my head; I'll drape myself in my lamé gown and spill my silver tunic over my shoulder, so that it sparkles vengefully in the midday sun. Then I'll bind my throat and wrists with diamond strings; I'll dress exactly as I used to when I was still Isabel Luberza and you were still alive, Ambrosio, the town spilling itself into the house to attend our parties, and I clinging to your arm like a jasmine vine to the wall, yielding my perfumed hand to be kissed by the guests, my delicate creamy hand which had already begun to be hers, Ambrosio, Isabel la Negra's; because even then I could feel the tide of blood rising, soaking my insides with Cherries Jubilee.

It wasn't until Isabel la Negra pounded vigorously on Isabel Luberza's door that the prostitute reconsidered whether she was doing a sensible thing in coming to visit her. She had come to talk to her about the business of the house they had inherited jointly. Ambrosio, the man they had both lived with when they were young, had died many years ago, and Isabel la Negra, out of consideration for her namesake, had not pressed her claim to the portion of the house that legally belonged to her. Isabel Luberza was living in the house, and it would have been inelegant to try to evict her. In any case, Isabel la Negra had wisely invested the money she had had from the mortgage on her part of the house, so that her mind was at rest as to not having made a poor business deal. She heard that Isabel Luberza was a bit mad. Since Ambrosio's death she had locked herself up in the house and never went out.

She had come to her rival's house thinking that so many years had gone by that all resentment should by now be forgotten. The widow was surely in need of rent money that would assure her a peaceful old age, and this would perhaps spur her to agree to a business deal. Isabel la Negra was very interested in becoming Isabel Luberza's partner. Her brothel had been so successful in recent years that she needed to enlarge it, and it would, moreover, be convenient to take it out of the slum, because in San Antón it lacked prestige, and even gave the impression of being an unhealthy establishment. But her yearning to live in the house, her dream of sitting out on the balcony behind the silver balustrade, beneath the baskets of fruit and garlands of flowers, answered to reasons deeper than economic expediency. She knew she suffered from a nostalgia that had become incandescent over the years, burning in her heart like a childhood vision. In this vision, which flashed back to her whenever she walked past Isabel Luberza's house, she'd see herself again as a young girl, barefoot and dressed in rags, looking up at a tall, handsome man dressed in white linen and Panama hat, who stood leaning out on the balcony next to a beautiful blond woman, elegantly dressed in a silver lamé gown.

That vision was the only grey cloud, the only elusive thorn that disturbed Isabel la Negra's contentment in her approaching old age. It was true; she was now a self-made woman and had achieved an enviable status in the town. Most society women were jealous of her, because, with the recent crash of the sugar market, the old families were now ruined and had only the empty pride of their names left to them. 'They haven't even enough money to take a little trip to Europe once a year like I do; they can't even afford the copies of my designer clothes,' she'd tell herself with a smile. Her importance in the economic development of the town was universally acknowledged. She had lately been the recipient of numerous prestigious appointments, such as honorary member of the Lion's Club, of the Chamber of Commerce, of the Banker's Trust, but she felt there was still something missing. She didn't want to die without having at least tried to make her secret dream come true: to imagine herself young once again, dressed in a sumptuous lamé dress and standing on that balcony, next to a man with whom she had once been in love.

When Isabel Luberza opened the door, Isabel la Negra went weak at the knees. She was still so beautiful, I had to lower my eyes; I almost didn't dare look at her. I wanted to kiss her eyelids, tender as new coconut flesh and of a bevelled, almond shape. She had braided her hair at the nape of her neck, as Ambrosio told me she used to wear it. The odour of Fleur de Rocaille, her overly sweet perfume, brought me back to reality. I knew I had to convince her that I was being sincere in seeking her friendship, that I would honour my contract with her as a business partner. For a moment she stared at me so intently that I wondered whether she truly was mad, whether she truly thought of herself as a saint, as they said in town. I'd heard people say she lived obsessed with the idea of redeeming me, and that she'd subject her body to all sorts of absurd punishments for my sake. But it didn't really matter. If the rumour was true, I was sure it would work in my favour. After staring at me for a moment, she opened the door and I went in.

When I walked into the living rooms I couldn't help but think of you, Ambrosio, of how you'd had me locked up for years in that shack with a zinc roof. There I had been sentenced to spend my days, milking the boys you yourself had introduced to me. 'Please do my son's friends a favour Isabel,' you'd say. 'Damn it, Isabel, don't be hard-hearted, you're the only one who knows how to do it, you're the one who does it best.' You'd tell them 'sure you can, son, why not, just let yourself go, that's all, as though you were skiing down a mountain of soapsuds without stopping,' so their fathers could sleep peacefully because their offspring had not turned out to be gay sissies with porcelain-splintered butts, because they were manly machos, thanks to the coupling of Saint Dagger and Saint Pussy. But your friends could only prove this by sending their sons to me, Ambrosio; and they knew I'd only take care of them if it was you who brought them.

And so it was that, just to please you, Ambrosio, I began to kneel in front of the boys, like a priestess officiating at a sacred ritual. My hair would blind me as I'd lower my head to sheath their penises, like tender lilies, in my throat. Until one day I got to thinking that I wasn't really spending myself with those teenage Romeos because you had asked me to, Ambrosio, but that deep down I was doing it for my sake, to pick up an ancient, almost-forgotten taste, that leaked out in bittersweet streams down my throat: the taste of power. Because in teaching those boys how to make love, Ambrosio, I also showed them what a real woman is like. A real woman is not a sack of flour that lets a man throw her on a bed, just as a real man is not a raping macho, but one that has the courage to let himself be raped. So I devoted myself to teaching the boys how to share a pleasure without having to be ashamed of it; I taught them how to be generous with themselves. Once they left my bed they could rest easy as to their future performances; they could parade confidently before their girlfriends like strutting young roosters. After all, someone had to show young men how to take the initiative; someone had to show them in the first place, and that's why they all come to Isabel la Negra – sinful like the slough at the bottom of the gutter, wicked like the grounds at the end of the coffeepot – because in Isabel la Negra's arms everything is allowed, son, nothing is forbidden; our body is our only paradise, our only fount of delight, and Isabel makes us understand that pleasure can make us live forever, can turn us into gods, son, though only for a short while – but a short while is usually enough, because after having known pleasure no one should be afraid to die. So be quiet now, my son, be still; nestled here, in Isabel la Negra's arms, no one will see you, no one will ever know you were merely human. Here no one will see you, no one will care that you're trembling with ague in my arms, because I'm just Isabel la Negra, the scum of the earth, and here, I swear by the holy name of Jesus that is looking on, no one will ever know that what you really wanted was to live forever, that what you really wanted was not to die.

When you began getting old, Ambrosio, luck turned in my favour. You thought I was taking my duties with the boys too seriously and that they were meeting me secretly, perhaps even paying me more than you did, so that I would finally prefer them to you. It was then you had your lawyer write up your new will, in which you left everything you owned in the world to your wife and to me.

Isabel la Negra stared at the sumptuously decorated walls of Isabel Luberza's living room and concluded that it was the perfect atmosphere for her new Dancing Hall. She could finally move out of her sleazy whorehouse, where it was so difficult to make business prosper. As she admired the gilded *fauteuils*, the brocaded sofas, and the crystal chandeliers, she felt convinced that if the Dancing Hall remained in the slum, no matter how much she invested in it, it would always remain a gimcrack joint. But here, in this elegant setting, and as Isabel Luberza's partner, everything could be different. She could hire half a dozen professional models and charge at least a hundred dollars a night. She made up her mind to get rid of all the old whores with musty cunts and wrinkled breasts, and decided to invest in new down pillows and Beautyrest mattresses, discarding the old Salvation Army iron cots. She was, in short, set on a first-class establishment, where one could wine, dine and dance to one's heart's delight.

When the women finally finished their tour of the house, Isabel Luberza shook her visitor's hand courteously, and in doing so took a few steps toward Isabel la Negra. She stretched out her hand and touched the procuress's face tenderly with the tip of her fingers, as though she were a soothsayer and were about to solve the riddle of life. Just when I was about to leave, she surprised me by kissing my cheeks, and then bursting out in tears. I felt a terrible pity for her, and thought, You must have had a heart of stone, Ambrosio, to torture her the way you did. Then she took my hand in hers and looked curiously at my nails, which I had just polished that day with Cherries Jubilee.

She's varnished her nails the same colour as mine but it doesn't surprise me, Ambrosio, there are so many things on this earth one doesn't understand. I couldn't figure out, for instance, why you'd not only left her half your estate, but made her co-owner of this house, where you and I had been so happy. The day after the funeral, when I realized the whole town was on to what had happened and that I was being slandered to bits, I walked through the streets hoping Isabel la Negra would die. But then, after she tore down the shack where you used to visit her and she built the Dancing Hall with your money, I began to feel differently about her, and finally realized what she'd meant to us.

The first year of our marriage, when I learned Isabel was your paramour, I thought I was probably the unhappiest woman on earth. I always knew when you were coming from her house; I could tell by the heavy way your hand fell on my neck, or by the way you dragged your eyes over my body like burning sparks. It was then I had to be most careful of my satin slips and French lace underwear. It was as though the memory of her rode you when you weren't with her, and she'd sit on your back and hit you mercilessly with arms and legs, tormenting you so you'd go back to her. So I had no alternative but to stretch out on the bed and let myself be made. As you bent over me, I'd keep my eyes wide open and look out over your shoulder so as not to lose sight of her, so she wouldn't think I was giving in to her, not even by mistake.

Then I decided to win you over through other ways, Ambrosio, through that ancient wisdom I had inherited from my mother, and my mother from her mother before her. I began to place your napkin in a silver ring next to your plate, to sprinkle lemon juice in your water goblet, to spread your linens on sheets of zinc under the glaring sun. I'd then place the linens on your bed when they were still warm with sunlight. I'd spread them inside-out and then fold them right-side up, thereby releasing, to please you when you'd finally come to bed, a subtle essence of roses. I'd place our monograms, intertwined like amorous vines, under your bare forearms, so they'd remind you of the sacred vows of our marriage. But all my efforts were in vain. Diamonds sown in the wind. Pearls thrown on the muck heap.

Thus, Ambrosio, as the years went by Isabel la Negra became for us a necessary evil, a tumour that grew in our breast, but which we nursed tenderly so that it wouldn't be bothersome. It was at dinnertime that her presence was most clearly felt. A fragrance of peace would then waft up from our dinner plates, and as the icy beads slowly ran down the sides of our water goblets, it seemed as though happiness would remain forever poised on the fragile edge of our lives. I would then begin to think of her gratefully, reassembling her features in my mind in order to see her more clearly, in order to imagine her sitting next to us at the table. It was she that brought us together, Ambrosio; she that made our marital bliss possible.

Since I'd never seen her, I invented her to my heart's content. I thought of her as bewitchingly beautiful, her skin dark as night when mine was milk at dawn, her hair a thick rope braided around her head when mine lay stylishly draped, like a soft golden chain, around my shoulders. I could almost see her strong teeth, which she rubbed daily with baking soda to whiten them, and then I thought of mine, delicate and transparent like fish scales, barely showing under my lips in a perpetually polite smile. I thought of her eyes, soft and bulging like grapes, set, as a negro's eyes are wont to be, in a thick, sluggish custard, and I thought of my eyes, restless and sparkling like emeralds, always coming and going through the house.

Thus the years went by, Ambrosio, and thanks to Isabel la Negra I began to feel useful again. Thinking of her made me acutely aware of the importance of my duties as a housewife. I would then measure the exact amount of flour and sugar in their jars in the pantry; I would carefully count the silverware in the dining-room coffer to make sure none was missing. Only then would I lie down peacefully next to you, Ambrosio, knowing that I'd done my duty and had looked after your assets.

I thought I'd lost the fight until a few minutes ago, when I heard her knock on the door. I knew it was her before I opened it; she had telephoned to say she was coming, and so I'd had time to prepare myself emotionally, but when I saw her I went weak all over. She looked exactly as I'd pictured her. She had lavender eyelids and thick, plum-coloured eyes, which made me feel like kissing them; she wore her hair undone, and it rose over her shoulders like a smoking mane. I was surprised to discover how little she'd aged. And when I thought of how much she'd loved you, Ambrosio, I almost felt like embracing her, like telling her, 'Let's be friends, Isabel, for God's sake, let's forgive and forget.'

But then she began to sway her hips provocatively in front of me, balancing herself back and forth on her sparkling red-rime heels, her hand on her waist and her elbow askew so as to flaunt before my eyes the stinking hole of her armpit. The terrible shadow of that armpit hit me square on the forehead, Ambrosio, and suddenly I remembered everything I had suffered because of her. Beyond her stinking armpit I glimpsed the open door of her Cadillac, a piece of her chauffeur's gilded buttoned jacket. So I flung the door open defiantly and asked her to come in.

I'd been waiting a long time for her visit. She's already successfully replaced me in all the social activities of the town, in which I used to preside holding fast to your arm like a sprig of jasmine. Now she's come to claim this house, where I've fought to keep your memory alive during all these years. She'll grab on to your mementos, the relics and memorabilia I've been saving for years, until she's taken them all, until she's sucked from them the last drops of your blood's dust. Because until now these events have all been shrouded in mystery, and

I haven't been able to fathom the meaning of so much suffering except through a glass darkly, but today I've begun to see clearly for the first time. Today I'll confront the perfect beauty of her face to my absolute sorrow in order to understand. Now that I've drawn nearer to her I can see her as she really is, her hair no longer a cloud of smoke raging above her head but draped like a soft, golden chain about her neck, her soft skin no longer dark, but spilled over her shoulders like dawn's milk, a skin of the purest pedigree, without the merest suspicion of a kinky backlash, now swaying back and forth defiantly before her and feeling the blood flow out of me like a tide, my treacherous turncoat blood that has even now begun to stain my heels with the glorious, shocking shade I've always loved so, the shade of Cherries Jubilee.

Translated by Rosario Ferré and Cindy Ventura

MATTHEW KRAMER

———————

Sunset

———

for my father

Unlike her, she told me, I wasn't old enough to remember the British Empire. Unlike her. This was true.

I wasn't old enough to remember that time after the red had steadily seeped its way through all the leaves of the atlas, such a strong and inexorable colour, nor old enough to recall a battered globe with a heavily rouged face, just before its abrupt erasure.

It was interesting to consider how that might have touched her. If she were, say, eighteen in 1949. (I choose that year because there'd been an uncle who rode on the Indian railways. I choose eighteen even though I'm certain she was never truly young, but rather sank into middle age, that boggy, impassable terrain, early, and stayed put.) And it was interesting also to consider what views and expectations – personal as well as historical – she might have had at that fragile age.

But did she know these were my thoughts while she sat opposite, closed up around her bag as if I might snatch it? After all, I was her sleek new solicitor, as remote from her as a sports car, and it wasn't part of my role to think such things. But still she went on, referring to the *British Empire* as if something still lived and pulsed in those stiff, gilded words – although I strongly doubted any family of hers ever held shares in it – and implying also, it seemed, that I wasn't old enough to remember anything that mattered.

Well, perhaps she was right. And I wondered if the railway-uncle's vision had been expanded by all those miles of endless track. Otherwise what was ever the point of crossing and recrossing a continent? Her father, she explained, could have joined him. She still had the younger brother's invitation. A few excited words on the back of a postcard. One of those old-style postcards with crimped edges. Which you've probably never seen, she said. But her father knew his responsibilities. And stayed where he was, in the pit he'd already dug. She really was anxious to talk.

Her hair was so threadbare, the white shell of her head was visible through its strands, and her anorak (which she'd refused to remove) had the colour of muddy, trampled, soaking grass. I found myself looking at the hand which gripped the conference table while she spoke. This hand was a different colour to the naked dome peeping out from under its unravelling covering of hair, the gully between each tensed finger jaundiced, the hand's back daubed with a bark-coloured constellation of spots. I found something admirable in that trembling hand. It had had to come a long way – not physically, but in every other sense – to finish up fixed to my table, like some small, tenacious animal which had leapt from undergrowth, and bitten deeply into the wood. And it clung there, shivering. Shivering persistently, but unconsciously, determined not to be shaken off until this small woman with the eggshell scalp and oversized anorak had received from me justice.

This was the first problem. Explaining that I was not a source of justice. But she kept on saying, *Do you think it's right? Do you think it's right?* as if she had only to convince me for everything to become right. Suddenly and totally.

With these cases, you usually never get to see – let alone touch, absorb – the houses, the settings. They become, somehow, insubstantial, unreal even, so often distorted, stretched and heightened by the decorative overlay of words the speaking mouth of the client opposite lays down, like a rich impasto. And so it was the febrile force of this speaker, almost swallowed by her anorak, face barely rising above its maw, ballooned her home for me into some ridiculous gothic edifice, steepening the stairs, lifting and narrowing the windows and gables, creating implausible passageways – until in the end I envisaged something fit for ravens to perch on, giving the creeps to its bleached suburban neighbours. It was bravura stuff, if spoken too fast – she could not advance on one front only – and, undeniably, she had the guts for Attic tragedy.

A spill of tea (for the drinking-hand also shook) had meanwhile touched the two unused sugar cubes on her saucer. These droplets ate deep into the upper face of each cube, turning their glitter brown, as if the crystals had begun to rot before my eyes. Then she laughed at me – I was caught unawares – and for the first time saw properly her incomplete teeth; every second one was the colour of teak.

I hadn't been listening to her, so I didn't know what was the joke. But I tried to smile anyway, a controlled smile, nothing too casual or relaxed, and said, Yes, I see, while linking my hands, knowing I had to keep a lid tightly pressed on this meeting, and stay rigid in my manner, as the only possible check on her. For she kept on saying, *Do you think it's right? Do you think it's right?* and I knew that what she was really looking for (that day) was an ally. She didn't want legal advice on her Green Form. She wanted a crazed and out-of-tune duet.

He keeps on asking me when am I getting married, and leaving the house. HE. *He keeps on telling me I should be married.* HE had tribal scars which gave her a turn the first time she saw them, picked out by the hallway bulb on that terrible night. When he first appeared, and told her, 'I am a professional man.' *First he told us that he had bought the house (I know why he came at night; we were all in the hallway, Hetty and me in our nighties, at that time Mr Scone was* eighty-three*), and then he said he was a professional man. Whenever we have an argument he tells me he is a professional man. Well, I told him, I am a professional woman. And do you know what he did? He laughed, and said it was time I got married. I won't have him talking like that to me. I won't have it. We were all there in the hallway. Do you know how late it was? Quarter to ten in the* *night. Mr Piercy was seventy-three at the time. He was shivering from the cold.* And then I looked at her own endlessly shivering hand, compulsively trembling the conference table to which it remained affixed.

She was still asking, *Do you think it's right? Do you think it's right?* I tried to imagine the tribal scars, three parallel ridges on either cheek of the professional man. The way she spoke, there were old people in their hundreds palpitating with cold in the hallway that night, massed in their threadbare nighties and pyjamas, undergoing a stern appraisal by their new landlord. In fact she gave their names. Five protected tenants in all. And Miss Bone only peeped out, into that benighted hallway; she was too frightened to leave her room.

They had all gone now. Except her, and her friend. Hetty. Who was doing the extra-mural degree. Her friend had lived there for eighteen years, since her husband died. *I type her essays for her, on my Olivetti.* They fortify each other, I learned. Next time she would bring Hetty with her. I took the full name. She was in the hallway that night? *Of course; she was our spokesman. She speaks very well. She is taking an extra-mural degree in history.*

HE had been waiting for the others to grow old, old and confused, and for his children to grow up, she explained. For seven years he had patiently waited ... *He infiltrated his children into the upstairs rooms, that's the word, infiltrated them in. Once they were old enough; as those rooms became empty. Miss Bone died. I know why. She was so sad at the end. Mr Piercy is in a home now, and doesn't even recognize me. And Mr Scone, he disappeared. How can a man of eighty-three disappear? Have you ever known a man of eighty-three to disappear? Am I right?* No, I had to admit. I had never known that happen before. *And now the children are in their rooms. If you can call them children. They are all so big; and they have no manners. Not one. And now* he *is infiltrating himself in. With her, his wife. Do you know,* she said suddenly, *I even had to have a boxing match, with his wife. Like this.*

And up came her fists, together, poised just in front of her face. There were defiant pinpricks of light in her eyes, and on her face a tightly pleased, but grim smile.

We both looked at those fists. I think she was almost as surprised as me to be gazing at them, an unsteady phalanx of speckled knuckles. They trembled before her eyes, but she kept them there; insisted on keeping them there even as their trembling increased, became a tremor in both forearms, as the effort told on her. What had been meant as a dashing, insouciant gesture now required her undivided attention. And as the vibration beneath the skin grew, I think she found herself compelled to meet the challenge, by not now – whatever happened – dropping her bunched and bony guard. She could have been an old pro, remembering better times. I said, yes, yes, but please, don't tire yourself.

'I did, you know. I did.'

And, still trembling, down they slowly came. The veins on both forearms were alarmingly pronounced.

She now elaborated on, for my benefit, this process of *infiltration*, as, year by year, the others, the old people, growing confused, their bearings lost, in quiet succession melted away; and their rooms fell empty . . . There was even Black Magic. *Yes. I'm serious.* At an early peak in the war's febrile graph. *After the Council imposed a Control Order. He says it was a Management Order. But it was a Control Order. This is a matter of record.* If she was right, it meant he'd been barred from the house. (Her papers filled a small suitcase and two plastic carrier bags, all of which she'd brought with her. County Court pleadings. Stacks of tattered, stapled affidavits intemperate with allegations and denials of harassment and neglect. My predecessors' files. Letters and more letters. Warnings. Notices. Court Orders. The fall-out from a private prosecution in the magistrates and a counter-private prosecution in the same place. The waste product of a guerrilla war: I was going to have to read all that.) But we were talking about black magic. *A tall stranger came to the house,* she said. *The wife brought him. I found out later he was their nephew, from Henley-on-Thames.*

I followed him and took his car number. He walked round the house twice. All the time they were talking in their language. Then he stopped opposite the front door and broke an egg. There were strange red marks on the shell. Then he crouched and placed the shell on the ground, and encircled it with small stones.

'I see,' I said.

'Mr Bollard, the Tenancy Relations Officer at the Council told me, he said we were being subjected to Black Magic.'

'I see.'

And so she went on. *They are from the Gambia. The couple. I think* he *came to take accountancy exams.* She *has hair like black candy floss. They let the children run wild. In the upstairs rooms. I hear them from my room, from my kitchen. The doors are all left open. Where Mr Scone and Mr Piercy and Miss Bone used to live.* And perhaps she even imagined, for an intense moment, their tremulous ghosts, hovering pale and disconsolate in their nightwear while the television (or so she told me) screamed at its highest volume, *though they aren't listening to it, they're in the other room listening to music, but they leave the television on, they leave it on all the time, and then when they do go to watch it, they leave the music still playing, in the other room. And they cook as well, the children cook. I hear them fighting in the upstairs kitchen.* (Her own little kitchen is downstairs, connected to her room.) *The parents are in another, nearby house, mostly. But the children bring food from there, in these big pots, and heat it. So I go out of my room to open the window on the landing. To get rid of the cooking smells. But then they creep down the stairs and shut it . . .* So when she'd hear them retreat, back to the noise, she would slip back out again and quickly reopen that window. But only for the children, whispering, to return a little later, once she was safely back in her room – though with her tensed ear now applied to the door (they didn't know this) – and close it. She'd hear their triumphant, mocking laughter (she told me) as they ran away.

Do you think it's right? She couldn't stop asking me that. *Do you think it's right?*

It was out of this there came the boxing match. *I was slan-*

dered. She said I hit her daughter. I did not hit her daughter. I restrained *her daughter. From closing the window. I know my rights* . . . And then she blinked. Suddenly, curiously, still; the rage had exhausted itself, the nervous effort of so much speech had sucked up all her anger. She was unexpectantly becalmed; and as surprised as me, I sensed, to find herself that way. Briefly emptied. Passive. I could see that she was unfamiliar with this feeling. It had stolen up on her; she didn't know what to do with it. *Yes, well*, she said, finally, starting now to fidget with her handbag, opening the thing, peering down, her low-ered head presenting to me the eggshell dome emerging through its decimated hair. The oversized anorak now seemed even more incongruous, huge on her as a gorilla suit. I waited. This new activity absorbed her, so I leaned back, using this opportunity to thrust out my tired arms and relax them. The attendance note I'd taken was solid, unbroken – the lines of frantic writing dragged across and across each page by her voice appeared dense and impenetrable as barbed wire. But she was reviving now, was looking up, at me. Her moment of calm (I could tell) had passed. That thin mouth opened.

I sit in my near-empty flat (which I seem always too tired to furnish), slumped and resting, irregularly dozing, drifting all the while in and out of the news, those bold harsh images from the TV in the furthest corner, fragments of whose stories brush me. Near by are her suitcase and the two carrier bags. I can, in fact, smell them. It is a distinctive and unattractive odour, compounded by time and persistence, by the packing together so close of all that accumulated and over-fingered paper. The supermarket carrier bags in particular look strangely out of place on the pure glass table-top. As if she's crouched there herself, arms around her knees, a shabby, bedraggled gnome who's hopped in from my garden.

There were dreary exchanges of solicitors' letters. I took her to see Counsel. The gravitas of his height, his young military jaw and barrister's learning impressed her. I think she was excited that someone so elegant, in manner and dress, should take such interest in her. She telephoned me twice, saying we should go to see him again. He had important things to say. She was advising me now. She thought it would help us both. He definitely had important things to say. But, as it turned out, we never did attend him again.

He and *she*, meanwhile, had finally, irrevocably, moved in. Her phone calls now became more frequent. The situation had become *impossible*. It was *completely, totally impossible*. They were all there up on the first and second floors. *Cooking. Making noise. Shouting terrible things in their language.* She and Hetty, downstairs, quaked in each other's rooms. It was lucky they had each other. What would happen to her if Hetty was murdered? And always, all the time, she would ask, *Do you think it's right? Do you think it's right?*

But the fight, the fight in her that had animated our first meeting, that had definitely waned – only a little maybe, but the evidence was there (in her tone) of its dilution; the dilution of its former, almost gleeful, belligerence. There was no more grand talk now of affidavits and summonses. She was withdrawing, in all ways, back into her single room and its little kitchen, fortifying them, sealing her borders. Even in the words she now used the house slipped and dwindled, its walls moving closer, the high windows foreshortened, the swirls of dust slackening and settling. The ravens took flight.

I think she knew now they would not be selling up, moving on, whatever she did; and her gaze, gradually, unsteadily, refocused. It no longer encompassed the entire house and its pitiful, overgrown garden. Weekly, in her fitful calls to me, I shared its shrinkage, its narrowing of perspective; abandoning the upper floors, retreating down the stairs, until all her remaining energy was centred on the narrow, plain lavatory door across the hall from her tiny kingdom. There was a lock, and there were two keys . . . *Hetty has one and I have the other. We take it in turn to clean and air it; I put lilac in there*, she told me

almost proudly, *in a pot-pourri I bought in the market ... You
don't know what a pot-pourri is, do you?*

No, I had to admit. *No, no, I didn't think you would.* It wasn't
made clear why this was a failing, but it was, although one
which it pleased her for me to have.

'He says we shouldn't have our own lock on it!' I remember
clearly her dramatic telephone call when she broke the news.
She was alarmed. 'He doesn't have any right to, does he? I
know he doesn't. I know exactly what I'm entitled to in the
house. I have all the documents. I know exactly where my
rights extend. I know *exactly.* I have all the papers here, all the
documents.'

There followed several weeks of spasmodic negotiations
with my opposite number. Meanwhile I received almost daily
reports. *He says that he and his family should be allowed to use the
whole house. Why? They don't need to. Do you think it's right? Do
you think it's right?* Immediately prior to this time she and
Hetty, by a joint decision, had begun to observe a rule of chilly
silence. *And now they do as well.* Both sides would pass each
other on the ground floor with eyes averted. As if there was no
one there ... I imagined the frosty defiance of her and her
friend, moving soundlessly, chins erect, between their rooms
and that solitary door like members of a religious order, while
the children periodically rushed by between the first floor
landing and the open front door in great whispering surges,
only bursting into noise when they'd safely passed.

After that the violence began. Late at night a tapping sound
woke her. For a long time she lay there, in her single bed,
hair sprayed out around her, hearing that discreet, persistent
sound. Then suddenly she understood ... She erupted from
her room, hands in the air, nightie hoisted by the turbulence.
He looked round, surprised, down on his knees with a
hammer poised above their lock.

There were so many different accounts of what followed,
there's little point trying to disentangle them now. I did however see the imperfectly healed scars on his wife's face, weeks

later, at court. My client must have sank her nails into that woman's skin with extraordinary, berserk force.

Altogether there were three, maybe four, eruptions. Pitched battles in that long war. For a period *he* went nowhere in the house without a tape recorder attached to his body. The two sides circled each other and that sacred lock. At one point, three of them were bound over to keep the peace, all hustled into agreeing to that at the court door by their legal advisers. It seemed the best way to get everyone out of there quickly.

On that occasion his solicitor sent me one of the tape recordings. But all I could hear was inarticulate noise, a hoarse medley of banging, scuffling and clumping; she was said to have crept up on him while he made his second tilt at the lock, determined to replace it with one to which his family also had access. I did briefly hear her screaming, 'Help, Hetty, they're killing me, they're killing me!' before it all collapsed back into meaningless noise.

Then came the police raid. Three cars – almost a dozen officers – to arrest the parents and their eldest daughter. They arrived at dawn. Solid fists detonated against the front door in the spiky morning air. Solid uniformed bodies swarmed inside. Earlier there had been another confrontation. Supposedly the worst. She rang me later to breathlessly describe her alleged bruising. I listened. It took her a long time to detail it all, as if she were speaking to me while turning naked and grotesquely marbled by blows before a full-length mirror.

They were released on bail. As they came out of the courtroom after, I watched as their eldest daughter, graceful as a Modigliani, began to cry. I was standing about ten yards from them, weighed down by my documents case. An African woman, among the two or three who'd joined them from the public gallery, turned on her, was almost – it was strange – smiling. Smiling and shaking her head. 'You are a black woman!' she remonstrated. 'So why are you crying? Why are you crying?' Then this tall figure, her head and conical hair suddenly jerking back, as if now she were angry, repeated her original sentence with even greater emphasis. 'You are a *blaaak* woman!' There was no immediate follow-up to this pronouncement. It seemed intended to say all. The girl was still wiping her eyes, trying to smile. 'And now you know what it is like to be a *blaaak* woman.' And then she placed a strong ebony arm across the daughter's back, hand cupping, gripping the girl's shoulder.

I stood and watched their small group move slowly away towards the stairs to the exit.

Then I looked for her. She was lost in her capacious anorak, moving away at a different angle, gradually dwindling as she headed alone towards the opposite stairs.

It is still going on. The silence now between the front entrance and the staircase to the first landing is heavier, sadder, overlaid with dust. The two old women move quickly, quietly between their rooms and the disputed door when they cross the hallway. They have a haunted look. The original lock is still there, just. In a telephone conversation, off the record with my opposite number, we agreed it was better to leave it that way. For the time being, at least. And when I speak to her, she is still insistent, still implacable. (I see her drawn, chilly smile and her focused eyes.) How she insists. That space (at least) they will never share.

The Great House

'Of course,' said my titled host. 'Isn't the real thing, you know.'
I was surprised. From where we stood, on a baize knoll cresting the man-made lake, I'd been counting the pillars which shouldered its portico. The house had seemed to me the very essence of elegance and breeding, with its confident, grave facade. 'That got burned down, Mr Schoenbaum.'

'Oh, what a terrible accident,' I said limply.

'No accident at all. Grandfather torched it, don't ask me why. They found him, just where we're standing now, wearing an Uhlan's helmet and applauding the fire. Damn lunatic was shouting Burn Burn Burn.'

We walked back towards the house. For a man of sixty-eight, he had an enviable posture. It was hard, during our thoughtful return, not to draw unfavourable comparisons. I was thirty-three and five inches shorter. I was thirty-three with rather less hair. I was thirty-three and had begun to develop a small, but alarming paunch, sufficient in fact to fill both my hands when I dared check. Then he said (he must have been thinking about this all that time), 'Not had those sort of problems in your family then?'

'Well, until quite recently, we didn't really have anything worth burning down.'

'No. No, suppose not. Still, luncheon now. Then back to the books.'

'Yes.'

He was silent again, until, as we neared the house, he suddenly muttered, 'Bloody books . . . Don't know how you put up with them.'

'Well, I've always been interested in figures.'

'Yes, yes, suppose you'd have to be . . . So you never considered the army.'

'. . . No.'

'Always knew it was going to be accountancy?'

'Well, sort of, I suppose.' We were going up the steps now. To maintain the recovered momentum of the conversation, I added, 'No, I don't think the military would've been quite me.'

'I don't know,' he said, ushering me in. 'Plenty of short fat chaps in the army.'

We entered the hall. Muddy dogs milled around us benignly. I preferred not to consider what he must think when he thought of me. He, who could look at the world down a corridor of portraits, to each of which he was joined.

Head surprisingly alert, my host now crossed the hall, and I went with him, accompanied by his loyal dogs.

I sat down to eat with him and also his daughter. He and I seated ourselves at one end of the long table (he at the top, I on his right-hand side), but his daughter, with great emphasis, scraped out a chair at the other end, and immediately sank her head into a noisy tabloid-sized newspaper. She kept on turning its pages, always with tremendous and unnecessary force, going impatiently backwards and forwards through the rag while quite ignoring the silverware of her place setting, elaborate as a coat of arms. Instead she preferred to stab away with just a fork at food her eyes shunned. She ate appallingly, like a hungry refugee, remaining throughout furiously entranced by her little newspaper. She never once looked up, or at us.

Meanwhile my host talked suavely, charmingly, the accent rich and thoroughly polished, unconcerned by the dissociated noise his daughter made; he was unexpectedly, almost alarmingly, attentive to my tales from the world of accountancy.

'Ever gone shooting?'

'I've never fired a gun in my life.'

'Like to give it a try?'

Before I could answer, his daughter stood up, driving her heavy chair back.

'Why don't you come down here, and say hullo to Mr Schoenbaum.'

Head now thoughtfully dipped, she carefully folded her newspaper. Her hair had been dragged back from her face to conclude in a tight, dense whorl. It seemed a hard, self-punitive arrangement, emphasizing the face, its shape, the moulding of her head; a physiognomy deliberately stripped of anything that might soften or shade it. This was a head that meant business, just as clearly as her father's, draped in its patrician folds of skin, did not.

Now she looked at us. No, she looked at him.

'I thought I might introduce Mr Schoenbaum to hunting, shooting and fishing, in the course of his weekend with us,' said her father equably. 'He tells me he's never fired a gun in his life.'

The daughter merely stared, but no longer at him. Now her object of interest appeared to be me.

'Wouldn't you like to, Mr Schoenbaum?'

'Oh yes, yes,' I said hastily, still stupidly holding my knife and fork to attention, unable to decide whether I was meant to look at him, or at her.

'Indeed,' my host continued, 'I understand Mr Schoenbaum has even packed a Barbour, just for us. Brand new, I believe.'

'Well yes,' I said, then added, almost stuttering, 'I've never needed one before.'

'Well that's splendid, isn't it,' my host insisted, to his daughter; but at this she merely turned and briskly, wordlessly left the room. The grand panelled door banged to behind her.

'I hope nothing's wrong,' I said eventually.

He laughed, briefly. 'This is what happens when they get politics . . . Yes. When they get bloody politics.'

It was night-time. Having been urged by my host to explore, to explore and satisfy any curiosities I might have, I now stood in the lamp-lit library, looking up. Shaped like a chapel, with a lazy, buccolic scene that gleamed across the ceiling through its skin of varnish, it had three bulging cliff-faces of books, at the far end and on either side, their thousands of ribbed leather spines shoe-horned into a dark terracing of shelves. The long, fluted cloth of the curtains had been drawn, masking the windows. It was impossible not to be impressed.

I intended to go down the carpet-path to the far end, climb the small set of wooden steps placed there, and pick a volume from out of the cliff-face. I intended to do that, then make for myself a quiet place on the floor, tucked into the curve of the wall, as if I owned that great space. It seemed a harmless fantasy.

I was about to walk when two bare hands softly encircled my neck, and held it.

'Did you know that was my father's speciality? In the SOE. Creeping up on people, and strangling them.'

'No. I didn't.'

'Without making any sound at all.'

We both stood there; still curiously linked in that way.

'Do you like our library, Mr Schoenbaum?'

I was about to nod, but her hands made that impossible. 'Yes, I do,' I said.

'Is my father charming you?'

I hesitated.

'Is he charming you? I'm sure he must be. Do you have a weakness, Mr Schoenbaum, for the charm of the upper classes?'

'Well, I wouldn't say that.'

'You don't have a sweet tooth then for such rich and candied things?'

'Well, no, not really.'

'No?'

Her hands left my neck. The same hands now gently turned

me around. I was startled to see she was smiling. It was a not unpleasant smile.

'Haven't you asked yourself why my father is so nice to you?'

'Well, because he's, because he's – nice.'

Her friendliness, the unanticipated lightness in her eyes, which before I'd missed, nonplussed me. I may even have gawped.

'Try again.'

'I'm his new accountant?'

'Because he *despises* you.'

'Oh.'

She was still smiling. 'Why do you think you haven't argued with him. Not once. Since you came here. Why does he never seem to disagree with you . . . on anything?'

'I don't know. I just thought we got on.'

'Oh come on, don't be so obtuse. It's because you're *beneath* him. He wouldn't argue with *you*. My father would only argue with someone he perceived as an equal . . . You see,' she added, 'you don't know my class. I *do*. And I hate it.'

'Oh.'

'I think it should be destroyed. As soon as possible, in fact.'

'You are very radical.'

She now pulled me towards the door. 'I would like to apologize. I didn't mean to be rude before. When you were eating. It was my father. I only meant to be rude to him.'

'I see. I just happened to be in the . . . target area.'

'That's right. You're learning. What American Imperialists would call collateral damage.'

'American Imperialists. That's a rather old-fashioned expression, isn't it?' I'd relaxed and was now, albeit in an exploratory way, beginning to enjoy this exchange.

'No. Of the moment,' she insisted as we left the library. 'Right now. Of the moment.'

We went out with the guns. We walked in silence, through

long grass. Up and into evaporating mist. At that early hour, the house, its great and quiet rooms, had borne down on me, dispassionately impressing its complex seal, with renewed force. I was still thinking of its chill, remote presence as our advancing bodies swished uphill, furrowing the high, saturated grass.

When we left the house, I had said, 'I'd prefer not to kill anything,' and he'd murmured some reply, words commensurate with, indistinct as, that vaporous morning's reticence and hush. But now a suspicion was thickening, intensifying inside me, that my host's designs were indeed on things very much alive.

Birds. Startled. Rising densely, suddenly, then thinning to a spiral of disappearing wings.

But he didn't fire. In fact he did not even lift his weapon, which slumbered on, angled downward, the heavy butt snug in the nook of his arm.

I also had started out like that, armament cradled, but now was tightly, anxiously clutching the rifle he'd loaned me, as if we had just faced off an attack.

'No, no.' My inexpertise amused him. He manoeuvred the gun, demonstrating how it should be held.

'Know what my daughter thinks?'

'No.'

'Thinks I'm corrupting you.' He shielded his eyes; slowly wheeled his gaze. '. . . Late children. Always a mistake.'

He was surveying his lands. I wondered what he thought as he did this. I wondered if he felt his proprietorship of his land as unproblematically as his proprietorship of his body.

Without really thinking – the gesture seemed indeed to have sprouted out of politeness – I now shielded my own gaze. And joined him in his slow act of surveillance.

'Well? What did you kill?'

'I missed, as it happens . . . Deliberately.'

'You don't want to leave, do you?'

145

'What do you mean?'

'Inside. You don't want to leave.'

'I wouldn't say that.'

'Are you so dim-witted? Can't you understand. It all starts here. The sickness, the mystification, it all starts here. Right here. Here is its source.'

'You don't think this is . . . a little extreme?' Her zeal perturbed me. It was two maybe three o'clock in the morning. I was cornered in the library, hemmed in by her vehemence, back against the bulging cliff of books.

'If you respect him, you tumble for the whole fraud. Where do you think our money comes from?'

'I know where your money comes from. I'm your accountant.'

She was roaming the library, an advocate possessed by the demon of her own righteousness. Her hair was drawn back even more starkly than before. She wanted, she was determined to beat her case into me.

'There are bodies under here, under our feet. Don't you know that? Down there. In the foundations. Hundreds, thousands, holding up this building. That's what it's built on.'

It was a gothic image. I thought of hands, hands in their hundreds, their thousands; they duly swelled into sight. Thrusting despairingly from the ground. So many stiffened, gaping hands: gloved in black earth, perhaps a fingertip or nail glinting through.

'And my blessed father. What do you think's behind him? Behind those effortless manners that please you so much, flatter you so much, because he condescends to lavish them on you. Nothing. *Absolutely nothing.* You're walking, talking with a cut-out, that's all, a painted canvas cut-out standing legs apart over its own pathetic diorama. Who passionately believes that he deserves whatever he wants – simply because of what he is . . . If you only dared to peer round it, to the other side, then you'd see. There's nothing . . . there.'

I had no idea what to say.

She was looking at me, studying me, smiling sadly. 'You just can't believe he despises you. Can you? . . . Oh. If only you knew. If only you knew how we talk, what we say – when you aren't there.'

'You mean you and your father?'

She appeared surprised. 'Me and my father? Do you think I would waste even a single word on him?'

I still had no idea what to say. The great house enclosed us. I thought of its dark, portrait-lined corridors.

'All right, I'm going to let you sleep now. But promise me one thing. Tomorrow. Ask my father who he really is. How about that. Just once, give him a surprise.'

I was lying stiffly in bed, unable to sleep. I suppose I'd fantasized, mildly, that this might happen. A soapy, indistinct fantasy in my room high up in that silent house; something just about fit to pass the time as the night dragged, and I was still awake, scratched at by useless, utterly banal worries, worries about ageing, about pointlessly, fruitlessly ageing at my regulation desk, dried into my swivel chair, turning bald as a polished egg gawping through spectacles. Maybe that was why she did it; had guessed and decided, out of some lordly, unbalanced caprice, to indulge my uninspired, already deflating fantasy; to apply her mouth to it . . . My door opened. Surreptitiously.

I was sure I disappointed her.

To begin with, it was a noisy, inconvenient hillock of a bed. And then she insisted on complete darkness. Not one shred of light was permitted through the curtains. At some point she tired of the bed, and we had to resume in the centre of the room. To get satisfaction, I was to search for her. (She thought up that game.) I picked up several bruises through collisions along the way. Briefly I even managed to lose her completely. Perhaps she left the room. I trod water. The darkness was so solid, so absolute, I began, ridiculously, to panic, fearing I'd gone blind. In the end she pulled me down and clambered on

147

top. I merely lay there; sweaty, clammy, difficult reality had entirely ousted the dextrous ease of fantasy.

After, we lay together, sedate as matching knife and fork in the bed, and whispered for a while in unvariegated darkness. She told me how twice, at fourteen, she had tried to kill herself. Why?

She couldn't tell me why. She spoke vaguely, formlessly, of feelings of unease, of disquiet; of a futility acutely, concretely felt, like some black inhuman wall. I wasn't impressed. This despair seemed altogether too grand for its cause. I thought rather of the diffuse, auburn melancholy of dawdling, drizzly Sundays; afternoons flat, without taste, torpid and drab, which had oppressed me so strongly at that age.

And felt tempted therefore to ask regarding the mechanics. To put technical questions. How had she tried to do this? What had gone wrong? What I really wanted to know was how deeply rooted had been her resolve. But in the end such questions still seemed unutterably cold, when I could feel her heat, her body heat, all along mine, and so I said nothing.

The next morning she wasn't there, having slipped away while I wheezed and snored. A departure as capricious as her entrance. I had expected that.

My host accompanied me across the great gravel bay of the forecourt to where I'd parked my car. In the shade of the curtilage wall we duly shook hands. Professional and client. He appeared, I thought, strangely perplexed. Finally he said, 'My daughter's broken the news.'

I swallowed spontaneously; was aware my mouth had opened, equally of its own accord, and now gaped moronically because not a single potential response would come to me. Her visit to my room had seemed so casually done, for passing amusement only, that I'd never once thought she would *tell* him. And tell him so soon after, as if admitting to some appalling lapse of taste.

'I was surprised,' he continued, speaking even more cautiously, placing down each word of that sentence with care, an entirely exploratory sequence. 'She can be so . . . flighty, you know; to be honest, never imagined something like that could be on her mind.'

I took this as meaning, although obliquely put, that he hadn't previously envisaged my sort of body might stir his daughter's interest.

I looked brazenly back at him.

'Now we have to talk business. How are you proposing to celebrate the marriage?'

'*The marriage?*'

'Look,' said my host, suddenly become the stiffly correct widower. 'It's out in the open now, so don't be so bloody coy.'

We sat together in a café in Covent Garden. She'd begun by telling me how she detested London. Too many dealers, too many brokers, too many slick and lustrous cars. She was wearing an aggressively pungent leather jacket and a khaki headband which appeared to lack any purpose. I'd armoured myself against the weather with a bulging mauve roll-neck pullover, which, immediately on seeing me, she'd vigorously attacked. After we finished our coffee, she was taking me to buy some proper casual clothes, including (I suspected) a pungent-smelling leather jacket. She'd insulted the pullover most imaginatively and I'd wilted inside it. Now, two or three times, she took my hand at exciting turns in her narration.

'He didn't know what to say. Do you know, until I came clean, he was afraid to tell his friends. Absolutely terrified. Couldn't do it. He never had any difficulty strangling people he'd never met from behind, but he still couldn't bring himself to say, my daughter's going to be the next Mrs Schoenbaum.'

'The first,' I said, idiotically, since of course she wasn't going to be any such thing, first, second, next or last.

'Yes,' she continued, 'I'm rather proud of my joke. I think I taught him a lesson. Don't you?'

'Why did you want to teach him a lesson?'

'I'm an urban guerrilla. Who's not yet ready to throw a grenade. So I threw that instead.' She was definitely high on something. It was barely eleven-thirty, but that something, I was certain, had been introduced into, was now adulterating her bloodstream. Poking from her shoulder bag, I spied the same tabloid into which she'd poured her concentration that afternoon when her father and I had been so emphatically ignored. I saw it was called *The Red Fist*.

I now noticed that her wild manner was beginning to attract attention from other tables. Despite the medley of noises in the café, her voice, that frozen, regal accent, broke clear of the confusion. Was clearly audible above it. For anyone bored with their own conversation, ours – or her part in it – was there to pass the time. But there was nowhere to duck for cover. I had to continue to sit upright, singled out for all to see in my mauve roll-neck as the involuntary straight man.

Then she laughed again. 'I'm sorry if I embarrassed you. But I just couldn't resist it. It was too good a joke to miss. Schoenbaum. It really is such a repulsive name.'

We continued after that to see each other. It appeared to amuse her. (Her father by then – apologetically citing delicate and personal reasons – had felt obliged to withdraw his retainer. So I'd nothing now to safeguard.) She would telephone me, usually at my office, informing me where and when we were to meet. I would leave the office early and go by car to collect her. She'd be standing, impatient and jacketed, on the kerbside. And already I would be thinking of how later I would drive from between the divided lips of her thrashing head – that summation of all those receding portraits – uncontrollable aristocratic yelps. I knew why I thought only of that moment, and not of any other. Only then, at that elongated instant, forcing and forcing, could the myopic accountant with the undeniable bald spot imagine himself in control.

I was persuaded to buy a leather jacket. I revolved before the mirror for her sake, deeply uncomfortable, before resignedly surrendering my credit card to the disinterested shop girl. Then we swished out together, identically clad.

This greatly amused her. In fact everything I did amused her. My appearance amused her. My name. Even the mundane facts of my job. It'd never occurred to me before that I could be so amusing.

I felt entitled now, sufficiently emboldened by my regular admission to that long, whey-skinned body, to scratch a little at her surface. Her father . . . wasn't this anger . . . wasn't it a bit ah excessive? She sprang back. From that mild scratch. Then delivered a confused tirade, it could even have been about class consciousness. Such words did not embarrass her. In the café those near us also flinched.

Twice she took me back home. To the great house. I'd been very reluctant, the first time, to go. Had even managed to hold out for a while, until one weekend she told me her father was away, in Scotland. And we went.

It was a lie. We passed an afternoon aggressively circling the grounds in our leather jackets, heads angled and pummelled by an appalling wind. I don't know if he was watching us from some high window.

The second time, she tried to persuade me to take a pill. Or a tablet. It certainly had the shape of a tablet. In the end, exasperated by my caution, she took it herself. I waited, with some interest, for the thing to take effect. But the consequences were not those I'd expected. She dwindled, faded, backed away; became in the end quite sad and passive. Her eyes watched me in a glassy, disengaged way; retracted and hunched like some gawkily perched bird, she appeared gripped by a terrible sorrow, but only for herself.

We dawdled in bed most of the following morning. From far off, in some remote and hidden corner of the estate, I heard at intervals the harsh report of a gun. Something, I didn't know

151

whether animate or dead, was being carefully shot by her father.

'He failed . . . with you.'

That early, she looked unpleasantly severe. I, doubtless, sagged and spread on the sheet, seeming as if I had been newly, liberally basted.

'Failed?'

'It would have mildly amused him to have you tagging at his heels this morning, the quintessential suburban man clutching at his new hunting gun, his evidence of elevation. But don't,' suddenly flattening her head to face me, 'don't take any pride in that. Your reluctance, that time, was no moral decision.'

'What was it then?'

'Cowardice, of course. You were just afraid to see blood.'

Needless to say, she was now tiring of me. While I – I was exhausted. I'd even been persuaded to subscribe to *The Red Fist*, though I never read it. When the heavy envelope arrived, I'd immediately slip the ridiculous thing into my kitchen bin. But we continued to meet. I don't know why. It just would happen. Then happen again. At random intervals, when the whim took her, instead of my flat she'd book us in for a solitary night at a London hotel. I would wait, a few yards behind her, sometimes equipped with nothing more than a toothbrush. Awkwardly twiddling it like the classic apprentice-adulterer (though I wasn't betraying anyone), I'd leave her to handle the receptionist. Which she did with relish; her voice painfully raised and porcelain for the time (always past midnight) and the abandoned, funereal mood of those lobbies, almost declaiming her name: 'Mrs Schoen-baum. Mrs Schoen-baum.' Then her father died. He left a beautiful will (from an accountant's point of view). And now he was safely underground, she – and she alone – had the great house.

It was a month after that, after trying and failing three times to push the necessary words out of my mouth and into her watching face – the attempt always turning to a gasp, a gulping for clean, neutral air to her evident mystification – that I finally sent the letter. It was brief, plain and concise. For a frightening week I then waited for the inevitable bombardment of telephone calls. But there was nothing. Like a stunned silence. Then three weeks further on into our abrupt separation, she rang me at work. I hesitated, uncertain whether to take the call. In the end, afraid of what she might otherwise say to the intrigued receptionist, I accepted it.

She was pithy and precise. She got straight to the point.

'You fucking yid peasant,' she said, before replacing the receiver.

A couple of months later, she tried (this was in the newspapers) to burn down the great house. I imagined that as originating, quite spontaneously, in some unconnected spasm of pique. But whatever the reason, she was less successful than her famous forebear, that ancestral memory dancing wildly before his five-storey fire in a spiked helmet, and managed only, in the end, to blacken and singe certain inner walls and curtains, the superfluous furnishings and frippery of that high, silent place.

The South

Shortly before I married Mari Cruz, when I was still a young and very clean man, we headed south.

I didn't know the South then. The world I knew was cramped and drizzly, always in shadow, dust thick on elderly mahogany, the light rationed. Mr Plantain had a waistcoat, a fob-chain with pocket watch, and kept a dark clogged pipe in the top drawer of his Edwardian desk. If I breathe in, I can still smell it now. They may have been wearing bum-freezers with fake epaulettes and smoking pot down the King's Road, but I was a morally upright, nascent gentleman and articled to this lean, leathery solicitor who stooped, gave off the odour of a musty bookcase, and appeared to fade in strong sunlight.

We took my spluttering little motor bike. At that time I had a freckled face and liked to smile at people. I stood up when my elders and betters entered a room. I was painstakingly polite, anxious to please and very English.

We drove across France. I was definitely, during those few innocent years, a charmed person. I was seen as fresh, boyish, earnest, likeable. Inwardly, I was still in flannel shorts.

Even the grudging, unsmiling Guardia Civil who manned the borders of Franco's Spain let us pass blithely through, the wheels of my Triumph Terrier bumping over pocked macadam, Mari Cruz clinging tightly to my back.

We were going to see her tyrannical father, that pocket *caudillo*, so I could ask for her hand. I had not yet slept with her (or anyone else) but underneath my boyish zest dark thoughts were now endlessly circling her like sharks in a confused, infuriated way. I knew I *wanted* her, but want and its corollary, the desire to take, were novel, indeed alien emotions for me then.

And eventually we arrived. Spain then was a parched, sour country. If the people were not darker than they are now, then perhaps I was fairer. I couldn't stop myself from trying to shake hands and prattling like a sidekick of Biggles, an Algy or Ginger among the natives. To the embittered Pedros and Juans and Manuels (for their life in those days was hard and its pleasures very few) I suspect I must have seemed scarcely human, like a hearty, heartless visitation from the world of celluloid.

We saw before us her home town. It was perched either side of a sheer gorge which pulled the startled gaze down level after level of stark white rock.

She led me to its edge. Sweating from the mounting heat, I stared down. Something contracted, or clutched unexpectedly, at about the level of my groin. A strange, needling contraction. It was the great gorge yawning vastly in the morning sun. I couldn't take it all in with my eyes, but, as if there were an older, darker man inside me trying to climb out, I was suddenly filled by a whispering urge to jump. Jump, and be quick about it, the gorge seemed to say. Jump. And damn the consequences. And it's true. Before I shook my head and shook out that insinuating voice, I did indeed want to obey.

Why should I have wanted to jump when I was a happy young man? For I was convinced that Mari Cruz was beautiful. To begin with, there was her mouth. It wasn't like an English mouth. Intrepid explorer of the bumptious freckled type that I was (who said gosh when surprised and didn't yet know pain), its dark labial architecture innocently fascinated and entranced me. Even though my three younger sisters, fair, also freckled, boisterous little women in pinafore dresses, were highly suspicious of it. *Their* mouths (practical and cheerful) were not like that. It was therefore, in their opinion, a showy and most dubious thing.

But I wanted to kiss it anyway, badly. Even bachelor Mr Plantain, who never usually appeared to recognize women as a different sex, had briefly stared at Mari Cruz when I first brought her to the office.

Her southern silences, the need for me always to prompt conversation, was seduction in itself. Perhaps because I was used to my garrulous sisters, like a trio of Beatrix Potter geese, and my parents also, my father leaning back, pushing at his sandy curls (which he'd passed on to me), apparently good-humouredly – yes, equanimity itself – at his lack of success in life, talking, stabbing perhaps at his newspaper, talking some more, my mother also, over her earnest if slapdash needle-work, the whole house too full of cheery freckled voices. That endless light chatter had startled Mari Cruz. We were (she told me) a *nice* family. But niceness can be a disturbing quality. And, in retrospect, it may even have unsettled others, our visitors. Niceness displaces, blankets *not-niceness*; but that only makes the thought that anger must, none the less, still be there, albeit buried deep down, more terrifying . . . After all, what is more frightening, more viscerally shocking, than the sheer rage of the *nice* man when it finally comes?

I was an object of curiosity for her fellow citizens. General Franco, *El Caudillo*, had already begun unlocking Spain's long cinnamon beaches for foreign exploitation, but the first juddering tourist buses were still some years away from Mari Cruz's proud landlocked town, and I was the only outsider to be found down among those sclerotic, inbred streets. The old peoples' hands and faces, the ancient walls white as eggshell, their closed shutters deeply bevelled with shadow, the sky bluer than any aryan eye – they all shared the same sunbaked hardness. We rattled among those streets on my splenetic little motor bike like a skittering marble in a stone maze.

They all knew I was English – and why I was there. Mari

Cruz had told me that in her town there were no secrets. And Englishmen for them (so slowly did news, the sense of historical change, filter down into such places in those days) were still jaunty, confident, pith-helmet and puttee-wearing types, superciliously ruling empires in great cheerful spasms of stupidity, undeservedly yet effortlessly blessed with fortune. They were ignorant of the dank, grimy truth (which no quantity of epaulettes, drooping moustaches, cravats, feathered hats, high heels for men and orange flares in maybe a dozen central London streets, like icing on a stale cake, could hope to properly conceal) and so viewed me instead as a flop-haired scion of empire.

Who was taking away one of their women. She may have been seen as a poor catch, too stubborn, too independent, too unashamed at her infection with unnatural foreign ideas. But she was still of their blood and their marrow, and so it was to their men that she, by rights, belonged.

But of course she did; she was already theirs, for there was something pliant in her, at a certain level, which I was still too innocent then to comprehend or (in my fastidious politeness) know how to – *let alone dare to* – get a hold of and roughly shape to my own taste and meek desires. But in the South they know how to do that (and so they had) – the crude but efficacious goading of the *corrida* as a prelude to the swordsman's final, all-important, blood-releasing thrust to kill.

In the Tableros' cluttered flat, on the top floor of a flaking building, they watched me eat. Near us, alone on its own little table, was a small, grubbily fingerprinted television set, its bifurcated aerial rising up like antennae. The modern world had recently begun to arrive and this was part of the advance guard.

From around the table came the sullen music of cutlery on plates, the sound of wine and water being poured, broad hands reaching out to take bread, surprisingly joyless voices. The leprechaun-faced grandmother liked me, I suppose because I lavished on her a tentative Anglo-Saxon deference and earnest courtesy (and she was used to abrupt, curt males pushing past to what they wanted); Mari Cruz's mother, I believe, felt likewise – but at the same time there was pale concern beneath her skin because she sensed Mr Tablero's silent, watchful, near-contempt. (I wasn't man enough in his eyes to merit the full-blown thing.) As for the aunt who'd come ostensibly to eat but really to spy, she also thought me less than a man, and kept on looking across at Mari Cruz's two elder brothers for confirmation of this in their faces. And they, loud and argumentative and brazen as they ate – to make it clear to me whose home it was, and who were the real bucks around here – found their sister's fiancée, it seemed, both enviable and absurd. Only Begonia, her sweet-faced little sister with the same ripe outcrop of mouth and eyes wide as tea-spoons, appeared to view me as a thrilling mystery ... Yet when I then took time to speak to her (ennunciating carefully with Mari Cruz translating) and she wriggled, smiling nervously at the others' faces in response to receiving the stranger's undivided attention, Mr Tablero's look of disdain simply thickened.

But that night, as I stood outside the bathroom holding my toothbrush, he unexpectedly appeared beside me – soundlessly stepping out of the corridor's gloom – and applied his hand, fingers like stone, to my forearm. As we were both monolingual, he then merely, tersely, nodded. But I believe what he meant to say by that was: *Si*. Though he thought me in many ways quite pitiful, I had, nevertheless (and certainly against his better judgement) passed.

Mari Cruz had been stubbornly determined that she was not going to be like *them*. Meaning first her mother and grandmother, then her family both as immediate unit and untidy extended clan, and finally her entire home town, that packed mound of red-brown tiled buildings so dramatically hacked in half by its huge inhuman gorge.

She was determined to be modern. She had spent hours alone with her tiny, treasured radio and its tinny, musical insurrection (from foreign stations), despising and disdaining the slow circular rituals of cooking and cleaning which her mother followed (and her grandmother also, before the stupefaction of age finally reduced the latter to helpless spectatorship from a nest of cushions in a low chair). Once her grandmother had even rounded on Mari Cruz when Mr Tablero, seeing a dirty plate on the dining table, had taken it into the kitchen. Wasn't she *ashamed* that a man *in her house* had had to do this? . . . And her brothers? I'd asked. *They do nothing*. It was usual for the young men of her town to be unemployed, except when annually hired to assist on the census. Still, the first tourists had begun to arrive and there were now Scandinavian girls in their shameless bikinis to be hunted and speared if they cared to catch the bus for the sea. But the tracking down of foreign bodies was not an option for a Spanish girl, especially not one with a stony, silent, brooding father who would stare at her over breakfast each morning, reserving the hardest stares for when she'd come back late from dances off the main square the night before. Of course, she went with the other girls; they moved in giggling, glittering feminine shoals for company and to protect their good Catholic reputations, but she knew he wondered obsessively (she later told me) what happened as those festive nights deepened and their tight all-girl formations began to loosen, fray and merge with the packs of circling males. After all, her father had once run with such a pack himself. He knew what happened in alley shadows, what wine and a protestation of love could procure when a couple had slipped from the noise into their own discreet cul-de-sac of emboldening silence. And so he stared at her over the broken bread and tomatoes beaded with water and she avoided his eyes. Timid but intrepid, she had already made it known – having now finished school with no prospect of further education, for her father would never countenance financing such a bizarre, unheard of thing – her remarkable wish to travel abroad, to go to London to find work as an au pair or chambermaid, and learn the English she had heard curled around her tiny transistor. (And over everything, in those days, there still loomed the vast black shadow of *El Caudillo* himself, Christian warrior and defender of the faith, even if now become a little unsteady on his actual fallible feet, and at school each morning the nation's flag was raised afresh before children in formation.) So it wasn't, I suppose, surprising how the other children resented this strange wish, regarding the high summit of her ambition as smacking too much, perhaps, of pride and disdain for her fellow townspeople, and they began therefore to point at her – she was only a little girl with long hair and a shy, heart-shaped face – and call her, mockingly, *la Inglesa*. The Englishwoman. And so she ceased drifting in those tight giggling all-girl groups, where anyway she'd invariably been the quietist member, almost obstinately marginal, her full mouth always seeming to be sulkingly downturned, though that was really its natural shape.

And instead Mari Cruz brooded on her hopes, going again and again to the town's only cinema, sitting by herself, separate from the rowdy clusters of youths in the back rows. And when she left to walk home alone in the evening cool, those same gaunt boys would point her out, jeering. Look, *la Inglesa!*

The days passed. I became a more familiar sight. I joined in the *paseo*, when the town takes to the streets before the evening meal and whole families drift formlessly in the tranquil light towards the main square.

Mari Cruz hooked her arm through mine. I looked down at her face, her head tilted back a little, cascading autumnal hair swept away from her pale forehead, falling in waves to a ringleted fringe below her shoulders, and realized (quite suddenly) that she was parading me as a defiant gesture. We were walking just behind her parents, her sister Begonia and that mean spirited aunt, and townspeople (both the gnarled and those as yet unblemished by the relentless southern sun) could watch us, note the irrefutable evidence of their eyes (the pale arm of that foreigner, this 'English gentleman' (so it's said), this *abogado* (so they say, but surely not, and yet it's possible) held, caught by that stupid little Tablero girl) and know she'd *beaten* them. That stupid Tablero girl (who my son and his son and both my nephews, so they say, kissed and groped and tongued and who knows what else when they were bored and drunk at the fiesta and had nothing better to do, who despite being small and timid thinks herself better than us, than this town) has found a foreign fool to take her away. To take her to London, which is a great and rich city. *Yes*, and why? Because they stole from other countries, all over the world, that is what it means to be an English gentleman – an elegant thief! *Heh*, so we didn't steal as well, when we had our moment? *Moment*? Two centuries you mean. The gold we took from the Americas. Yes, and look at us now, so much good it did us, well, that's Spain, isn't it. We know how to have a good time, sure, but that's all, not like the English, they are clever thieves, but we, we are such stupid ones.

Back in London, four months before we set off on my asthmatic motor bike, when she still wasn't sure, and would sometimes let me kiss her on secluded park benches and sometimes, instead, turn her head away, still undecided – well, once I'd said to her (exasperated, confused), Don't you like kissing? And she'd looked at me, and then, in apparent misunderstanding, said, You think I have never been kissed before? You really think so? And the way she said it, those words, her adult, weary, even incredulous tone, meant there was no need to say more. And another time, on the same bench, quite suddenly, after a long charged silence (and they were always charged, by her opaqueness and my consequent erotic expectation), she'd said, out of nowhere, quietly but emphatically, I think I'm . . . infertile. And some time after that, lying awake in my bed in the creaky, musty house in Finchley where I lodged, I'd abruptly understood. It was a sweaty, vertiginous moment, a surge of chill lightness against my chest – for she had told me (on an earlier occasion) in a resigned, yet matter-of-fact way, how it was they invariably married in her town; how, when the teenage boy had finally, clumsily managed to impregnate his teenage girlfriend and she was safely, respectably wed and installed in her new prison-home, her husband (still of course a boy) would return to idly passing time with his mates in the streets and in the bars. I'd listened calmly at the time, nodding sagely, quite unaffected – only for the connection to make itself *now*, with awful force, unlooked for, as I lay there, restless and unable to sleep.

But I was still too diffident (or nervous of the truth) to broach that connection with her. And yet, it had its effect. For two days later in that same park (my landlady like all landladies in those days forbade girls) I tried, roughly, emboldened for the first time in my life by real lust, to touch and palpate a breast – and for a while, incredibly, she let me. Under the soft cloth, the even softer skin, a shape which amazed me, conical, it seemed to run, slip through my hand. That evening was dark, drizzling, we were swaddled in heavy coats and scarves, while my hand moved, sliding again and again to its new-found possession's little puckered tip, my face pressed blind all this time into the thick collar of her coat. I was awed, but there was also a calculating, experimental, indeed *unmoved* side to that simple, repetitive exercise. Maybe, I thought, I was not quite the person I believed myself to be. Then I chanced to look up, see her face, tilted, somehow clenched, because of the cold and wet. It was not the face of a girl transported by her lover. If anything, it appeared bored.

And as we passed through the tight, inbred streets of the town, her arm through mine, everything below her waistline still barred to my earnest English hands, I found myself looking at those hard young men.

Had I made the right connection?

If so, which one had it been? Was *he* here?

Was *he* watching us?

A deputation came to the flat. I was invited to join the young men at football. Yes, would the Englishman like to come and play football with us? We know your Manchester United, very famous team, and your Liverpool also, very hard to beat. They stood, three of them just inside the doorway. One of Mari Cruz's brothers was there as well. Briefly they talked and laughed quietly among themselves before looking again at me.

I rose to my feet, freckled face smiling, widening, evincing my enthusiasm, my readiness and pluck. (My face was sunburnt, unlike theirs, which were uniformly, handsomely tanned.) But a part of me, a small but insistent part, was also thinking – as the eyes of the young men now took in Mari Cruz where she sat, silent in the motionless rocking chair, looking flatly, even coldly back at them – was it one of *them*? Am I going to play football with, well, *him*?

I didn't like this voice. I thought of my father. Such a voice could never, ever, have whispered inside his head. (No, not my father, prodding at his newspaper, laughing at my geese-sisters, ruffling his own hair, which was still like a boy's. I knew that, far away in England, while I faced the football players, he was doing all these things.) Then a hand tapped my arm. Mr Tablero.

He was holding a pair of old football boots. They were worn and battered, with grim protuberant studs. Clearly they had done good service in their time. I noted that each boot was scrupulously clean. Silently, he proffered them.

'Gracias, Señor Tablero,' I almost stuttered.

He nodded, once. Then turned his head to speak abruptly, authoritatively in Spanish to his son and the others.

It seemed as if they'd been waiting for me. Maybe two dozen of them, loitering in several knots along the edge of the dry pitch.

I approached with my escort, discomforted by the size and bagginess of the old black football shorts which Mari Cruz's father had also tersely offered me and which I'd felt obliged to

163

accept. I felt less like Denis Law or Greaves or Martin Peters, or whoever were the pros and starlets of those days, than a throwback, a Stanley Matthews, a sexless missionary who plays cricket with the dark natives to show them that, yes, he's one of them (when in fact he knows full well, having been so brought up, that he's white, Oxonian, *chosen*, and therefore, of course, human in a fuller, more profound way).

Now their scuffed leather ball was being casually kicked around. Two or three of the young men juggled it, using their feet and their chests and their thighs, bodies rhythmic and in control. As I approached, the ball was rolled towards me. I punted it back, grinning engagingly. Only one prospective brother-in-law was at my side (the other didn't like football).

The young men gathered around me. I compared their sun-browned legs, the muscular topography densely, blackly haired, with my own, scarlet and rose from sunburn. Several hands were offered to shake. A discussion I couldn't follow then ensued. I wasn't sure if this was an argument (though those who spoke did so emphatically, harshly) but from it I deduced who were the leaders, who the led in that small pack bursting with testosterone and incipient disappointment. (For the lives of their parents in that spectacular, eggshell-white town were poor and weighed down by a drudgery that they would also, in just a few years, inherit.) I realized now my prospective brother-in-law was not one of the leaders. He made his comments, certainly, but deferred to two or three of the young men who were taller, broader, and apparently unconscious of being gifted with lean, handsome faces. Was it one of them? I noticed how they all, if discreetly, eyed me. I wasn't sure if I could detect smiles, or rather suppressed smiles, in the shape, the apparent tension of some of those encircling mouths. What did they know that I didn't? Not to be party to a secret is powerlessness. My nice family, my relaxed, lethargic father, my three Beatrix Potter sisters, they didn't have secrets, well, not that kind. Our family was a surface without dank and troubling depths. And as those men surrounded me, no longer seeming so young, definitely full grown, the real thing, capable picadors and matadors to a man (I was sure), that strange, sick vertiginous feeling, a lightening even in the very ventricles of my heart, returned. And I found myself eyeing them, assessing *them*, their movements, their gestures, even though I wasn't meant to be a spy. Spies don't have tousled sandy hair and long flannel shorts and smiles which run from ear to ear. It was not in my nature, I knew that – and yet, once again, I felt it begin to unfold, that particular infection, to unfold and spread.

Then we were playing, the pack arbitrarily divided up by two of the leaders. I was the last to be chosen. My prospective brother-in-law was on the other side and took apparent pleasure in sliding in, feet first, to steal the ball the first time that I had it. They moved around me, seeming now far larger, faster, a rampaging herd, and the ball itself seemed to change, to become a vast solid cannoning sphere which flashed across me with a scary velocity I couldn't impede. Until, at last (when I thought it never would), the ball fell neatly to my feet and I began to run, the thing shrinking, dwindling all the time to something manageable, over which I could exercise control, and in my Stanley Matthews shorts, their hems frantic, ballooning as I ran and dashed and swerved, I passed two, three, maybe four of the young men and even managed then to shoot goalward, the ball rising, curving dramatically away from me with a power I didn't know I possessed.

Someone shouted, the words heavily accented, Manchester United! Bobby Charlton! Then we were surging, mob-like, the other way as the ball, at the feet of one of the leaders (Mari Cruz's brother pleading fruitlessly, forlornly for a pass), bounced crazily towards my team's goal.

Later we sprawled, sweating, on the parched grass. I was asked (my faltering, rudimentary Spanish, their randomly acquired fragments of English) about London. What did we do in London? Were the girls nice? How did I live? What was I? '*Abogado*,' said my prospective brother-in-law quickly. He said it as if he were vindicating his sister's honour. Meaning *that* is the kind of man my sister has. But perhaps they were thinking, well, if he really is, what kind is he, to be spending his time with that stupid, stuck-up Tablero girl? Then the conversation shifted, away from me, roughening, coarsening also (I sensed) from their laughs, the accompanying gestures. Girls' names were mentioned. Rosana. Maria. Mari Sol. Pili. Isabel. I never found out what these girls were supposed to have done or to let be done to them.

We drifted back to town. It was evening. Behind the gaping, shadow-filled gorge the sun had begun to set. A tangerine, blood-scratched sky. The lengthening shadows which followed us as we trailed back, the sense of another day almost gone (and with nothing really changed, nothing achieved) brought a wistful mood, it seemed, to the group. We talked less, and the ball was kicked ahead of us in a desultory, uncaring way. Manual and Pedro and Jose and Manolo and Stanley Matthews in his baggy improbable shorts.

I was taken by her father to one of the bars he favoured in the old town. I don't think he wanted to go just with me, but I believe he now felt, however reluctantly, that it was time for us to be together, and without the women. To be men together untrammelled by women. Perhaps so he could gauge of what material I was really made and at the same time leave me in no doubt as to the sort of stuff which constituted him. Mari Cruz passed on the invitation while he sat at the far end of the living room with his hard, unforgiving eyes on us. So I hurriedly nodded and smiled to show my assent, while already wondering how on earth we were to pass that time; wondering what I could hope to do or say which might amuse that bleak, suspicious face. Did this man ever laugh and, if so, what could I possibly do to lure from those severe lips even the adumbration of a smile, let alone the real thing? Perhaps he thought such expressions unmanly and found my own propensity for giving wide ingratiating grins suspiciously effete.

'What should I say to your father?' I half-whispered to Mari Cruz. 'What are we going to do there?'

'I don't know.' Her eyes moved to where he still sat, observing us together.

'But it's going to be awfully embarrassing,' I almost pleaded. She now became impatient. 'Don't be afraid of him.'

I hadn't expected that. 'Of course I'm not afraid of him. He's your father.'

And when, that evening, we left the flat to go down to the old town without the women, we received what I can only describe as a formal, indeed solemn, send-off from them. Mari Cruz's anxious mother standing at the door and the grandmother watching also, apparently understanding, certainly nodding and audibly mumbling, despite her habitual aura of stupefaction, from amidst her nest of cushions. Begonia too, standing close against her mother with those bright eyes once again wide as teaspoons. The non-footballing brother and the sceptical aunt formed a rival party at the back of the room, both bearing on their mouths the traces of smiles. (How I hated that – the trace of smiles, which seemed to confront me in their little whitewashed town wherever I went.) I'd wanted Mari Cruz, at least, to lighten the ridiculous tone – to maybe even wink at me, squeeze my arm, do something, anything, to remind us both that our real life was in London and that this was all an awkward dream which would soon pass, but she didn't. I could still see, on her face, the residue of her annoyance from our earlier exchange.

So I felt very alone as we passed, shoulder to shoulder, into the dark and crowded old town. Occasionally men of her father's age hailed him as we marched along and received in return a sour nod. Did I embarrass Mr Tablero? I tried to stiffen my back and harden my features.

It was a cave-like bar of sawdust and trestle tables, a shining wall of bottles with lurid, multi-coloured labels behind the loud sweaty barmen, tumescent sausages dangling like zeppelins from the rafters at one end. We found a private corner in the smoky confusion into which we squeezed. The rough skin of Mr Tablero's forearm brushed mine. I had never been so close to him before. Looking at the skin of his face, thick as saddle leather, I could tell he had never been handsome, even as a young man, and, more importantly, that this must have rankled with him, a piquant, vinegary resentment. I still knew very little about him. I knew he worked in a factory, but had no idea what it was he did there. I knew he had made Mari Cruz's mother cry one night for his hoarse raised voice passed easily through their bedroom door, and Mari Cruz had translated fragments of their dispute for me, her tone at once flat and sad (I suppose because she had heard all this before, and many times). Among the charges he had levelled at her weeping mother was that she had dried up; that the texture of her body was like the texture of *chorizo*. And apart from that, what else did I know? That he had played football with passion and a mean-minded intensity before he'd married and got a family, kicking the legs of silkier players and winning a certain reputation thereby. And that was it. We sat there, each with his small glass of beer and a dish of olives whose smell repelled me. He was evidently as uncomfortable as I was.

The silence between us now grew, became an invisible weight. I had no idea how to break it. Soon it had swollen beyond the point where some manufactured remark could make it implode, and rescue us. But, after a while, he nonetheless appeared to relax and accept this silence, leaning back against the cold stone wall and looking about him while eating olives and flicking away the disgorged stones with his forefinger. Once he caught me watching him. I hurriedly averted my eyes. It was hot in that overcrowded space and I was sweating freely.

Now, from time to time, I tried out my rudimentary Spanish. I complimented the bar and then the beer. He didn't react. I asked him if he liked olives. (That earned me a particularly incredulous stare.) Finally, at a loss, I told him (and surprised myself) that the girls were 'muy bonitas'. He gazed at me, saying nothing. Then, smoothly, he expelled a black olive stone from between his lips. Perhaps I had offered that comment too tamely, without the appropriate salaciousness, the knowing leer which would flavour my remark, italicize it as something to be shared between us as men who knew how to do the business. Perhaps he saw himself as a connoisseur of women's bodies, of their breasts and their legs, and felt that I, as a virgin Anglo-Saxon, had no business trespassing (and so feebly) on his terrain. Then a particularly striking girl of the tanned, curvaceous type likely to appeal to him passed beside us, her hip unwittingly brushing his hunched shoulder. His eyes were on her at once, then redirected to me. His mouth offered an odd, ironic grimace, intended (I knew) to convey his assessment – grudgingly positive – of her figure.

Without thinking, I clumsily grimaced back at him – and immediately felt the squeeze of an acute embarrassment. He must have felt the same, for he stood up at this and started, wordlessly, to push his way to the bar for a new round. Soon after, when another uninterrupted silence had begun to unpleasantly congeal, he finally lost patience. 'Si,' he said roughly, and rose to his feet. I obediently copied him, 'Si, hombre.' And with that he propelled me ahead of him and out of the bar.

We would be going home soon. I sat with Mari Cruz in the empty flat, discussing the logistics of our return. 'How does he feel about me now?' I asked.

'I think he likes you,' she said eventually.

I laughed. It was quite a sour laugh for me. 'No, tell me what he says.'

'Oh, I don't know.' Yet another of those dark flashes of annoyance. I leaned forward and tried to kiss her. She averted her face.

'You do want to go back?'

'Yes,' she said.

'You're sure?'

'What do you think, that I want to stay here? The people here are stupid.'

'That's why?'

'They are . . . small-minded.' Mari Cruz spoke those unfamiliar words with a disconcerting precision.

I took a deep breath. 'Are you sure you love me?'

I could tell she didn't like the question. 'Yes,' she said finally.

'You're sure?'

'Yes,' she said impatiently. 'Don't keep asking me that.'

I sandwiched her face between my open hands. She obediently, patiently cocked and parted her mouth as I lowered mine onto it, she shutting her eyes very tightly as I did so.

I kept my own wide open as our tongues moved. I wasn't sucked in. I could study the delicate lines on her eyelids as if both had been delivered up to my gaze, pale and enormous, through an angled magnifying glass. The dark brown eyes which they hid now seemed infinitely remote. We were embracing in the place where she had been born; where she'd once been a tiny, awestruck child on unsteady, inquisitive legs; the space where she'd grown and matured between her sad mother and terse, harsh-tongued father, surrounded on all sides by this town which she so violently, but quietly hated, and maybe also feared. And what I felt should be simple – what connected her to me – was, I knew, in truth sickeningly entangled. Later, as we sat outside in the dark beneath all those shuttered windows (behind which, she'd once told me, she always sensed eyes, nothing but eyes, and all so cold), Mari Cruz admitted, 'He is jealous of you, because he thinks you are lucky.' 'Lucky?' 'Yes. And he thinks he is not. He cannot accept that.'

On our last but one day, we drove down to the sea. I pushed my little motorbike as hard as I dared. I believe I wanted to frighten Mari Cruz as she tightly clung on – hugging, hunched, entrusting herself to me, face flattened against my back to avoid the whipping wind and grit.

And when we stopped, the sea ahead of us a vast dazzling bluegreen arc, and I turned my head, she was smiling, sweating, lips divided. I could see she was excited. I took off a driving glove and felt her heart. It had a vivid urgent thumping rhythm.

I let my palm rest there. Her eyes seemed – and for the first time in a long while – mischievous and alive. And suddenly everything appeared simple again, as if it might indeed be possible to be happy.

We walked down to the beach, hand in hand. Mr Tablero, if he had seen us, would have snorted and maybe silently jeered. The coastline, still untouched by development, ran for luminous miles. We removed our shoes and socks. I rolled up my trousers. We splashed our way along the sea's frothy margin. Seen from a distance, from high above the beach, we were the kind of couple her father would have envied. And, standing down there at the centre of that great and pristine space, I felt for a moment an overwhelming surge of optimism.

In the early evening, we sat with our backs to the vertical rock-face, an open bottle of wine lodged in the sand between us, and watched, largely in silence, the tide's gentle approach. After the wine had worked its way through me – a slow passage which left me feeling curiously weightless and cumbersome at the same time – I finally clambered heavily on top of Mari Cruz.

I felt her small body and the sand under me with a new immediacy, conferred by the percolation of alcohol. I wasn't sure what to do, but though her eyes were open and alert, Mari Cruz barely moved and showed no inclination to give my inexpert hands guidance.

I was pawing, limply kissing patches of her skin, my head no longer feeling so good, when I realized I could hear – whooping? *Cheers*? Yes, cheers, shouts, recognizable words of apparent ironic congratulation. And as I realized what I was hearing, I realized also that those sounds had been there, pressing on my ears but ignored, for much longer than I cared to acknowledge. I rolled away as their eyes converged on us like so many spotlights in the solidifying dusk. We had been caught; exposed, I thought, as two shameless (and most un-English) dogs, and, moreover (and this was worse), caught out as starkly lacking the easy competence real dogs would have brought to the task in hand. *Viva el abogado! Viva la Inglesa!* someone shouted. Mari Cruz was already on her feet, furiously brushing sand from her undone clothes. 'I told you they were coming. I said I could hear them. Why didn't you listen to me?' I sat there, now feeling decidedly sick, hunching over my knees, as those familiar voices and faces came towards us.

They were not unfriendly, merely amused. We had to join them – on that they insisted, in loud, good-humoured voices – around the fire they were to light that night on the beach. I recognized young men from the town amongst whom I'd inaccurately dashed on the football field, while some of the girls, I didn't doubt, were those who had been discussed with such interest and detail in the long, sprawling lull which had followed our game.

They had a guitar with them and, later, as the fire burned, the night now very black, they sang songs I didn't know in an increasingly mocking and drunken way. Then some of them rose to their feet and danced on the sand, dances which were also unfamiliar to me, and executed with the same odd edge of mockery – as if it would've been embarrassing for them to take at face-value steps once performed by their parents, and before them by wrinkled grandparents and of course long before that as well. Arms snaked and writhed, moving with almost contemptuous exaggeration. Thinking back now, I believe it even had something to do with Franco, yes, with *El Caudillo* himself, that manner they adopted, a collective exultant thumbing of their noses at that sick old man.

Two or three times I was invited to join them. But,

uncomfortable, my head now aching, I could only decline. And shortly after, without my noticing, Mari Cruz must have got up, for suddenly I realized that she too was moving, her mouth still sulky, lips so bold and pronounced in the firelight; moving against one of the footballers, one of those who had come to the flat to collect me and later dominated the afternoon of the game. He loomed over her, almost a foot taller, brown-skinned and strong.

I watched. I watched, trying to gauge each one of Mari Cruz's gestures, the changing shape of her mouth, the aspect of her eyes, as she danced with him. I was like a spy who is trying to decode the enemy's transmissions. When Mari Cruz suddenly, unexpectedly, smiled, and so broadly, so spontaneously, looking straight up at him, so I could see the whiteness of her teeth, I felt it as a terrifying stab between my ribs. The simplicity I had thought we'd got back, recovered for ourselves (and for good) as we walked alone along the endless empty beach, simplicity like a glass of the clearest water, that was all gone, once again – if it had ever been there – the glass rudely toppled, the water all drained away, back into the sand. And maybe by then I was the only one not dancing. And maybe by then it had become a celebration (no less) of her return, of the fact that Mari Cruz, even if infertile (as she was convinced they'd shown her to be, and shown her so peremptorily in some field or alleyway), had been reclaimed. After that the boyish freckled *abogado* could have her, his little, stuck-up trophy; take her away with him, back to the rain, on the pillion of his ridiculous undersized motor bike, and it would no longer matter – because she would remember that final night always, and with great vividness, each time afterwards whenever he placed a damp awkward hand on her. And suddenly I thought, unable to tear away my eyes from the spectacle presented to them, I hate the south. I really hate it. I hate it. I hate it. I hate it.

We were married. After the obligatory one week honeymoon

in Torquay, bachelor Mr Plantain, holding his pipe, looked me up and down for a long time when I returned to the office – what did he expect to see? – but otherwise said nothing.

SUZANNE CLEMINSHAW

Disillusionment of Ten O'Clock

The houses are haunted
By white nightgowns.
None are green,
Or purple with green rings,
Or green with yellow rings,
Or yellow with blue rings.
None of them are strange,
With socks of lace
And beaded ceintures.
People are not going
To dream of baboons and periwinkles.
Only, here and there, an old sailor,
Drunk and asleep in his boots,
Catches tigers
In red weather.

Wallace Stevens

Memories are like viruses. They infect whole families. I should know. I have been earning money as a bartender at weddings at the country club this summer. My friend Casey and I do it. We had to provide our own tuxedos and wear them, but the girls really go for them. And around one in the morning, it never fails, some red-faced uncle comes up and says he wants to take over the bar and that we should go dance with his nieces. There are always nieces. They all go to Mount Holyoke or Bryn Mawr and they have pinkish indentations across the bridges of their noses from the glasses they removed just before the wedding. Glabella is the word for it – the space between your eyebrows. It sounds sort of sexual and sort of like an isle off the coast of Italy. Just knowing this word makes these spectacle-less girls somewhat charming – knowing that they are probably more aware of their glabellas than girls with twenty-twenty vision.

I'm studying the classics at college. When I tell parents this at the weddings they look at me kind of strange, but also as if it's noble, like I joined the Peace Corps or something. Like it's something they're glad someone is doing but relieved it's not their kids.

I have to finish a paper for Modern Poetry this summer. It's on 'Disillusionment of Ten O'Clock' by Wallace Stevens. I got an incomplete for the course and the professor said he wouldn't flunk me if I get the paper into him by the end of July. I haven't written a word yet and this weekend is the fourth of July. My parents said they wouldn't ground me for the incomplete if I go to the library for a few hours a day to work on it. I sit in the reference section, thinking of the nieces and what they would look like sans taffetta skirts, sans glasses, perched on the dusty lectern that holds a mammoth Random House Dictionary, opened to the letter V. I never realized how interesting the reference section could be. I've been looking up the etymologies of words today. Virgin means man-trap.

There are always stories being told at weddings. After a few glasses of wine everybody remembers stories. Families have their own Greek tragedies but they usually run along the lines of family accidents. The time Matthew got his hand smashed in the car door on the family vacation, the time the McKnights' poodle scratched Missy's cornea, the time Uncle Bob got a suction-cup dart stuck to his forehead at Jenny's birthday party, the time Peter stuck an unstrung pearl up his nose. I guess this is the only common ground for all these cousins who haven't seen each other for a couple of decades. One of these wedding planner books was left on the bar one night. The first line of the page it was opened to said, 'Place distant cousins further away at tables in the nearest row on the far left or right.' Second cousins are a lot like Greek characters. They are the ones that send your family these long tragic mimeographed letters at Christmas-time telling you about cousin William's operation and cousin Bette's imprisonment. There are a lot of Hecuba-types amongst second cousins.

Where Streetsboro Road begins, at the exit off of Highway 77, there is a Moo Shu Chinese Restaurant with a plastic pagoda out front, the Atomic Bar that looks like a set from a sixties motorcycle movie and the No-Tell Motel with a flashing pink and black neon sign of a winking cat. Then there's a trailer park, with all these rusty trailers sitting on the pavement. You never see anyone outside of them and it makes me think of those places up north where whales go to die. Then there's a stretch of road that's just marshes on either side that developers always want to landfill and build on but environmentalists protest because there's some musk-rat that will go extinct if they do. After a few miles of these marshes the road gets all windy and overhung with huge trees that stand at the edge of the road like obedient dogs. There's a stoplight at the end of all these trees and this is where Ridgewood starts. Past the stoplight are eighteenth-century houses with plaques in front of them telling you how old they are. They are all painted white and have black shutters and there is a brick pavement out in front of them. Further along are shops contained within more eighteenth-century houses – there is Haddie H. Halpern's, a women's dress shop where there are huge stuffed pigs with gold rings in their noses under all the dress racks and velvet cushion seats in the dressing rooms. My mom used to take me in there before my voice changed. Once I saw Mrs Cutter run out of Haddie H. Halpern's in just her slip to talk to her husband who was standing on the pavement. She's very pretty.

Further on there are lots of gift shops with things made out of glass and wood in the windows and antique shops with Amish quilts and old clocks. There are also a ton of real estate offices, and the women who work in them are always marching up and down the pavement wearing suits of red or green or yellow depending on which real estate company they work for. They look like brand new items in a hardware store. You take a right just past the gazebo where there are band concerts and ice cream socials in the summer and you're on Ogilby Drive. You go past Ms Dimmer's house, who has hair the colour of flat champagne and wears silk robes all day out in her grape arbour and is pretty crazy – for instance, she can't stand the word 'succulence' and as kids we used to hide under her bushes and chant 'succulence, succulence' until she banged open her shutters and flung wineglasses of water out at us. I've felt pretty bad about this lately. The houses get bigger as you drive further down Ogilby – there is Mr Mastrioni's house that has gates and everyone says he works for the Mafia and his son told our class that they bury their victims face down so they can't haunt the killers, but he might have said this just to get popular. Further on is Mr Huxley's, he owns sports cars that sit in the driveway with grimacing grills and back ends that lift up in the air like the rear ends of mating baboons. You turn left at Mr Huxley's and then you are on Treelawn Avenue. Here the houses are large and sunken in among big elms and maples – the houses and trees on Treelawn seem to have some sort of communion, there is something pachydermish about them. If they were alive, they would be slow-moving and powerful and unaware of what is scurrying about at their feet. If you turn right into the driveway of 154 Treelawn, you are at my house. It is large and white with green-and-white-striped awnings over the windows. I used to eat pears under the Oriental plum tree in the front yard and pretend I was in China.

Casey is majoring in pre-med at Columbia. I grew up with him here in Ridgewood. He's always been into obscure diseases of the mind and body. Like in sixth grade we both pretended we were missing our left arms, which made lunch and scooter dodge ball in gym difficult. Then in tenth grade he put on that he had 'Tourette's Syndrome' and screamed 'Fuck you cunt' at the principal's secretary. He got ten consecutive Saturday detentions, but the teachers still liked him because he's so brilliant and all. Like he could probably figure out this poem in one hour and write twenty pages about it in the next but I'm basically pretty ethical about these things. In fact, I think I'd like to be a poet. I'd never tell Casey that, he'd think it's 'fruity' and not lucrative enough. You can be sure all the uncles know how lucrative Casey's profession will be – the nieces are marched up to him in an unending procession. Casey's goal is to have some obscure tropical disease named after him.

Why do the words in poetry sound so different than words on billboards, in advertisements or coming out of the mouths of people you know? The word purple in this poem sounds different from purple in everyday life. Purple in real life is a Crayola crayon, my father's deep purple leather chair, the ink they stamp on fresh meat. Purple in the poem sounds like it comes from some other place, far away from crayons or grapes, somewhere where it exists on its own, purely purple, without having to inhabit an object.

The uncles all hang out at the bar. Most of them are large with shoulders like bridges but there's always a little one stuck in among them like a sneeze. They are at that obscure stage in life – in between yelling 'Hey Dude' to their friends and wearing black socks and brown shoes down to the beach. They all bore each other like mad, choking back yawns like snakes swallowing mice, but they try to rise above it by acting boisterous and describing the hips on a new secretary with hand motions in the air.

Around twelve I was dancing with one of the nieces. There

were all these little kids running in and out amongst the dancing couples like stinging nettles, and then I saw Mrs Cutter. I hadn't seen her since I saw her in her slip outside Haddie H. Halpern's. She wore this dress with purple and yellow flowers on it, but the fabric was kind of see-throughish and when she moved, the flowers seemed to go from solid to liquid and back again – like they were freezing and melting and then freezing again. I've read that the Greeks got their idea for the shape of their vases from the shadows of women dancing on a sunlit wall. 'What are you majoring in?' the niece asked. I watched Mrs Cutter as she disappeared behind a row of black tuxedos. A little kid ran by and nearly knocked us over. 'What are you majoring in?' the niece asked again once we got our balance. She had this brand new notebook feel to her. I caught sight of purple and yellow in between black suits. 'Huh?' I asked. '*What are you majoring in?*' I couldn't get sex off my mind for the rest of the night. All the big vases in the room started looking like Venuses of Willendorf.

It's hard to think poetic thoughts in Ridgewood. I'm not just procrastinating. I think you need a clean fall of vertical light on everything – clean blue, clean white, clean curves, clean angles. In Ridgewood there is too much bric-a-brac. There are cupolas and shutters and door wreaths and flowers. Tons of flowers. Did the Greeks have flower-beds? I can't imagine it. Geraniums are like caged animals. Geraniums are a hindrance to the mind.

I remember seeing Mrs Cutter one winter. She was in front of me at the traffic light in a blue convertible. Its top was down. And it was snowing. Just a light snow. There was a pinkish glow to the flakes from the red light. The snow was falling gently upon Mrs Cutter's bare head – almost as if someone was placing each flake there in some sort of arrangement.

At the Ridgewood Public Library there are glass cases full of objects at the entranceway. There are Indian head nickels and Mrs Maddie Cohasset's widow's ring, which is onyx and opened part way to show the piece of hair off her husband's head who was killed in the Civil War, and also an indentured servant's contract with the red seal of the King that looks like melted red licorice. And there's this big soup tureen, with painted Chinese pagodas and trees and little people moving over bridges and a typewritten card under it that says, 'This soup tureen was used in the service of luncheon to Mrs Mamie Eisenhower when she visited Ridgewood in 1965.' It's kind of creepy and Egyptian – all these artefacts of Ridgewood. It's like no one is sure the past actually ever occurred so they have to prove it by displaying all these things in these glass coffins. All these commemorative plaques and historical items in Ridgewood get on your nerves after awhile – you start to feel like you're living in one big sunken Spanish galleon.

Later on that night, the night Mrs Cutter was at the wedding, I saw her out by the pool. It was drained, I guess because they were going to clean it, and the lawn chairs were sitting aimlessly around it like bison panting around an empty watering hole. I went up to her and said hello. 'Don't you love aquamarine?' she said, looking down into the pool. 'Yeah, I guess so.' I didn't really know what to say. 'Not just the colour. The word. Aquamarine.' She sat down at the edge of the pool and let her feet dangle into it. 'Aquamarine,' she said into the pool, and it echoed a bit. Her voice sounded like a clear stream running over smooth pebbles. I sat down next to her. I tried it. 'Aquamarine.' It sounded great. I realized it must be my favourite word. When you say it, you can feel yourself submerging into its complex turquoise depths, bubbles rising at each consonant. And I wasn't even drunk. Mrs Cutter must have been reading my mind because she looked at me and said, 'I'm not drunk.' 'I didn't think so,' I said, even though I guess I did. She kicked her feet against the pool wall and the flowers on her dress danced around. I wanted to ask her something but I couldn't think of a question. Someone called my name and I remembered I was supposed to be working.

'None are green,/Or purple with green rings,/Or green with yellow rings,/Or yellow with blue rings.' I used to picture blue rings coming out of President Nixon's mouth whenever he spoke. Watergate was on television all the time one summer when I was little. It was on all day long and then at night too. I'd be in bed and I could hear President Nixon's voice on the television downstairs. I'd picture the blue rings rolling outwards from the television set. They never seemed to dissipate, like smoke, but wheeled behind the furniture and up the stairs to spin like tops in the corner of my bedroom. It's funny how language can be a force like electricity or gravity – the way it pulls on you, how it can cause chemical changes, blushes, yawns, shivers.

Mrs Dawson came up to me tonight. She used to babysit for me when I was little. She got stuck on the subject of how I used to suck my thumb. About how I was eight years old and still sucked my thumb. How I put my left thumb in my mouth and then rubbed my nose with my left index finger. She demonstrated this. All the uncles laughed. Then Mrs Dawson wanted me to demonstrate how I used to do it. She said she tried to put oil of cloves on my thumb to get me to stop, but nothing, absolutely nothing could stop me. She reminded me of my sister's music box that played 'Blue Danube' over and over unless you closed its lid. She plants rows of geraniums in front of her house.

'From whence hast thou come and whither thou goest?' Socrates reminds me of the uncles at the weddings. He is always nosing into other people's business, wanting to dredge up their pasts and corner them about their futures. I wouldn't want to get into a conversation with Socrates. People at weddings are always asking you, 'What are you going to do?' It is a terrible question. It gives you this unsettled vertigo feeling. I wanted to be a Pony Express rider when I was little. I remember seeing an old ad for riders in a history book. It said you had to be willing to risk death daily, that you needed to be young, skinny and an expert rider, and that orphans were preferred. Who could resist this? But I guess as you get older you start worrying about breaking your legs and stuff. Heraclitus saw organisms as storms of fire, but everyone seems to simmer down after a while. There's some guy, Boris Ulla or Olla, who is a fish-frightener. He frightens salmon. It's true. These domesticated salmon don't learn fear in the laboratory they are raised in so Boris has to teach them to be frightened before he releases them into a natural stream. This is what Boris 'does'. I wonder what the uncles are afraid of. They don't seem to be frightened of anything – they have the same elephant attitude as their trees and houses. But I don't think they would be Pony Express riders.

'The houses are haunted by white nightgowns.' I have looked up haunted in the dictionary. It means to visit often or continually, to recur repeatedly, supposedly frequented by ghosts. There is an upright Steinway in the corner of the library that I think is haunted. It bears the inscription: 'Played by Sir Robert Winston on his visit to the United States, April, 1940.' It is made of cherry wood and depending on the light, I can see different figures traced in the grain: first Oriental men pulling carts, then plum trees with laughing branches. They have the motility of clouds. Because it is humid, the piano gives off a deep brown smell, the smell of shadows. Plants communicate through smell; they can warn each other of poisons and insects. I wonder if inanimate objects can do the same, hot rocks in summer, the insides of old pianos, suitcases in closets, books packed together tight. I wonder if everything is haunted, if everything is talking behind our backs.

Around two in the morning the parents leave the reception.

They are slightly drunk and swaying in front of their newly-polished cars shining under the streetlamp like huge metallic June-bugs. This desolate look sometimes flashes across their faces, like they have arrived after a week's train journey only to find an empty station with a broken timetable. But then I guess they think 'tomorrow' and they put their car keys in the lock. I sometimes try to picture the bride and groom in the hotel room later that night. I never completely imagine the ACT, but I see her on the bed, cocooned in her white stockings and him, lit by the supermarket light of the bathroom, his tuxedo tie undone and hanging around his neck like two black goldfish, his mind thinking the Far Eastern thoughts of a new husband.

The library has the smell of old school buildings. You wonder if learning gives off a smell. The librarian is this man with long fingernails. You can hear him flipping through books. Clip, clip, clip. He has an unnatural skin colour because he is never out in the sun. He reminds me of those phosphorescent jelly-like things you find under old piers at night that no one knows the name of. But I like him. There is something foreign about him, even though he's American. It is interesting to watch him move – the cuffs of his trousers lift up to cling to his socks for a moment and then drop down against his shoes. It is funny how a detail like that can make you feel for a person.

This poem makes you notice colours more. Purple grapes, purple nights, blue towels, blue gardens, yellow skies, yellow eyes, green celery, green salamanders, red stop signs, red nail polish, white houses, white tennis shorts, white lawn chairs, white cake, white wedding dresses. Casey once told me that there is nothing perfectly white in nature.

I keep thinking about Mrs Cutter out on that pavement in front of Haddie H. Halpern's in her white slip. The mica in the pavement was sparkling and it made it look like her feet were sparkling too. She was angry. You could tell by the way she was standing that she was angry. It was a very sunny day. I could see the shadows of her legs under her slip. The ancients thought that anger could be a form of art.

I went walking through the neighbourhood last night. It was late and all the lights were out. Everyone was asleep. You wonder what these people dream about. That line about baboons and periwinkles has really gotten to me. It's been running through my mind all week. It's been like a mosquito buzzing in my ear. 'People are not going to dream of baboons and periwinkles. People are not going to dream of baboons and periwinkles.' These lines are like checkmates in chess or something. They just leave you stranded. All the lights were out down our street. I thought of all these people turning their pillows over to the cool side. My mother used to tell me to turn my pillow over whenever I had a nightmare, because then I'd get the good side. I still do it sometimes, although I don't have nightmares much anymore. It was so quiet on the street. It's strange to think of everyone going into their own private trance every night. It's like everyone's diving into a private grotto and then they resurface in the morning and have their coffee and get in their cars and go to their offices without a thought about the strange place they just came from. I read that under the Sahara desert are all these small seas and rivers, where all these multi-coloured and unknown fish live and swim.

One of the uncles got extremely drunk last night. Casey and I found him in the hallway leading to the kitchen. He was walking as though the hallway had stairs. Casey got a hold of his shoulders and led him over to a chair. 'Come on sugar shoes,' he said real gently. Casey and I are used to dealing with drunks. 'Life is a series of endless yellow hills young man,' the uncle mumbled at Casey's fly. Uncles start to talk in proverbs by the end of the night. Casey and I call them the 'Unclilian

Dialogues'. One of them stayed in my mind though. 'The man who asks many questions may seem stupid for a moment, but the man who asks no questions stays stupid all his life.' The thing was, the uncle who said this said it in such an exclamatory way – you could tell in the way he said it that he thought in exclamation points rather than question marks.

Your body is always lagging behind your thoughts. I sit in the library and my thoughts go zooming, but pretty soon my body drags them back down to the hard yellow wooden chair I always sit in. Casey is always saying we should get back to our limbic system, the ancient reptile brain, and think fierce wild animal thoughts. He usually makes this point in reference to one of the nicer-looking nieces, but I think it would be a good idea all around. Casey is also into how our bodies are full of memories. He's always pointing out aspects of people that he feels fell behind in evolution. Some uncle has a gibbon hand (an elongated palm and short fingers), another orangutang arms. He says there are vestiges of evolution all over our bodies – the third eyelid at the corner of our eyes, the muscles used for smiling being once the muscles used for snarling. They seem like price tags left on clothing. Most of these people at the wedding are Protestant, but most of them would say they believe in evolution. I don't think they really believe in it though. I don't think they believe that they are animals.

Weddings are like painting a scenic background for LOVE. The background really starts to overshadow the original intention if you ask me. I can't believe how thick these wedding planner books are. We used to have a print of Fragonard's 'Progress of Love' in our bathroom. I used to think this was what 'love' was – blue-grey trees in the background haunting roses in the foreground. Everything gets so concrete as you get older. When I was eleven Casey told me that having an orgasm was like a dozen great sneezes all at once. It ruined it a little.

*

Mrs Cutter was in the library today. She knows the librarian. He was looking something up for her in the card catalogue. Click, click, click. I could see the parting in his hair as he leaned over the file. It was all crazy and jagged and meandering like a South American river. He said something to Mrs Cutter and blushed and she laughed. Her laugh sounds all shiny and new like patent-leather shoes. He helped her get all these books and then she sat down at one of the long yellow tables and looked at them. I don't see many married women in the library. Or men. Usually just students and children. I was going to go up and talk to her, but she seemed so absorbed. She had a little notebook and a pencil and she was writing a lot. After a few hours she left and I went over to the table she was sitting at. I could smell her perfume. The books were all about gardening. 'Horticulture and You'. 'Basic Pruning for the Beginner'. I closed the one that was still open on the table and looked at its cover. 'Petunias and Geraniums: Happy Bedfellows'.

I have decided to look up each word of the first line of the poem – 'The houses are haunted by white nightgowns' – in the dictionary. If I can just make the words concrete then maybe the meaning will follow. But it just ends up making a new poem:

> A particular person or thing
> By how much,
>
> Or a building to live in, a shelter
> To cover
> and exist,
>
> and visit often or continually,
> repeatedly occurring and
> supposedly frequented by ghosts.
> Near
>
> and following in a series

in another dimension.
Having the color of pure snow or milk

A light colored part,

Pale, wan, like a loose gown
worn to bed by women or girls.

You realize, though, that you could look up all the words in the first line and get all their definitions, and then look up the definitions of those words in the new line and then look up those definitions, ad infinitum. It gets you dizzy just thinking about it. There is no end. It's like a mirror facing a mirror. I drove by Mrs Cutter's house today. She was out in the front garden. She was out there talking to her housemaid. She had white gardening gloves on and a white skirt. But you couldn't see her legs through it. All around them were cartons of red geraniums.

How Many Miles to Babylon?

My name is Harry. I'd much rather be called Mark. Or James. If I had a one-syllabled name perhaps I could close in upon myself, coiled in a shell like those cretaceous creatures adhered to the bottom of boats that you do not quite believe are alive. And my name ends in 'y', the letter invented by the old mystic Pythagoras and symbolic of the forked path. Virtue or pleasure. True or false. One or many. The devil or the deep blue sea.

I live in a three-storey brick Georgian house outside of Canton, Ohio. I inherited it from my Uncle Harvey when he died five years ago. The house and a large red Cadillac complete with stray earrings snapped to the sun visor and almost twelve cases of Chivas Regal and two cases of Dandee salted peanuts. The rooms are large and the walls are covered with maps. Maps of the world drawn by Strabo and Herodotus and Ptolemy. And dozens of medieval maps with their scarlet towns, green seas and blue rivers, and their vermilion words: zephrous, boreal, austral, meridional. From out the rear windows of the house you can see railway tracks which wind through the backyard in a one-armed embrace. All along the tracks are long reeds and cat's-tails and skunk cabbages because the ground is marshy. Harvey told me that there were patches of quicksand as well but Harvey liked to tell tall tales. He also told me he once saw escaped convicts walking along the rails and I imagined them lying in wait under the skunk cabbage and marshy water, breathing in air through the long reeds, or sinking slowly down under the quicksand.

Harvey died of a heart attack. He used to do a funny thing. He placed a pair of Oxford shoes under the curtains of his study to make it look as though a burglar was standing behind them. He did it to scare himself. He believed it helped his heart – in line with the idea that small doses of poison eventually create a strong resistance – and felt that small shocks to it would make him immune to the big attack. Nevertheless he had a major coronary in his study and from where he fell it could have been from the shock of the shoes.

Harvey lived like an Assyrian king, all his actions beset by auguries. He looked for signs in the flights of birds and the ripples of water. I found him eccentric, maybe even a little insane, but now I wonder. The ancient Greeks studied mathematics to better understand astronomy. In order to become astrologers. To predict the future. So from the beginning, numbers which seem so solid and elemental as atoms have been forms of magic, of soothsaying. Harvey practised bibliomancy. You open a book at random and read a few lines and the lines you read are a clue to your future. I opened one of Harvey's books today, at random, and read this line from Augustine: 'If the future and the past exist I want to know where they are.'

I have a ritual. It is important to have rituals. Even the planets in space have rituals. It is what keeps them afloat. If they stopped their grand ellipsing they would fall. Fall for centuries, millenia, through black basement-dark space. This is my ritual; I step into it every day like a newly pressed suit. I wake up and walk through all the rooms of the house. I like to see them in the first morning light, in their idol stillness. Once in my own house, when my son Luther and I were playing hide-and-seek, I found him under a coffee table with his ear pressed against one of its legs. 'Daddy, the table doesn't breathe,' he said to me, eyes wide. There are different kinds of stillness. The curtains at the window. The telephone on a table. A chair in a corner. Still tulips in a still glass. And sounds outside can make these things more still – a car horn or an airplane flying overhead – so that everything in a room seems suddenly to hold its breath.

After I have walked through all the rooms, I make myself a cup of tea and walk into the backyard and sit under a large oak tree there. I look out at the train tracks. The trains no longer run. It is summer and living things are all about and underfoot. I list all the living things in the backyard. I list them alphabetically. Ants, beetles, caterpillars, centipedes, crickets, crows, frogs, grasshoppers, mice, mosquitoes, snails, spiders, wasps, woodpeckers, worms. I watch the clouds go gallivanting by. Luther wanted to have clouds as pets. In the summer when it was still light out when he went to bed, instead of reading a story we would watch the clouds and pick which ones might be good pets. We imagined them whispering through the summer windows, elephantic or giraffic, leonine and delphine, and bouncing along the ceiling and nudging wetly at our ears. Perhaps a few moody ones would gather darkly, thinking their tempest thoughts, brewing a storm in a corner. When I finish my tea, I look at the leaves in the bottom of the cup. They gather in the same animal shapes as the clouds. I do not know how to read tea leaves. But even if I did, I would not know what questions to ask them.

Mr Yoder, the man who lives next door, is trimming his hedges. He must be in his seventies now. When I was a teenager and living with Harvey I avoided him. His house sits up on a slight incline off the road with a roof that looks like a mashed trilby, and he has gout. There is some myth embedded in boyhood America that men who live alone on top of hills are scary creatures. Also, Harvey told me that he had a poisonous garden, that all the plants in his garden were poisonous – jimsonweed, nightshade, oleander, red sage, rhododendron. Harvey liked to pull my leg. I give Mr Yoder a little wave and walk to my car. He has invited me to dinner and I know I must go over soon, but the thought of it seems impossible. What would we talk about? He doesn't ask what I am doing here. Why I have returned. He is too polite. Just as I am starting the car, I see his hobbling figure in the rear-view mirror, flapping something white in his hand. I stop the engine and get out of the car.

'I got this here letter for Harvey the other day.' He's holding a neat white envelope in his dyspeptic hand. He wears thick glasses, and his eyes look like green fish gills encased in glass paperweights. He doesn't give the letter to me. He is as unsure as I am as to what you do with a dead person's mail. It sits, in his open hand between us, malign as a dead pigeon set on an Italian doorstep. A plane passes overhead and we both watch the thin, neck-arching line it makes across the pure blue sky. I take the card from him. 'Yup,' Mr Yoder says, acknowledging that I have done the right thing. Mr Yoder yups a lot. He yups to himself while he's out trimming his hedges, watering his petunias. It has the same earth-affirming sound as the crickets and the blackbirds.

I tear open the envelope before Mr Yoder has time to leave because I don't want to be alone with a letter to a dead man. It is a birthday card. On the front is a watercoloured fishing scene. A man in a straw hat sits on a pier in bold sunlight. A shack with a tackle and bait sign at its door. Inside there is simply 'Happy Birthday' written in joined-up Hallmark writing, and underneath it is scrawled: 'Another year Harv, have another beer! Going fishing, Fred.'

'A birthday card,' I say needlessly to Mr Yoder who is quite obviously reading it as well.

'Yup,' Mr Yoder nods and rubs a line of chrome on the car with the sleeve of his plaid shirt. 'Yup.' The sun shoulders its way out from behind a large tree and shines heavily on us, as obtrusive as a fat person on a small elevator. 'Come to dinner tonight Harry. Around eight,' Mr Yoder squints up at me. There is no way out. 'Sure Mr Yoder. I'd like that. I'll bring the whiskey,' I say, my voice cheerful.

I get into the car and back out of the driveway. I am on my way to the County Building. This is another one of my rituals. I sit for an hour in the County Building's waiting room. It is long and high-ceilinged like a train station. There are murals on the wall that depict Indians and cowboys and corn and rivers. Deer and antelope playing. Skies not cloudy for days. No discouraging words.

What I like most about the waiting room is the sound of machinery. Typewriters and electric pencil sharpeners and xerox machines and telephones. Elevator doors opening and closing. Clear ringing metal sounds like an orchestrated chart of elements. To me the sound of machinery is the most sooth-ing of sounds – the lawn-mower, the electric can-opener, the power saw – music of the spheres on a small scale. I also like the sound of shoes against the tile floors. The shellacked lacquered steps of high heels, barrelling black Oxfords, pussy-footed loafers, all entering and exiting, exiting and entering. I like to think of all these variously-shod feet as machines. Machines for locomotion. Machines for shuffling, shambling, gallivanting, rambling. Listening to the dinging of elevator doors, the ringing of telephones, the tinging of typewriters, is listening to the sound of the present. Tinging, dinging, binging – everything in the County Building is saying here, now, now, here.

Just as I am sitting down on the bench, Carol goes clicking by in a dress like a shot of tequila. I give a low whistle and she stops, sees me and comes and sits down next to me. Carol is a secretary at the County Building, and I went to high school with her here in Canton. We didn't know each other then. No one knew me. I kept to myself. But we recognized each other the first day I came to the County Building and we had a chat. Caught up on things. I made up some vague story about putting Harvey's things in order.

'So Harry, did you bring me some candy?' Carol says and laughs. She likes to pretend I am a dirty old man even though we are the same age. She thinks I am courting her, that I come to the waiting room to see her. This is partly true. But not the whole story. I do not think she would understand my thing about rituals and machines. She re-crosses her legs and I think of how her skin is like peach sorbet. I think that if I listened to the hollow behind her knee I might hear the sea. 'Nah, you're already too sweet a thang,' I drawl to her. She has a bottle of glue in her hand, the amber liquid kind with a rubber red lid that resembles the tongue of a dumb animal. She waves it in front of my face. 'I'm going to glue your lips shut, bad boy,' she teases, but I can tell her heart isn't in it. She is frustrated with me. She asked me out a few days ago and I made up some excuse. She is confused by my presence. I am confused by my presence. But I cannot stop myself from coming here. It is the ritual. I am too afraid to break it.

Harvey said there are places where portents linger and I believe this to be true. There is a liminality to certain places, places where the arrow of time lingers, noetic, and rocking like a small boat on heavy seas. The word 'forever'. The word 'enchantment'. Say these words many times and they become a beautiful incantation. My wife and I honeymooned in the Galapagos Islands. A strange choice. On a boat with ten other people. Mainly scientists and historians. On black lava-covered beaches we saw fat, barking sea lions that bore a strange resemblance to nineteenth-century statesmen. Blue-footed boobies doing their high blue-stepped mating dances, lizards outrageously crested and spiked reminding me of griffins-basilisks-hydras and other ancient exaggerations. Huge turtles still as stones with unblinking siesta eyes. Birds and reptiles and insects all on the verge of extinction. They reminded me of Leonardo's orinthopters. A good idea but made for the museum rather than real life. I could picture them all tumbling over a huge cataract of water continually spilling voluptuously over the edge of the flat earth. Once in the middle of the night there was a knock at our cabin door. I opened it to find one of the historians. 'The evolution of the vertebrae eye sent shivers down Darwin's spine,' he said con-spiratorially to me over the glass of whiskey he had in his hand. I could think of nothing to say. We stared at each other for several long minutes. Then he took a large swig from his drink and turned abruptly to the blurry porthole behind him in the corridor. He stood very still, with his back to me. I finally closed the door.

Once Luther and I caught a couple of huge wood spiders in our garage. We put them in a small terrarium and sealed it tight. I told Luther to catch some flies for them. Luther didn't have much luck with the flies, and then we forgot about them. The next day after I made some coffee I went and looked in the terrarium to see how they were doing. I thought I would probably let them out. But they were gone. One long brown leg was left. And a wisp of webbing in the corner. The ipsey wipsey spiders had climbed out the water spout, except that there was no spout. The terrarium was still sealed tight as a drum. I asked my wife if she had released them. 'No,' she said, barely looking up from the paper. My first thought was that they ate each other. Which is, of course, impossible. Spiders cannot eat each other and disappear without a trace. The more I thought about it the more frighteningly odd it seemed. I chased it out of my mind. I told Luther that the spiders looked hungry and so I let them go. But maybe I should have told him what I found. The whole situation had the logic of a nursery rhyme. And children understand that logic. There are a lot of wide open maybe spaces in their minds. Luther might have been able to explain it to me.

Luther and I were standing at the corner of a busy intersection and a woman came up to me and asked if I had change for a dollar, quarters for a parking meter. Does it matter that she was good-looking? Well she was good-looking. She had a Southern-quick voice and look-away Dixieland eyes and she was snapping gum in her mouth that tinged the air with peppermint and I pictured her perched on a detective's desk, talking fast, lipsticked words. And I was smitten by her elbows. Actually the little crease in the arm just before the elbow that only women have. Sometimes it fades as girls grow older, but sometimes it remains a deep cleft. It is something that should have a name, some word with -issimo at the end of it. I know I digress. But what else is there to do when everything is rent asunder? Digression is the vine that helps you cling on. I cling to those elbows, set at their jaunty hypoteneuse angles, and to the line of silver bright meters standing in their cadet rows in front of me as I disengage my hand from my son's to feel in my pocket for quarters. It does matter that she was good-looking. Not because I would not have done the same, searched for coins in my pocket for a lumberjack-shirted cowboy or a blue-rinsed widow, but because in the end everything matters. Every little goddamn thing matters.

My mother died when I was fourteen, of a female ailment that everybody was too embarrassed to describe to me. My father and I lived on in our house, bumping into things as if the furniture had all been rearranged. My father often murmured 'excuse me' to a side-table or an armoire. I gave up all my friends. The first week after my mother's death they all sur-rounded me, in a huddle, gawky as ostriches and silent. I took to reading aimlessly, anything, on the davenport in the sunroom. My father hired a cook named Elgar when, in the second month of our state of desuetude, my trousers kept falling down due to our corn flakes and how-was-your-day-fine-silence suppers. Elgar made us huge pancake and sausage and egg breakfasts every morning and stood between us, frying pan and spatula in hand, ready to fill in any spaces on our plates that we'd cleared. I felt too tired to fight with her, and I was a bit afraid of her. Her name bespoke Hunnish origins – I could picture her priestess sisters in some dark age tobogganing down snowy slopes on shields, heads of their foes hanging from their belts, trumpets, tumult. Yet also in her flat brown eyes, eyes that had the false depth of highly pol-ished wood tables, I could sense cold gloom, pine tree forests, shadows, wolves, loneliness. I didn't want to give her trouble.

My reading became more focused. I read only detective novels. My head filled up with convoluted plots, accomplices and alibis. I took to following people. I can still smell the wet moss of trees I hid behind, the hard diamond smell of hot concrete. My favourite person to follow was Mr Mars next door because he had a hawk face and walked to work and was therefore an easy target. And because he always carried a brown paper envelope with him which he deposited in the mailbox on the corner. I decided it was a drop-off point. Once, when the envelope stuck in the mouth of the mailbox, I retrieved it and went off in the woods to read it. It was a letter to his mother, and he told her everything he had eaten that day, and when he had gone to sleep and when he had woken up, and who had been kind to him and who had been unkind, and what he had watched on TV. I suddenly didn't want to be a detective anymore.

Until I noticed my father looking out the window with a half smile on his face, or laughing at nothing in particular while we were watching the news. It made me suspicious. Then he started taking walks after our enormous Elgar dinners. I followed him. He'd walk up to the top of the street and then turn right. Pull down the branches on a dogwood tree and smell the blossoms. He would stand there for several minutes smelling them, and once I thought 'This is my father' and it made my legs feel weak. Then he would twist some of the blossoms off and walk to the very end of the street where a small house painted jade green stood. There was a flag-pole in the centre of its lawn. My father would stand for several minutes looking at it. I often thought he might salute. Then he would put the blossoms in the matching jade green post-box and turn around and walk home. Then one Saturday evening he walked there and didn't stop for the blossoms or to look at the flag-pole, but walked straight up to the door of the house and rang the bell. A woman came out and they kissed and she kicked her leg back like those women in old movies. Before I knew what I was doing I was on top of him, punching him, kicking and crying. He didn't even seem fazed. He just kept saying, 'Hey. Hey there.' Some neighbour came out and pried me off him. My father got up and wiped his bloody nose with his handkerchief. He wouldn't look at me.

Soon after I went to live with Harvey. It was my decision. My father didn't argue with me. He drove me there in silence. It was not an uncomfortable silence. Out of the corner of my eye the bandage on his nose – which I had succeeded in breaking – looked like a huge white beak. And I pretended I was not with my father. That I was with a top notch informer, alias 'The Beak', who was bringing me to meet with the city's top crime boss. Days later, lying in bed at Harvey's house I couldn't sleep because Harvey's house at night smelled of empty old desk drawers and the empty bowls of unlit pipes, smelled so strongly of this that I thought I would choke, and somehow it smelled of my father's loneliness and I wanted him to talk me into coming home, but he didn't.

After I leave the County Building I drive to the natatorium. My next ritual. It is a one-storey sandstone building set in the middle of an uncertain field. Flowers, loud and reckless, are scattered amongst the weeds like a marching band that has lost its leader. I walk through the steamy glass doors and the frigid smell of chlorine hits me like the north wind. Just inside the glass doors sits Nancy, of high-piled red hair, who used to be a Weekie Wachee mermaid in Tampa, Florida. She exchanges my dollar for a locker key and a towel and a small piece of heaven. I can't imagine that the Empyrean could do better than this – row row rowing your boat gently down the stream of morning glory – birdsong-bluesky water. I change into my suit and enter the swimming pool area. A few boys from the swim team are standing at the far end. They have gleaming slicked-seal hair and their mouths are stained bright red from the powdered jelly they have been eating for bursts of energy. Their voices ring in the humid air, seem to strike like small pieces of sharp mica against the tile walls. But as soon as I dive into the pool everything becomes silent, mooncalm. Time and gravity fall away. I watch one of my hands push through the water in front of me, white and amphibious. When I was very young I fell into a neighbour's swimming pool. I couldn't swim, and so I started to drown. My mother jumped in and saved me. But before she did, instead of feeling horror, I remember feeling as though I was encased in a robin's egg, blue and holy and hushed. When I rise to the surface I hear someone calling my name. It is Nancy. She has changed into a lilac bathing suit and is standing, hands on hips, at the other end of the pool. I swim over to her.

'I want to practise holding my breath,' she says, and holds up a stop watch. 'Would you time me?' Nancy likes to practise holding her breath in case she decides to go back down to Tampa again. The Weekie Wachee mermaids perform at a huge amphitheatre, behind glass walls, and underwater. They do all sorts of ordinary things – combing their hair, walking around, putting on lipstick – but all underwater.

I take the stopwatch from Nancy and sit at the edge of the pool. She jumps in, says, 'Ready' and sits cross-legged on the bottom of the pool. I watch her slow-motion red hair fanning out from her like living coral, water shadows beating lovely scales against her skin. For a moment I believe she really is a mermaid.

My wife and I drifted dreamily through our honeymoon like a couple of sea anemones in a small tank, occasionally nudging each other and then drifting apart. I wasn't a talker and she wasn't a talker. It was part of what drew us together. During the whole trip I felt as if I was a few feet off the ground at all times. Not from happiness so much as disbelief. You see I didn't quite believe my wife existed. I kept expecting her to walk out of the frame of the picture. I tried to weight this down with the heaviness of memory. I would stare at her for long moments until the image of her turned hard and metallic, deposits of rock ore in my mind. At first she took this for desire, for infatuation, and said, 'What?' her eyes mischievous, a smile twitching on her lips. But soon she became impatient with it. 'What,' she said, the word like a heavy stone thrown in water. So I stared at her when her back was turned to me. When I think of that trip, I see the back of her head languorous on a deck chair, the nape of her neck as she is taking pictures of islands, the back of her knees climbing up rocks. I see this in the milk and moonrock hue of old movies. After our honeymoon I continued to do this. I was always standing behind her, trying to fix her in my mind, figure out what I had. It is very hard to hold on to the things we have seen. Perhaps if we could remember everything we have seen we would recognize the auspices and portents of our future life. But we are dissolved in invisibility as in water. The seen goes tumbling voluptuously over the edge of the flat earth.

I lost touch with my father. He sent me cards for every holiday. Even St Patrick's Day. At first he signed them 'Dad' and then after a few years, 'Your father'. I kept them in my top desk drawer until they overflowed and then, instead of moving them to a bigger drawer, I kept stuffing them in until they became mangled and the drawer stuck. Once I awoke in the middle of the night from a nightmare and thought for an instant the desk was a huge rabid dog, the cards the froth at its mouth. I took this to be symbolic, and wrenched the drawer open with such force it fell clattering to the floor, awakening Harvey who came and stood sleepy in his bathrobe at my door while I shoved all the cards into a garbage bag. When I was finished, Harvey took the bag from me and walked down the hall with it. Then when the cards came I didn't open them. They sat in a neat stack on the foyer table, crisp and white and ecclesiastic.

Harvey and I lived our own separate, alone lives. I didn't bother to make friends in Canton. I lived in my film noir detective fringe world of silhouettes and shadows. I imagined myself lying face down drowned in a pool like the poor dope in *Sunset Boulevard*, and the image pleased me. I walked the streets looking for barflies and expensive mistresses. I could create week-long ruminatory plots just by seeing a woman light a cigarette or speak on a telephone. I imagined them all carrying guns in their handbags. I saw them standing at the foot of sweeping stairways that had the frightening immensity of tidal waves at sea, speaking to dark-suited men, their repartée stiff as arithmetic in the air between them. Harvey dated women who fed my film noir fantasies. They would wake me at dawn with their laughter, having run drunken and evening-clothed through Harvey's lawn sprinklers. Or I'd find one passed out on the couch, a high-heeled pump dangling precariously over the armrest like the long black note at the end of a song.

You cannot tell me you would have acted differently. You will not know until you have let go of your son's hand, its backward trajectory drawing the opposite arc of his forward arrowed, final motion. The self is not a stable entity. See how you fall apart at the apparently solid seams when a love affair goes wrong. The outline dissolves. Like Zeno's arrow, you are still and you are in motion. You will never know where you are. You will never know if you have been moving or if you have been still.

The only time Harvey and I had conversations was when we were sitting on the porch at night, watching the trains. The sound of the trains was like the sound of the sea and we were like a couple of sailors, telling our stories, listening to the tides break. Except that I didn't have stories yet. I listened to Harvey's stories. I don't remember them in much detail, but they had to do with destination. The word destination sounds like it is made up of railway cars, a caravan of camels. Harvey had a favourite book called *The Roads to Discovery* that had Ptolemy's map of the world on its cover with the inscription 'Hope went before them and the world was wide.' It had chapters on Arab wayfarers, Vikings sailing the northern seas. Bartholomew Diaz reaching the stormy cape, Sir Walter Raleigh searching for El Dorado, Mungo Park and the Niger, Livingstone's last journey. Harvey spoke of the daemons of the meridian, horse latitudes, golden reliquaries holding saint's hearts, papal menageries, Barbary pirates, Islamic influences. I listened to him for such long hours as the trains went by that the stories of the great discoverers superimposed themselves onto Harvey's stories of his own life, and I would see him pith-helmeted and monocled and full of gin and the far flung Empire stretched on a palanquin. Or weak with ague and fever, crossing the Mongolian steppes and whispering confidences into a Tartar emperor's ear. Or scratching into the South American sands the sign of the cross with his own blood, whispering 'Jesu'.

Harvey also told our futures while we watched the trains. He threw bones from our chicken dinner on the ground in front of us and read their configurations. The number of blackbirds on the telephone wires, the number of railway cars passing, the number of stars we could see in the sky all measured out our future. The smell of Mr Yoder's poisonous garden hung spicy in the air. We watched the lights from the last caboose fall off the edge of the horizon.

When they pronounced Luther dead, I got into my inherited Cadillac and drove to this house. I did not contact my wife. The police would do that soon enough. I cannot explain. And I do not expect you to understand. If you did understand I would be suspicious of you. I would ask you what you expect to gain by being sympathetic, compassionate. Then I would take you out to the railway tracks, past the skunk cabbage and the reed-breathing criminals and show you where the rails meet at the horizon. This is why, I would tell you. I'm going to find where it connects.

After I return from the natatorium I begin my next ritual. I

204

pour myself a large glass of Chivas, get a handful of peanuts and take a look at Harvey's maps. I study their red Heraclitan boundary rivers running through prairies and steppes, veldts and savannahs, boreal forests and tundra. The lands are leek green, hunter green, bottle green, pistachio, verdigris, or citron, honey yellow, beige, fawn, caramel. The seas are cerulean, azure, lapis lazuli, cobalt, indigo. It is hard to describe the sensation of distance. I go out on to the back porch. The sky looks like honeymoon sheets, rumpled and tinged with violet. The trees brush their cathedral arms against the windows. The train tracks are still, yet they seem to be moving towards the hypothetical vanishing point, penicillin sharp. A mathematical theorem states that the surface of a sphere is finite, yet moving over it you will never find a boundary. It will seem to go on for infinity.

I arrive at Mr Yoder's house a little early with my bottle of Chivas, eager to get the evening over with. I have never been in his house before. In one glance I can see that he lives the life of a man who has never married and had children, and therefore has the luxury of deeply embedded habits that are rarely, if ever, disturbed. Habits that take on the solemnity of a religion. You can see it in the way the furniture is placed, the magazines are stacked. We have a drink and he asks me about my life. And I lie. I find myself telling fabulous tales about my travels and women and illegitimate children to whom I send anonymous cheques. We have more drinks, and dinner, and I tell him about the shores of the Caspian Sea, rich yellow land, and lions drinking at Lake Banguvedo, and a monkey named Greensleeves. I do not know why I am lying to Mr Yoder. He would probably be a good confidant. The more I lie the more weightless I feel. I can feel myself floating higher and higher until I am touching the ceiling and looking down on Mr Yoder and myself. I think of the Indian rope trick, where the conjurer throws a rope up into the air where it remains taut and firm while he climbs up it, then he pulls the rope up after him and disappears. We have finished my bottle of Chivas and have worked our way well into a bottle of Mr Yoder's whiskey. Mr Yoder starts to tell a joke about a Russian, a German and an American and then gets tangled up in the punchline and stares at his shoes. 'I need some air,' I say. 'Yup,' Mr Yoder answers and follows me to the back door.

Then we are out in the fresh, dark night and we half walk, half stumble down the small incline towards the railway tracks. Mr Yoder kneels to the ground and puts his ear to the earth. Then he looks up at me slyly and says, 'Listening for Injuns,' and laughs. I pull him to his feet. 'Let's go for a walk,' I say, 'let's go see where the tracks meet.' Mr Yoder falls into stride beside me. The cat's-tails brush our legs and I imagine the thrushing sound to be the exhalation of convicts beneath the reeds. I wonder if we will hit a patch of quicksand and sink soundlessly down, further and further, until we reach equilibrium and become still, in a heavy, shrouded sleep. Every night before Luther went to bed we recited the same nursery rhyme.

> 'How many miles to Babylon?' I'd ask him.
> 'Three score and ten,' he answered, sleepy.
> 'Can I get there by candlelight?'
> 'Yes and back again.'

Oh Blessed Fall

Names are like doors. They connect your inside to the outside. And if someone knows your name, you exist inside of them because your name is floating around in their brain. I didn't know Dante Cavenetti knew my name. He is in my science class. He asked me for a pencil the other day. He said 'Haddie, do you have a pencil you could lend me?' He has these revolving door eyes. They revolve from sad to happy to bored, all in about two minutes. And he wears a gold cross around his neck. He is Italian and Catholic. I've decided to study religion. I've decided to become Catholic.

My best friend at school is Stephen. He lives in my neighbour-hood. I have known him since I was about two. My parents say that Stephen is a BAD INFLUENCE. I suppose he is in a way, but I don't like people who are good influences. I never learn very much from them. Stephen's always teaching me things. How to make wine, how to write odes about various parts of the human body, how to develop insouciance. Once he taught me how to be a cat burglar. We both dressed completely in black and rubbed charcoal on our faces and climbed around the roofs of a few houses. It ended in catastrophe. Stephen fell through the Ashtons' skylight and nearly killed himself. We got our pictures in the paper. In it, Stephen's head is all wrap-ped up in bandages. I'm standing a little behind him, wearing my black turtleneck and knit hat. I still had some charcoal on my face, which, in the picture, makes me look like I have a skin disease. Stephen, on the other hand, looks like Charles

Boyer in that film where he loses his memory and all these blonde-haired women who use cigarette holders try to help him get it back.

Stephen gave me a gold cross and some rosary beads. He got them from his mother's jewellery box. He said she never uses them. She is a fallen Catholic. She fell when she met Stephen's father, who is Episcopalian. Stephen thinks his mother would be happy for me to have them, even though he hasn't asked her. He says that the rosary beads are probably like pearls – if you don't use them they lose their lustre. Stephen said he might go Catholic too. He likes the words stigmata, blasphemy and sacrosanct. He said he'd like an excuse to use them more often.

We learned about phobias in psychology today. Vertigo interested me in particular. It is a sensation of dizziness derived from great heights.

Dizziness is a gilded misery. When I think of the earth moving at 64,800 miles per hour, I get this feeling in my stomach like when you're on an elevator and it drops suddenly. I wonder if the earth and the sun and Venus and Neptune are all falling and we just don't know it. If we can't feel the earth moving we wouldn't feel it falling. When you wonder about something it makes you catch your breath. Like a trapdoor opened beneath you. And you start to fall.

Leonora, our cleaning lady, had a religious vision when she was twelve. Her daddy worked as a porter on the Southern Pacific railroad and she was riding on the train with him as she often did when her mama had a headache and Leonora seemed on the verge of stirring up a hornet's nest. Out the window there were rivers, bridges, trees – it became a kind of rhythm with the clicking of the train. River, bridge, trees . . . river, bridge, trees . . . river, bridge, trees. Then everything opened out on to a field of daisies and the train stopped. There was an announcement that they would be stopped there for at least an hour, so Leonora's daddy let her get off and run through the daisies. A line of trees stood at the edge of the field and Leonora said as soon as her feet hit the ground she ran towards them, they beckoned her like a song. When she reached them, she saw a stream running below them, so clear the stones on the bottom shone like new silver nickels. Leonora climbed down to its banks, took off her socks and stood in the cold eel-slick water. Schools of minnows darted around her ankles. Dragonflies buzzed near by, and since she knew they stitch your eyelids shut, she closed hers tight. That was when she heard the bells. Thousands of bells tolling so loud they seemed to be inside the dome of her head, clanging at her temples. And when she opened her eyes she saw below her in the stream an enormous golden cathedral. It seemed to be a thousand feet below her in the water, but rising at each toll of the bells. The golden light began to blind her with its brilliance, and then a dozen angels swooped around her head in an iridescent glimmer and she felt herself rising out of the stream and up above the trees. The next thing she knew her daddy was carrying her back to the train. Raindrops, big as grapes, in the now darkened sky, hit her face and mixed with her ecstatic tears.

The first crush I had was on this monk in an El Greco painting. He's at the Cleveland Museum of Art. I first saw him when I was about seven. He's in this room full of paintings of people suffering. All their mouths are open and their eyes are rolled upwards and their hands look arthritic. They remind me of people in aspirin commercials. The painting of the monk is in between two huge paintings of suffering people. He is very tall and seems to be both sitting and standing at the same time. He has long white fingers that rest on the arms of a big black chair. They seem very alive. His face is long and pale and thin. He is so serene. Looking at him after seeing all those grief-stricken people is like diving underwater at an overcrowded pool. His eyes are the best part. They are brown and deep – they are like long dark passageways into the cave where his mind lives. You can get vertigo looking into his eyes.

'Where did you get that cross?' my mother asks suspiciously. My parents say that they are Episcopalian. But they are basically pagan. They get real edgy around anything religious.

Dante has this walk. It's nonchalant. I secretly practise it. You've got to completely relax your shoulders and let your head hang back a bit. My brother James and I used to pretend we were the 'Backdoor Cats' in the Purple Pit jazz club. We wore old Frank Sinatra-style sunglasses and had little pieces of rolled paper sticking out of our mouths. We played Dave Brubeck albums and grooved. Dante walks like he's walking through the Purple Pit jazz club. Like he's wearing a sharkskin suit and gliding through its smoky dark cavern rooms with that martini walk actors in technicolor films have. And everyone there knows him, but he's too nonchalant to acknowledge them.

You get vertigo looking up at the stars, but then you also get it when you look closely at something, like the palm of your hand or the grain of a table. In both instances you lose yourself. Maybe that's what vertigo is. When you feel yourself disappear.

'The wise find pleasure in water, the virtuous find pleasure in hills.' My grandmother's always sending me these fortunes. She has Chinese food sent to her house all the time. My parents try to get her to stop because the monosodium glutamate is bad for her heart. She's addicted to it though. She carries little packets of soy sauce around in her pockets. And when my parents take her out to a fancy restaurant she takes Mr Ching's soy sauce out of her pocket and pours it all over her lobster thermidor. She's a bit of a Buddhist. She has a big blue Buddha on her dining-room table. He's got a placid smile and his pupils are at the outside corners of his eyes. My grandmother says this is because he is looking outwards, towards eternity. I turn him away from me whenever I eat there. Those eyes make me nervous. Eternity can make you nervous. It can make you disappear.

Sometimes I close my eyes and picture Leonora when she was twelve, running through the daisy field towards the sunken-cathedral stream. If I concentrate hard I can hear the wind rustling the daisies. The whispering of celestial secrets. Little green grasshoppers ping out on to her path. She brushes bees from her bare arms. There is a hot yellow smell. In religious paintings there is usually a foreground of warm animal brown and distances of cool, silvery-elegant blue. The colour of tomorrow. Sometimes I picture Leonora and her daisy field in the background of some religious painting. Blue train, blue daisies, blue trees, blue stream – everything inside the rarified air of a prayer.

I used to imagine staircases in everyone's ears, winding down further and further to end in a great symphony hall in the middle of their heads. The light from the science classroom window makes Dante's ear glow pink and see-throughish with the delicacy of a newborn animal. 'Potassium sizzles when it gets wet.' Mr Havish, our science teacher moves over to the chart of elements. His fly is undone again. Every time he turns to point to another element, the cloth on his pants gaps open, the brass of his zipper gleams. There is a potent spell cast by staircases.

Leonora plays all these religious records while she cleans the silver. There is one that I particularly like. It's *Alabama Truth and His Eternal Mercies*. There is a picture of them on the cover. Alabama Truth is wearing a pale blue tuxedo with a ruffled shirt. His mouth is open and there are little streams of sweat running down his face. The Eternal Mercies are wearing chiffon and kneeling behind him. Their voices sound like they are coming out of a steamy bathroom. Leonora and I like to dance to one song in particular – 'Jesus Loves His Little Babies and Leads Them Down That Hallowed Road to the Kingdom of Joy and Happiness'. Leonora moves her hips like they are going to melt right off of her and tosses her brown arms over her head like wild snakes, the rings from all her boyfriends glittering in the air like magic dust. 'Oh the Kingdom!' she growls and tosses her head, 'Oh the Glory!' I catch sight of both of us in the mirror on the side table. Her hips and arms are a tornado blur. Mine look like they are attached to me by metal hinges.

'Benissimo. Abbiamo noi la biancheria ma i miei bambini chiedono se c'e' anche la televisione.' I am in the library, reading a book on conversational Italian. Someone named Signor Bianchi is saying that he has bed linen but his children want to know if there is a television as well.

According to Christian theology, there are nine principal vices to which humans are subject: tristia, philargyria, fornicatio, superbia, cenodoxia, gasturnergia, aredia, ira and taedum cordes. They sound like those ancient diseases that made people's faces go yellow. I picture Dante saying these words over and over, like an incantation. He is lying under mosquito netting in some remote hospital. He is clutching a gold cross in his long white fingers. His face has gone yellow.

Stephen and I are standing on top of the Terminal Tower in Cleveland. We are trying to get vertigo. It's all windy and cloudy out, which makes me feel like we are in a black and white film. Higbee's department store is off to the left. Stephen's mother is in there shopping. There are trees in the windows with pink and blue Easter eggs hung on them. What would it feel like to arise from the dead? Actually, there don't seem to be that many ideas around about what happens to you after you die. The Catholics and Leonora think you go to heaven or hell. My parents think you decay and become part of a tree. I don't know what the Buddhists think. I'll have to ask my grandmother. I stick out my breasts and yell 'Buongiorno Roma!' into the wind and feel like Gina Lollabrigida. Stephen holds me while I lean real far over the side. I get whirlwinds in my temples.

I heard people having sex once. We were in Niagara Falls. My brother and I were sharing a hotel room. We were watching *Columbo* and all of a sudden I heard the bedpost next door banging against the wall. Then all this heavy breathing. 'James, listen,' I whispered to my brother, who was sitting on the floor next to the miniature bar, trying to open the lock with his penknife. 'I think someone's being *murdered*.' James turned the volume down on the TV and listened. Columbo was circling a dead body, scratching his head. Some woman in a bouffant hairdo was looking dubious next to a grand piano. 'Idiot – they're fucking,' James said in disgusted voice. This was the beginning of his being-disgusted-with-me phase. 'It sounds like a fat man trying to squeeze himself through a window,' I said. My brother rolled his eyes and turned *Columbo* up so loud I thought my teeth would shatter in my head.

I'm reading Thomas à Kempis' *The Imitation of Christ*. He has all these great titles to the chapters like 'On Guarding Against Familiarity,' 'On Avoiding Vain Hope and Conceit,' and 'How Man has no Personal Goodness of which to Boast'. This last one mainly consists of a disciple talking to the Lord about what a nothing he is and how great the Lord is and how he doesn't find anything fun or joyous except lying prostrate in front of the Lord and talking about how he doesn't take any pleasure in creatures. He ends saying, 'Oh Blessed Trinity, oh my God, my Truth, my Mercy to You alone let all things ascribe all praise, honour, power and glory throughout the endless ages.' I love these words – Trinity, Truth, Mercy, Grace. They seem to sound different with capital letters in front of them. They almost have a taste in your mouth – an old, regal taste, like you're licking something dusty yet sweet. Oh, and I forgot. This disciple also likes to be smote. Whatever that means. I have to look it up.

Aren't lips strange? Are there any other animals that have lips like humans? All of them are so different. In the Bible, Luke judges people by their mouths. Leonora's lips are large and thick and soft. I could imagine it would be pleasant to walk barefoot across them. Mr Havish, my science teacher, has lips that look like an old sofa, one that is all sunken in at the middle from too many people sitting on it. Dante's look like he plays a reed instrument, maybe a flute. Someone told me that Eskimos sit cross-legged, facing each other, open lips to open lips, blowing into each other's mouths, vibrating each other's vocal chords. I wonder what it would sound like to blow on Dante's vocal chords. I wonder if it would sound mystical and religious, like echoes in the halls of monasteries.

'Nel mezzo del camin di nostra vita, mi ritrovai per una selva oscura che la diretta via era smaretta.' I am standing in James's room, reciting from this book by a writer who has the same name as Dante. The poetry is lost on my brother. 'Go away before I bruise you, Haddie,' he growls. 'Vivo in Italia. Milano e' grande come Roma. Lavo tutto a mano. Ti fermi da Mario?' A large algebra textbook hits me on the side of the head.

Smote means to be struck. With powerful effect.

In fifth grade they herded all us girls into one science classroom and all the guys into another. We were shown these films about our periods and the structures of our vaginas. The woman narrating it had a voice that sounded like lemon furniture polish. In outline form the vagina looks like one of those antelope skulls they find out West. It's a little eerie. Then they gave us little pamphlets that demonstrated how to use a tampon. We all carried them around with us all day like secret talismans. The guys were in the other science classroom with the gym coach. Stephen told me he explained wet dreams to them. Wet dreams. I couldn't get those words out of my head for the rest of the day. It sent these little sparks, like fireflies, running through my veins. It also sounded mystical to me, like those dreamy landscapes of waves by Chinese painters. The whole rest of the day, in fact, seemed mystical. It was the beginning of May and the first lawn-mowers could be heard on the school grounds. Their summer sound made everything seem to be in slow motion. I couldn't pay attention in class. The lawn-mowers seemed to be purring wet dreams, wet dreams.

My mother screamed this morning. I've never heard her scream before. I bought a bottle of Loreal's Midnight Black hair colouring at Saywell's drug store yesterday and did my hair last night before I went to bed. I had it up in a towel all night and I must admit it gave me a shock when I looked in the mirror this morning. My face looks pretty pale beneath all this black hair, but also wonderfully tragic. I practised this look in the mirror. With the cross around my neck and rosary beads clutched in my hand and my eyes kind of glazed over a bit, I look like I'm undergoing some unfathomable religious ritual. My mother is yanking at my hair. She is still screaming. I think of suggesting she read Thomas à Kempis' 'On Avoiding Rash Judgments'. But I don't. My psychology teacher told us you can't scream and think at the same time.

Fishermen in Italy hang live lobsters from church rafters so that the death throes will excite them in their reverence for the mass.

My mother is driving me to Sergio Visconte's hair salon. It's up in Cleveland. We have Easy Listening 105 on the radio and there is an instrumental version of 'Volare' playing. I pretend we are in a little white Fiat driving through Rome. I stop tapping my feet when my mother gives me a look. Sergio Visconte is known to do matching hairstyles on women and their dogs. It's true. It makes for a very interesting atmosphere. There are pictures of poodles and chihuahuas on the wall, next to pictures of their owners. The resemblance is often striking. One pair is especially similar – it is a woman and her pet Afghan. They both have long, flowing, sexy auburn waves. Even their noses look the same. Which, I guess, Sergio had no part in. When we get there, Sergio shoves my head under the sink and commiserates with my mother. Then I'm stuck under a dryer for about an hour. Next to me is a llasa apsa. When we leave my hair is dirty blonde and poofed out about ten inches from my head in that horrible hairspray style male hairdressers favour. I look like a Chow. I hate that Sergio. He isn't even really Italian.

Some monks in the fourteenth century decided to count up all the angels. At that time they numbered 301,655,722. I wonder how many there are now. Leonora's always talking to herself. Except she says she's talking to angels. She calls them by different names: Sachiel, Behemiel, Shakziel. She says her favourite one is Nathaniel, the angel of fire. 'That's the element I feel closest to baby!' she says and jiggles her hips a little. I asked her what they look like. 'They don't look like nothing sweetie. They just *sound* you out.' She draws the word 'sound' out like it's taffy. At night I try to listen for them. They say there are sounds too large to hear, like the earth moving, and sounds too small to hear, like your cells rotating. I wonder how big angels are. It would take you two whole weeks to count from one to a million. There are millions of stars. And you can't hear them.

Large numbers can give you vertigo.

*

I am sitting behind Dante today. I am staring at the nape of his neck. It seems so vulnerable and secretive. You hardly ever see the nape of your own neck. And you'll never see your own heart. Mr Havish asks Dante a question. 'Uh. I dunno.' 'Come, come Mr Cavenetti. Think a little, will you?' Mr Havish leans back against his desk with a smile and his fly splits open like a smile on a second mouth. 'Uh, paramecium, like, split in half to reproduce.' The ends of Dante's words trail off like sheep being led over a cliff. We are learning that with sex came death. Before sex, things divided to produce more of themselves. What would it feel like to divide? I wonder if there is a certain frisson to it. A certain ooh la la.

My brother is driving me to the Cathedral of Tomorrow. I saw him smoking pot with his friends last weekend and I'm hanging it over his head in order to get favours from him. Leonora took us to the Cathedral of Tomorrow one Sunday years ago when my parents were away. We sat in a huge domed hall. The preacher asked if anyone had sinned before. My brother and I raised our hands. We had painted stripes on the neighbour's snotty white Abyssinian cat the weekend before. No one else raised their hands, and the preacher called us up to the podium and personally blessed us. Then there was silence while everyone said a prayer for us. Leonora wept.

We pull into the car-park. There is a gift shop here I want to go to. James won't come in with me. He's slouched behind the wheel with a look of eternal suffering. He could learn something from the Christian martyr Archbishop Vladimir who had his clothes stripped off by seamen and was beaten and then showered with taunts and insults. Or the martyrs of Lyon, who, after whips, many beasts and the iron chair, were at last thrown into a net and cast before a bull. I go inside. There is a big woman standing in the corner. She has a name tag on that says 'Sister Thelma Roosevelt'. Her slip is showing beneath her dress. She calls me 'honey' and tells me to look around. There are lots of gold crosses, St Christopher statues to hang from your rear-view mirror, tapes of the Cathedral of Tomorrow Singers and large gilt-framed pictures of Jesus, who has soft, flowing brown hair and eyes like a doe. There is a tape of hymn music on and Sister Thelma Roosevelt is humming along to it and swaying slightly. She sounds like the motor of heavy farm machinery. I browse a bit. Then I see what I want. It is a plastic bas-relief of the Virgin Mary. You can hang it on your wall. And there is a lightbulb inside and an electric chord coming out of the back so you can plug it in. Mary's eyes are kind of slanty and she has a low-cut blue dress on with great billowing folds. She looks a little like Sophia Loren. Sister Thelma Roosevelt demonstrates to me how it works. Then she says she'll throw in the lightbulb and one of the postcards of the Cathedral of Tomorrow Singers for free. You can tell she is used to wheeling and dealing. I have some trouble lugging it out to the car. Mary's about three feet tall. 'You . . . are . . . so . . . fuck . . . ing . . . weird,' James says between clenched teeth, and then peels out of the car-park.

Stephen is teaching me how to flirt. I am winking at him. I am not getting it right. Stephen is acting like one of those petulant French dance coaches. 'No, no, no!' he says, completely exasperated, 'Like *this*.' He tosses his wavy blonde hair and winks his right eye behind a lock of it. Stephen has great hair. Sometimes after he's just washed it, it looks like the hair on the Metro Goldwyn-Mayer lion. Who invented the wink? Who thought it would be a sexy idea to close one eye and keep the other one open? In the Sermon on the Mount it says that it is better to have one eye, because with two you will be cast into hell-fire.

I wonder what the difference is between what you see outside and what you remember inside. And if you become what you have seen. People have different weather in their eyes. Some have storms, some a sirocco blowing, some Indian summer. When you are with different people it is like being in different weather. And different landscapes. Some people make you feel as though you are on undulating green hills with lazy clouds in the sky, with others you feel like you are in a deep forest with a light rain and everything's pungent and spicy. Others are hot dry tundras with a shimmering gold horizon. When I look into Dante's eyes I feel like I am on a rocky, cave-encrusted coast.

'Now that's what I call decoration!' Leonora is standing in my room with her hands on her hips, admiring my Virgin Mary. She doesn't like my parents' taste in furnishing. When she's in a bad mood she talks to our furniture instead of angels. 'You bad old chair! Someone should knock the silly old stuffing out of you!' Whack goes the feather duster. She finds one of the sofas sarcastic. 'Don't be giving me that slimy old stare, Mr Davenport, you aren't going to be moving when I kick that smirk off of you buster.' At night, with just the light from my Virgin Mary, my room is hazy blue. I lie on my bed with my arms crossed at my chest and pretend I am one of the statues carved on top of a Roman sarcophagus. I make my face completely expressionless, until it feels like stone. I picture Dante carved on top of one next to me. The blue light is coming from a tall, stained-glass window. We are so completely sacred.

When you look at someone, you no longer own yourself completely. There is the you looking and the you in their heads. There is the you you want to be and the you they want you to be. There is the you of the past, the you of the present, the you of the future. When you think about it, it is like being in a room full of mirrors. The original you disappears amongst all the other yous. It seems that you can get vertigo from anything if you think about it long enough.

'All composite things decay. Strive diligently.' I got another fortune from my grandmother today. Sometimes she also sends me these little stories called koans. You are supposed to rotate them around in your mind all week until you understand them. One goes like this: A man asked his master, 'Do dogs have Buddha souls?' And the master replies, 'Moo.' This one gave me a headache. I prefer the Bible to Buddha. There is a lot happening in the Bible all the time. There are natural disasters, and wars, and people being smote. Buddha sits.

Dante has been saying 'hi' to me in the halls. It makes my heart jump up into my head and whirl around like a wild bird. I wonder if the heart is the seat of the soul. Except I don't feel like it really belongs to me – its sacred red chambers, its distant congo beat. It doesn't seem real. None of my internal organs do. They don't seem to be *mine*. They lead their own lives.

Stephen and I are going on a quest. He's really getting into religion with me. We are at the mall. Stephen says that shopping is a religious experience. He also says that jewellery shops are a great place to experience vertigo. All that gold does make your head spin. Apparently gold is mentioned hundreds of times in the Bible. The salesman asks us if we need help. Stephen wants to see a ruby ring. The salesman has clear nail polish on his fingernails and a disgusted expression on his face. He's wearing a gold bracelet. Stephen tries on the ring. It is a woman's ruby cocktail ring with lots of diamonds. He holds it up to his face. 'This is religion,' he breathes. Actually, he reminds me of that painting of Pope Leo X. Pope Leo X is wearing this velvet cape and a ruby ring. It's not quite as flashy as the one Stephen has on. After we have annoyed Mr Gold-Braceleted Salesmen sufficiently, we walk down to Saks. Some guy in an Easter Bunny suit seems to be following us. Maybe it's security. People in stores never trust Stephen.

At Saks, all the salesladies wear grey smocks with 'Saks Fifth Avenue' embroidered in gold on their lapels. They look like custodians at a museum. In fact there is a museum quietness to Saks. As you walk through the doors there is a sudden hush that is almost physical. It's like entering a church. I head for the shoes. I learned my appreciation for shoes from my mother. The salesladies are always ABSOLUTELY DELIGHTED to see her. She keeps her shoes in boxes in the closet. There are foreign names printed on all the boxes. I love looking through them all. They are like exotic animals. The black velvet pumps with little diamond squares at the toes seem to have come from a jungle; the parakeet green ones with the gold buttons look as if they might change colour depending on their surroundings. I browse among the new selection they have at Saks. Then I try on all the ones with Italian names. When the saleslady starts to get a wild look in her eyes, I leave to find Stephen. I find him in men's toiletries. The Easter Bunny is at the counter next to him, looking at men's talc.

What makes a 'thing' sexy? I am looking through my mother's lingerie drawer. Everything is lacy with scalloped edges. Maybe it's a thing's shape. Like my mother's shoes. They have a dip to them like Leonora's hips. Maybe it's when a thing seems slightly alive. When I slide open my mother's closet door her dresses sway and rustle, like there are birds captured underneath them.

It is Easter Sunday. I am at church with my parents and my brother. Even though they are pagan, we go to church on Christmas Eve and Easter Sunday. Our church is Episcopal. Everything here is drained of colour. The church is white. The pews are white. The minister's face is the colour of water stains on old ceilings. He seems very depressed. I wonder what Leonora's up to at the Cathedral of Tomorrow. They are probably saving someone and weeping and singing. Everyone there has that 'Where will YOU spend Eternity' look in their eyes. And the music from the huge organ cartwheels around the room, and the preacher's voice boomerangs off the walls, and the whole congregation stampedes down the aisle like it is one big exclamation mark at the end of Amen. Even the building, with its turrets and steeples and buttresses is shaped like one big hallejujah. I guess the sense of the sacred has a lot to do with location.

A miracle occurred today. Dante asked me to the junior high dance, which is the day after tomorrow. I was at my locker. I didn't even hear him come up. He said, 'Haddie, do you want to go to the dance Friday?' Real nonchalant. I had this stupid pencil in my mouth. And the thing was, I forgot I had the pencil in my mouth because I was so flabbergasted. So I said 'Yeah, sure' trying to be nonchalant back, but it came out all lispy and spitty because I was talking through this damn pencil. So he said, 'Great. I'll meet you there.' And walked away. With that martini walk. I stood looking into my messy locker for about ten minutes afterwards. Dumbfounded. Clutching my drooly pencil in my hand like it was some sort of relic.

When I tell Stephen, his mouth drops open in mock despair. He holds one hand on his hip and the other against his cheek and exclaims: 'Oh my little one has grown up *too* fast!' Sometimes he really annoys me. At times like this I wish I had a girl as a best friend.

I've been playing my parents' Enrico Caruso albums in my bedroom all day, trying on different outfits for the dance. I sing along to 'Vesti la glubba' and think of all the tragic things that could befall us before we get married at St Mark's in Venice and have fifteen children. Enrico Caruso's voice sounds like an overly-rich cake with lots of Italian biscuits and candied fruit stuck in it. Actually, the idea of God and heaven and angels is like an overly-rich dessert.

My favourite cloud formations are in the sky. Cumulus. And they are tinged with pink like those clouds in children's psalm books. I sit on my bed, waiting for it to get dark. Even my Virgin Mary light is off and as it gets darker her face seems to shrink. The large elms lining the street outside appear blue in the half-dark and are swaying slightly in the wind. They are reflected in the long mirrors of the closets that run the length of my room. In the cold glass I imagine the branches becoming divers in blue bathing suits, continually jumping into the blue depths of the street. I go to the closet and feel for the silk dress I am going to wear. I already have my stockings and shoes on the bed. I pull off my jeans and shirt and carefully roll on the stockings and fasten them with the garters. They feel so sexy they make me dizzy. Then I step into the dress and zip up the back. It has a swishing sound. It's a swishing sound like those drum brushes just before the first notes of 'Volare'. The material of the dress and the stockings is so very smooth; wearing them makes my room seems coarse and childish.

This really lame band are playing 'Miss You' by the Rolling Stones. I am standing next to Dante and his group of friends. They are talking about all the beer they drank at various parties. I can't seem to stop smiling. My cheeks are starting to ache and I feel like the muscles in them are going to give out any minute and my face will fall like a soufflé. I see Stephen out of the corner of my eye. He is wearing a Spanish jacket and a string tie. He looks ridiculous. Which is probably his intention. And he's with Missy Sabrina Carmichael. Who I can't stand. She wears plaid headbands. And monograms on everything. MSC. She should just get herself cattle-branded on the forehead. Stephen walks over to me. 'Stop smiling!' he shouts over the music. 'I can't,' I say, smiling. No one ever laughs or smiles in the Bible. I think of mentioning this to Dante, but just as I open my mouth he asks me if I want to dance.

I am in the bathroom. I am sitting on a toilet with the lid closed. I needed some time alone to let my face relax from all the smiling. Dante doesn't seem very religious. Or Italian. I asked him what he thought of the Christian martyr St Polycarp and he said 'Huh?' Then I asked him, 'Who do you like better, Sophia Loren or Gina Lollobrigida?' And he said 'Who?' When I left for the bathroom I said, 'Arriverderci for now,' and he said 'What?'

The band is packing up. Everyone is kind of milling around, blinking in the bright lights they just turned on. The girls' corsages are all dying extravagant deaths, their stemmed necks either thrown back in a sort of ecstatic agony or bowed over like dying saints. Dante and his friends are laughing about yet another beer drinking episode. Then Dante turns to me and says, 'Well, Haddie, thanks for being my date. I had a nice time.' Then he shakes my hand and kisses me on the forehead. And before I know it, he's weaving nonchalantly through the crowd and out the door.

I am walking home. Stephen's father kept trying to get me into the car with him, Stephen and Missy, but I insisted on walking. It is very dark out. There are lots of stars. I wish we could hear them. I wonder what they would sound like. What does God have to wonder or think about? If He created everything, if He knows how everything works, then what does He think about all day? There's this man, Mr Forester, who comes to all my parents' cocktail parties. He knows the manufacturing processes of everything – shoes, plastics, soup. And if you get stuck next to him, he'll tell you about them. The whole process. From start to finish. If you could speak to God, maybe you would be disappointed. Maybe He would tell you how amoebas, giraffes and star nebulas are made. And you'd be disappointed.